Ana's
Dream

For Barbara —
a special friend

Barbara Boudreaux
January, 2006

Ana's Dream

Barbara Boudreaux

Ivy House
Publishing Group
www.ivyhousebooks.com

PUBLISHED BY IVY HOUSE PUBLISHING GROUP
5122 Bur Oak Circle, Raleigh, NC 27612
United States of America
919-782-0281
www.ivyhousebooks.com

ISBN: 1-57197-446-6
Library of Congress Control Number: 2005901095

Printed in the United States of America

To musicians everywhere, who enrich our lives beyond measure

Chapter One

IN THE GENTLE sunlight of early morning, Noelle Wright, feeling isolated and vulnerable, held herself stiffly erect on the rear seat of the long, black Lincoln Continental with its state seal on either front door. She tapped nervous fingers on the leather seat to a jittery rhythm she heard only in her head. Her eyes were drawn to bright splashes of color from wildflowers, poppies, and blue lupine growing profusely between a double row of ancient oaks and meandering free-form into the meadow beyond. *How lovely it would be,* she thought, *to wander there aimlessly in the sunshine—preferably alone—and to sink down in the midst of all that vivid color and perhaps to take off her shoes.* She sighed.

Light and shadow flickered between the giant oaks like an old-fashioned Nickelodeon film. Even with the car windows closed, the humming tires were a soothing background sound that varied in pitch each time the surface of the highway changed.

In the dusty area beside the highway, an agricultural worker in shabby clothing and a battered baseball cap pulled low over his eyes trudged along with his head down.

She supposed that he had no desire to attract attention from people who traveled in cars with official seals on their doors. Most likely, he had missed his morning ride to the field where he should have been working by that hour, and now he had to hoof it. *Latino,* she thought, *working the fields that so many U.S. workers shun.* The work was hard and so often back-breaking.

Her thoughts turned to Angelina and her three little ones—Luis, Maria, Miguel—and their tiny, faded-pink stucco cottage behind that forlorn pepper tree. She had not met their father, but she supposed that he would resemble the worker they had just passed, since he also worked the fields. She wondered if his children had received the clothing she had bought for them and whether he resented that, perhaps fiercely. If the clothing was too small, she also wondered whether they would abide by her request not to squeeze into it anyway. Not likely.

The two men in the front seat were talking shop in lowered voices. She picked up the morning newspaper she had brought along and scanned the headlines. "Balkan Tension Increases." "Japanese Economy Slows Again." "Italy Will Name New Leader." Nothing new there.

As she turned a few pages, the pavement smoothed out, and the sound level of the tires dropped a few notches so that bits of the conversation in the front seat floated back.

"That stagehand," Los Angeles Police Lieutenant Donal Fitzgerald, at the wheel, was saying. "Rotten luck that we'll never have a chance to question him."

"Well, I'm sure he had no intention of going out that way, poor sod," D. E. S. Allbritton said. He rode beside Fitzgerald in the passenger seat and was an insurance investigator on assignment from the Oxford Agency in London. Noelle missed their next few comments, but she began to listen more carefully when she picked up Allbritton's next question that ended with the word "record."

"Oh, just light stuff, I would think," Fitzgerald's deep voice rumbled. "A couple of D.U.I.s, one disturbing the peace, rowdy behavior in a public place, and so forth."

Noelle had the sudden feeling that she was being observed, and she looked up quickly to catch Fitzgerald's eyes on her in the rearview mirror. She dropped her eyes again to her newspaper, turned a page that she didn't read, and listened closely.

"The manager, Marshall," Fitzgerald said in an undertone. "He's up to his ears in casino debt. Something to check out there. Motive, possibly."

Allbritton nodded and said, "Right. My thought precisely."

Noelle again sensed Fitzgerald's eyes on her, and her uneasiness returned. As considerate as they were to keep her informed, she felt that there were things they knew that they weren't telling her. Fighting off stress, she closed her eyes and put her head back against the seat. Oh, would this hazy cocoon of anxiety in which she had been suspended for the past weeks dissipate any time soon? She wanted to get back to living her normal life and stop being constantly on guard, at the beck and call of police investigators, insurance adjusters, and worst of all, the relentlessly intrusive media. Memory was vivid of that first early morning call on the morning after when this clipped British voice, sounding distant, said, "Dr. Noelle Wright, please. Evan Frobisher, *London Times*."

She sighed again. Who would ever have dreamed that she, who was innately fond of peace and quiet, would find herself trapped in the middle of a sensational incident that involved the brazen theft of a priceless Guarneri violin followed by a violent death? It had captured the avid fascination of music circles worldwide and thrust their peaceful city of San Sebastian—where a few cars broken into constituted a crime wave—into dead center of a maelstrom? And was today, finally, the day that they might hope to see the ending of this bizarre affair at a nondescript music store in one of the seediest sections of east Los Angeles?

She sat up restlessly and unbuttoned her jacket, wondering again if what she had chosen to wear was appropriate. But how did one know what to wear for a rendezvous with a thief who might turn cranky without warning and fire potshots at the three of them? For her, that would be a first. After changing her mind three times, she had settled for a pearl-gray linen suit with a black silk blouse that had been one of her favorites because it accented her hazel-gray eyes and short, dark hair. But what did that matter today?

How much more frightened she would be without the protection and guidance of those two sharp professionals in the front seat. After tension-filled weeks, she considered them to be friends she could count on. From this perspective, she studied them, unobserved. Opposites in appearance and background, they worked well together and obviously respected one another.

The broad back of the driver filled the jacket of his standard dark blue suit that made him seem to be in uniform when he wasn't. Large, scarred, strong-looking hands rested easily on the wheel. From that angle, Noelle could more easily see the dark red scar she had noticed before. At that point, she realized that he had lost the lower tip of his left ear in whatever action that had caused the scar that spiraled down his stocky neck and disappeared under the collar of a starchy, white shirt. Noelle shuddered. Whoever had caused that scar was going for the jugular. Fortunately for Fitzgerald, he had missed by a half inch, yet Fitzgerald continued in police work seemingly undeterred. *It goes with the territory,* she thought. And yet, he retained a surprising kindness and compassion.

Their conversation had turned to hobbies. Fitzgerald explained his tiny lapel pin shaped like an old steam train. "I began with one engine, one car, and just a bit of track," he said. "And before I knew it, I had a bunch of cars, and the tracks had escaped from the spare bedroom and sprawled all over the upstairs hall, until now, it's all I've been able to do to get to bed without breaking an ankle." He chuckled. "After a bad day downtown, I put all the engines and cars on intersecting tracks and create this gigantic train wreck." They both laughed.

"You're not planning to become a railroad engineer on retirement, I hope?"

"Can't promise. Been a railroad buff since I was ten, when I didn't get the model train I was hoping for at Christmas."

Allbritton, much taller than the lieutenant and more athletically slender, had a fine voice that had attracted Noelle from the moment she met him. It was rich, mellifluous, rising and falling, as good music does. He said, "Well, we all have our hangovers from childhood, I'm convinced of that. Mine is marching bands, flags flying, and people in gaudy uniforms with tons of gold braid." He held up a forefinger. "And, of course, the *flügelhorn.*"

"What the devil is a *fooglehorn?* Never heard of it."

"*Flügel.* There's another L in there. A German word. The horn's like a bugle, only with keys and sometimes in three pitches. In the U.K., we only use the middle one in B-flat, and then it's for brass bands, military events, royal ceremonials, grand affairs of that nature. The horn has a fine, pure sound. I get called on to play now and then, but not often enough to suit me. Still and all, I have to keep up my practice and maintain my *embouchure*—my lip—just in case. Wouldn't want to make a fool of myself in front of the queen or even any of the less-admirable royals in their magnificent hats."

"And you still play this . . . horn?"

"Practice every morning when I'm home. Drives the household straight up the wall, but I pretend that I don't notice. After all, it is my house. Only my six-year-old daughter loves the sound as much as I do. Whenever I practice, she puts on this little red jacket she has, brass buttons right down the front. Don't know where she ever got it. She pops herself at the end of my bed and waves a ratty, red-and-blue pompom in perfect time with the music."

The tone of his voice rose and fell with his enthusiasm.

"The best thing was when an old friend in the music publishing business in London came across an original piece for *flügelhorn* composed by the great Henry Purcell in the mid-seventeenth century. It came up for auction, and I just had to have it. Spent quite a bit too much—more than I could afford—but it's the second treasure of my life, after my daughter, of course."

Eavesdropping, Noelle was fascinated. She had never heard him mention his horn. She tried to imagine him blasting away on it, and she wondered if he played it while still in his pajamas. Or perhaps in a nightshirt or his underwear? The rather wicked thought crossed her mind that there was something hilarious about imagining otherwise dignified people in underwear of stripes or plaid. Or was he dressed as she saw him almost daily, in one of his well-tailored Bond Street suits with pristine white shirt and proper tie, every fair hair on his head brushed into place and looking as if he had it trimmed daily between breakfast and lunch?

She resisted the impulse to giggle at these mischievous mental images and was therefore caught off-guard when he suddenly looked at her over the back of his seat. His blue eyes glittered with suppressed humor, as if he had been reading her mind and enjoying it. He asked, "And how are you doing back there, Madam President?"

Days earlier, when they had been alone, he had told her that he would always treat her professionally in public because the Oxford Agency took a very dim view of any fraternization between investigator and client, but when she recalled the serious personal conversations they had shared over coffee and croissants at her kitchen table, she felt her face flushing. She returned his smile. "I'm doing very well," she said. "But tell me more about this . . . horn you play. I've never heard you mention it."

He grinned, "I can't play it for you because it's back home in my closet behind my favorite slippers. I've always thought everyone should be able to make some kind of music. Do you play? Piano? Piccolo? Tuba?"

"None of the above." Noelle laughed. "But I do play cello. Not professionally, of course." She loved playing Schubert's songs with words she improvised according to her mood at the time—romantic, philosophical, nonsensical. Avery had joined in this game with enthusiasm, and some of their creations became wickedly ribald. Without warning, her eyes filled with tears at the memory of playing for Avery one evening in front of her fireplace.

Allbritton, a sensitive man, sobered and turned away immediately. Fitzgerald, also sensitive in his own way, glanced at her again in his rearview mirror. "Not nervous about this, are you, Mrs. Wright? You won't be in the slightest danger, I've seen to that. We'll be fully covered by some plainclothes guys from L.A. Metro in an unmarked car directly across the street. I can reach them on my mobile at a second's notice."

"No, no," she said. "I'm fine. I was thinking about something else altogether."

"Well, that's good then. You two will stay in the back

room of the music store. It's a little grubby but safe enough. This guy's got a one-way mirror in the door so he can watch the shop while he's working in the back. You can see everything that goes on."

She nodded. "Yes, fine. I'm sure you've thought of everything."

"You don't need to do a thing," Allbritton added. "We wanted you to be there to represent the symphony association, as one of the injured parties."

She nodded again and began to feel like one of those little dolls called Bobbleheads that have big round eyes and large heads on springs so they nod brainlessly back and forth, agreeing with everything. The highway broadened to become an elevated freeway, and traffic grew even more congested. At the next branch, Fitzgerald veered right. Noelle bit her lip, and her stomach convulsed when she read the directional sign that indicated "Downtown Los Angeles—35 miles." So, they had arrived.

Chapter Two

THE DAY THE extraordinary event began was an ordinary day like any other. A Saturday morning rehearsal was scheduled for the San Sebastian Symphony. Backstage it was almost dark, and sounds were muted. The musicians waited, passive yet expectant, alert to the tips of their fingers, seated on the lighted section of the stage within the massive acoustic shell. They had already tuned, and the concertmaster was in his first chair position. It was just prior to 9:00 A.M., and they were ready to play, as their contract required.

Ana Iliescu Breckenridge slipped in quietly from the bright sunshine outside and closed the heavy stage door without a sound. She knew how to be silent and she knew she had to make it to her assigned seat onstage before the conductor did so she wouldn't face another tardy deduction from her payroll check that was meager enough to begin with. She was still burning with resentment about the behavior of her car, an aging Renault that she barely managed to drive. Because it usually failed to start without numerous tries, she was almost always late for rehearsals. Bystanders dispensing free advice often suggested that it might have something to do with the battery, but she knew nothing of that, and she had no money to deal with it, whatever it was. Perhaps it would go away.

She placed her violin case on one of the long tables provided backstage for the musicians and softly tuned. There was just enough light filtering between the sections of the acoustic shell for her to move silently among the other instrument cases left carelessly open and it took her only a minute to find an available block of rosin for her bow, to which she helped herself. Although rosin was not expensive, she had no money at that moment and she was sure no one would mind.

She heard the rapid steps of the Austrian music director Lucas Richter approaching from the dressing room area. She stepped back into the shadows and he passed her without looking in her direction. She fell in behind him and slipped into her seat—second row, outside, first violins—a split second before he turned and mounted his podium.

He was not fooled. After a long pause to let her suffer in suspense, he glared at her. Tapping his baton on the edge of his music stand, he pointed it at the personnel manager—who might have been generous with Ana—and then at her, waggling it a little. *She's late again! Mark it down!*

Ana bent her head and turned the pages of her music, ignoring the curious glances of the musicians around her. Actually, some were sympathetic but she saw them all as judgmental. Sometimes she hated Richter. She had tried all of her charms on him when she first arrived, but he had been impervious and cold toward her. She suspected that he didn't fully agree with the decision of the audition committee when it had approved her to fill a temporary vacancy in the orchestra, and she thought that this hostility probably related to the fact that she had never attended a recognized music school of any kind. Her mother had tutored her from the age of four in their cramped apartment in their Soviet-bloc country.

Her beautiful mother, Lucienne, a tiny, green-eyed blonde and a vivacious, fun-loving tease, was also a fine professional musician who had played for years with the State Philharmonic and the Theatre of Opera and Ballet of the Socialist Republic. Everyone loved Lucienne, especially the males around her, and she had loved a number of them, literally, in return.

So what if Ana's technique differed from that which Richter personally favored? *Well, too bad! My mother is every inch the musician you are! Pompous ass!* she thought. In spite of everything that had happened between them, Ana was intensely loyal to her mother and proud of her. She thought of her then and wondered where she was and how she was surviving. Did she have any more money or clothes or food than Ana did? There had been no word from her mother for more than six months. Ana worried.

On the podium, Richter arranged his scores and watched the large clock until it showed exactly 9:00 A.M., as their union contract required. Sharply, he tapped his music stand and raised his baton. The musicians raised their instruments. "Berlioz, please," he said. "We'll begin at number twenty-one."

The music soared around her, and for a while, nothing else mattered. As she always did, she entered that private space that nonmusicians can never understand. In a newspaper interview, the orchestra's concertmaster said it best, "I cannot imagine my life without music. It's all I've ever wanted to do, and it brings my greatest happiness. We musicians sacrifice a great part of our lives, time, and money, or endure the lack of it. When frustration or discouragement suggest considerations of another livelihood, the thought is only fleeting. A musician plays because he *must.*"

About half an hour into the rehearsal, the horn section

began having problems. Richter's blond head reared up, and he rapped again on the podium. The music stopped.

Ana let her eyes roam around the orchestra as they waited. The sections ranged back from the podium like spokes on half a wheel. Violins sat in left front, where the audience could see their bow arms moving in perfect unison. Second violins came next, then violas. Cellists sat to the far right, and their fingering along the strings of their instruments was readily visible to those in the audience who were fascinated by this. Behind them, the string basses stood to play but had tall stools behind them in case they needed them. Extending the spokes of the half-wheel layout, behind the strings were the woodwinds— flutes, clarinets, oboes, English horn, bassoons. And at the back, the brass—trumpets, French horns, trombones, tuba. Percussion was at left rear with the three big copper timpani attracting a lot of attention unless the orchestration called for a stately harp, which always drew so many eyes.

As always, Ana felt alienated from the other musicians, like an outsider who didn't quite fit in and perhaps never would. She had no special friends among them, although she had been playing with the orchestra for more than six months. She kept her distance.

How smug these Americans are, she thought. *So confident of their own rightness in all things, so self-satisfied, certain that the rest of the world comes in a weak second.* She had often wondered if any of them had grown up hungry, wearing cast-off clothing and barely surviving in a dumpy fourth-floor walk-up flat, as she had. Sometimes she hated all of them, too, even while she longed for a friend among them.

Richter, dissatisfied, had the horns repeat the same phrase over and over again. She shut it out. She had no interest in what the horns played. Only the strings—the heart of the orchestra, her mother always said—were important to her.

She intercepted the suggestive glance of the principal violist whose section was opposite hers. Phil Mathiesen, with his bulging eyes and somewhat fleshy fingers that made such full, rich sounds on the strings of his instrument, was one of the few orchestra members who had made any effort to be friendly to her. But she sensed that it was the wrong kind of friendliness. Too much was sensual in his crude jokes. She resented the fact that he felt free to make those kinds of remarks to her, as if, after all, who was she—a little nobody from some loser of an Eastern European country about whose exact location he couldn't care less.

As a section principal, he was automatically a member of the audition committee that had approved her for the temporary position in the orchestra, and she supposed that he thought she owed him something for that. Not that she was some kind of a blushing virgin, but still, she would make her own choices and would not let anyone pressure her. Coldly, she avoided his glance.

She smoothed out a tiny wrinkle in her leather miniskirt where her violin had been resting. The skirt and matching knee-high boots were her pride and joy, because they announced to the world that perhaps, in spite of what they might think, she was a bit special. Slowly, she inched her right foot forward until she could admire, yet again, the rich, gleaming brown leather of the tapered boot on her slender foot. Never had she thought anything so elegant would belong to her. Her shoes had usually been handed down from her mother as soon as her feet grew to nearly her mother's size. Lucienne loved shoes avidly, and the two of them had often gone scrounging for used ones in the stalls of the old section of the city. "Look for leather only," her mother always said, "even if they don't fit exactly!"

Ana's provocative mouth, with its full lower lip, curved in

a tiny smile. She remembered how proud Emil had been on that magical, sunny day in Frankfurt when he had bought her the skirt and boots. He knew what a big event that was for her, and it made him happy to be the one to make it possible— although this was an extravagance he could ill afford. In the brief times they had together, they had been silly and giddy, laughing at every foolish thing they saw or invented. He was so much fun to be with, and he had a lively imagination. She could easily have fallen in love with Emil, and she sensed that he was already quite a bit in love with her. He was so handsome—tall and blond, lithe and muscular at the same time, affectionate and considerate.

On the down side, he already had a wife. *Fat Gerta,* she thought. *How I hated you!* Ana got to keep the leather skirt and boots because they were much too small for Gerta, but Gerta got to keep Emil, and Ana was left with no one, again. So, who won?

She came back to the present to realize that Mathiesen's eyes were still fastened on her with a knowing smile. *Buzz off, you lech!* she thought.

At the break, she drifted out into the warm sunshine with the rest of the musicians and went to her favorite spot around the corner of the brick building near tidy beds of blue pansies and golden marigolds, where almost no one else ever came. She pressed her back against the warmth of the bricks, closed her eyes, and wished desperately for a cigarette. She was out, as usual.

A slight breeze ruffled a sheet of paper on the sidewalk, and she opened her eyes to recognize the brilliant scarlet background of a promotional flier for the coming appearance there, in three weeks, of the latest concert sensation—a young violinist named Daniel Lessing. She still found this hard to believe, although inevitable, when she thought about it. She walked over lazily and picked up the flier, even though she already had five of them in her tiny apartment—including the one mounted on her bathroom mirror to which she directed sensual glances and sometimes pressed a lipstick kiss.

He didn't seem much changed from when she had known him five years earlier in Prague, except for a few added pounds that his undernourished frame could handle. Dark eyes with incredibly long, thick lashes reflected that same dreamy look and the familiar flicker of light she remembered, small as the flame of a birthday candle. She had never been quite sure from where that tiny glow originated and what it meant—excitement, anticipation, happiness at being alive, love of the music he was capable of making, or what? He had seemed to experience every emotion more profoundly than she did. He was more readily aroused and more quickly pleased, as if his nerve endings were quivering and exposed, waiting to be assaulted and gratified. But she herself could never permit her emotions to be so exposed, so vulnerable. If one didn't care too much, nothing would hurt too much. She had learned that years before, and she never forgot it.

She and Daniel had known each other for a brief but passionate month after she had gone with her friends to Prague. Her vindictive Aunt Marie had thrown her out of their apartment in the old city. She was living on her own and supporting herself, as her friends did, with whatever music gigs came their way and trying, on a daily basis, not to starve to death.

She was barely sixteen, and he was a couple of years older. Daniel was a skinny kid from Israel with a huge musical talent that she recognized more than he did. His vitality and eagerness attracted her from the beginning. He seemed younger than he was, behaving as if the whole world was waiting to be discovered and experienced by him. His parents, devout Orthodox Jews who lived by the admonitions of the Torah, had tightly controlled his life in Israel. They had built thoroughly structured lives around their only son as soon as they recognized his startling precocity when he was three years old. He had lived an isolated and protected life, the center of their hopes and dreams. He was to study very hard, with no distractions and the best teachers they could afford until, with luck, a rich patron would discover him and help him go to New York to finish his studies and become a concert artist— one of the best.

The master plan collapsed when his father died at thirty-eight, suddenly and shockingly, from encephalitis. His unworldly mother was left with Daniel and two younger daughters to support without the means of doing so. She had never worked outside her home and rarely left it except to attend synagogue or shop at the market. She turned to Daniel. He was now the head of the household and must take charge. She would do whatever he decided. He tried, bravely, but he was as unworldly as she was. His father had firmly controlled every aspect of their lives and made every decision. Eventually his mother decided that he needed to leave Israel, at least temporarily, to find work in other cities with active music centers. She let him go with tears and lamentations, praying for hours on end.

In Prague, his path crossed Ana's, and she was instantly attracted to him because he was so funny in enthusiasm appropriate for a much younger person. A Ferris wheel? What was that? Could they ride on one? He never had. Movies, rock concerts, dances—they were all new experiences for him that his father had mostly forbidden in his past. He was out early every morning, alone or with Ana, exploring the city's high and low spots, meeting strange new people, talking eagerly to everyone he met, savoring exotic foods, or riding streetcars to unknown destinations. And if they got lost, so much the better. It was more fun.

They laughed a lot and had a fine time, pooling their limited money for food and fun and their rented space at the youth hostel. It was the first time either of them had been in love, and they were like a couple of spring blossoms, frolicking in the breeze in a delicious, liberating, intoxicating freedom that neither of them had known before.

The halcyon interlude ended abruptly. His mother wired him that they were about to lose their modest home because she couldn't make the payments on it. He must come back and take charge. She was totally unable to help herself or her children. She spent her days praying and weeping, neither of which helped. Sadly, with tears in his eyes, clinging to Ana, he bid her *au revoir* and promised her, "We will meet again."

After a perilous year, his luck changed. The aging violin virtuoso Phillipe Breton, who wanted to retire but longed for a protégé to nurture to take his place, discovered Daniel playing with a small orchestra in Tel Aviv. Within weeks, Daniel was shipped off to New York for accelerated study with Breton, followed by admission to Juilliard and four more years of arduous study. He made his sensational debut at Carnegie Hall, followed immediately by a contract with Olympia Artists Management and performances scheduled with the London, Berlin, Chicago, Philadelphia, and Hong Kong symphony orchestras. His sheltered life changed overnight and became supercharged, electric. His new celebrity transformed him.

Daniel and Ana lost track of one another, and all she knew of him then was what she read in the newspapers. She often wondered if he remembered those intoxicating weeks in Prague. Probably not. She guessed that he now ran with the

Beautiful People and that he would remember her, if at all, as a pale moth among the butterflies.

She sighed but then giggled out loud when she recalled his wild careening over the streets of Prague when he had discovered rented roller skates. He went off at full speed, jumping curbs, missing pedestrians by inches, slowing down by grabbing at light poles as he passed them, and calling to her, "Follow me!" He laughed wildly at his near misses, sometimes singing at full voice and eventually, in exhaustion, collapsing headlong on whatever grass was available. He had joyfully survived roller skating, another first for him, but she imagined that now he rode in black limousines, guarded by a stern minder, a chaperone of sorts, hired by his manager to protect and assist him, but to control him as well.

She folded the flier carefully, stuffed it into the small back pocket of her leather skirt, and returned to relaxing with the sun on her face. A husky male voice whispered into her ear, "Hello, doll face. I've got something nice for you." Reluctantly, she opened her eyes.

It was Tommy, one of the stagehands, with a scruffy cigarette dangling from his moist lips and one hand behind his back. She smiled at him, and he brought his hand around to offer her a greasy paper bag containing half of a frosted doughnut. She was hungry, as usual, having had nothing for breakfast so she took the doughnut and finished it in two bites, licking her lips afterward.

He said, "I thought I could save a whole one for you, but those guys ate them like a bunch of pigs. Want a smoke?"

She held out her hand, and he gave her a hand-rolled cigarette and lit it for her. She gave him a teasing glance. "Only you, Tommy, bring me these good things. But don't get yourself in trouble."

He shrugged, "No sweat."

As generous as he was to her, she found his personal appearance distasteful, his stringy hair unkempt over a dingy T-shirt that was too shrunken to cover a fleshy roll of fat that bulged over the belt that barely held up his greasy blue jeans. She realized that he wasn't devoted to the idea of daily baths, either, and she hoped he wouldn't begin to expect a greater show of appreciation from her for his little gifts. She moved away slightly.

"Hey, Annie," he said, "tell me something." He drew a crumpled page from the morning newspaper from his pocket and spread it out over his hand. "This guy that's coming here, the violinist they're making such a fuss about? I've been readin' about him and his fiddle. So how come it's worth such big bucks and all? What makes it so much better that yours? Looks exactly the same in the picture."

She was irritated that he wouldn't leave her in peace for the few minutes remaining of the break. She didn't feel like listening to his stupid chatter. She kept her eyes shut and turned her head slowly from side to side in the sunshine, so her long hair with the least bit of curl at its ends brushed across her shoulders in a way that felt sensual and pleasing. She opened her eyes slightly to see that Tommy was still there and waiting for her answer. Well, fair was fair. She replied in a monotone that rose barely above a whisper, "Because, Tommy, it's a Guarneri. One of the finest instruments ever made. You see?"

"Yeah, yeah, I got all that from readin' the paper," Tommy said. "But what I'm askin' is *why* it's so much better? What makes it worth all that dough? Why don't they just make a bunch more just like it?"

She sighed. He was so hopeless. "Well, Tommy, it's like this. A long time ago there were three Italian families, Stradivarius, Guarneri, and Amati. They called them 'master violin makers.' They had their secrets, and they took them to the grave. Lots of people have tried to equal their work and they still try, but so far, no one has come very close. Naturally, every serious musician dreams of having such an instrument, but there are only a few left in this world. They are priceless, better than gold or diamonds because you can always get more of those. Daniel Lessing has a Guarneri, but on loan only. Not really his, you see?"

"Secrets like what? Couldn't other guys learn to do it, whatever it was, and make a friggin' fortune?"

She sighed deeply. He was like a pesky child with his stupid questions, but she wasn't quite ready to brush him off. "Many people have had this idea, Tommy, but making a fine instrument is very complicated and calls for a special talent. It's not as simple as building a cabinet and stretching strings over it. It takes about eighty pieces of wood of many kinds, some not so available now, and a special glue they made for themselves. Nobody has been able to figure that out, either. A good soloist, on his way to the top, will mortgage his life for an instrument like that if he can find one, because it will make his career."

"Criminy, it must make a guy nervous to carry something like that around!"

"They never let it out of their sight. It becomes like another arm, goes everywhere with them."

From the corner of her eye, she spotted the violist Emily Murphy drifting around the corner of the building, looking innocent but watching them and sniffing the air for any telltale aroma. *Well, hello there, Fat Emily.* she thought. *Out for a little spying for your boyfriend?* Ana's eyes hardened, and she looked the other way.

"Gotta go, Tommy," she laughed mischievously. "Thanks for the chewing gum." She escaped to the rehearsal hall, hoping she had annoyed Emily, who was always hanging around the manager like a little toady.

It was during the last half-hour of the rehearsal that she became aware of two people seated at the back of the darkened auditorium where the lighted exit sign gave off a dull, red glow. After a few moments, she had the eerie feeling that they were watching her or someone seated near her on stage. The man appeared to be concentrating on the music, his head bent forward. He wore his fair hair in a short brush-cut, military style, and gold-rimmed glasses reflected the stage lighting whenever he turned his head toward his companion. He wore dark trousers and a white shirt open at the neck.

From this distance, the girl at his side appeared to be much younger, almost child-like. She wore a T-shirt with some kind of an emblem on its front and a baseball cap perched on a mass of wildly kinky red hair. She held some kind of folder or portfolio supported against the seat in front of her. At the next interruption in the rehearsal, Ana studied them more closely and realized that the girl was sketching on a large paper pad.

Ah, she thought, *publicity or promotion people.* She lost interest.

The rehearsal came to an end, and she was outside walking toward the parking lot where her aging Renault had begun dripping oil on the pavement. Suddenly, the girl was walking with her, keeping step, side-by-side. The man with her had stopped at a little distance and seemed preoccupied with lighting up a cigarette.

"Hi," the girl said cheerfully, blocking Ana's passage. It was now easy to see that the black lettering on the girl's shirt read "Salzburg Festival," with two violins crossed artistically in the center. The girl was petite, but up close, Ana could see that she was not a child. She had tiny lines at the corners of light-blue eyes that reflected an anxious look, and a small frown made a crease between reddish eyebrows. She seemed nervous, blinking her blue eyes repeatedly. She held out a freckled hand. "I'm Beth Godwin. Hope you don't mind if I was sketching you? You play well. My husband and I just love the orchestra. Here." She thrust a sheet of sketching paper toward Ana. "It's for you."

Ana was wary, but she accepted the sketch and was surprised to find it a very good likeness. It was the first time anyone had ever sketched her. The girl was clever and had a definite talent. It was certainly Ana, in profile, her long brown hair falling across cheek where it caught the light, her head bent into the chin-rest of her instrument on her left shoulder. The chiaroscuro of shadow and light gave the sketch three intriguing dimensions. Ana checked to make sure that her bow was held correctly with her wrist unbent and level with her arm. Yes, very good. The artist had captured a faraway, veiled look in her eyes.

Ana was flattered and impressed with the accuracy of the artist's interpretation. Also, it was obvious that Beth knew a good deal about music and musicians. "Thank you so much," Ana said. "It's quite good. I may really keep it?"

"Of course. You make a pretty subject, and it was fun to do it."

Ana rolled up the sketch and held it lightly under her arm. She held out her free hand. "My name is Ana. Ana Iliescu . . . Breckenridge." *For now,* she thought.

Beth shook hands and looked behind her for her husband who hadn't approached them but held his head turned toward them. Ana had the distinct impression that he was listening to every word of their conversation and that the girl knew this and expected it.

Beth pursed her lips and blinked rapidly. "Well, look," she

said, "my husband and I love classical music, and we often play quartets, just for pleasure." She made a little face and wrinkled her nose. "We're amateurs, but we're not too bad. Right now, we're short a violin. Would you be interested in potluck dinner and quartets tonight at our place? It's not far from here, and we'd be pleased to have you."

Ana hesitated. She didn't know them. The girl seemed likeable, but the man turned her off. He seemed arrogant and rude. "Sorry," she said. "Maybe some other time."

"But . . . " Beth looked toward her husband and shook her head very slightly, and he quickly joined them. "Hello. I'm Karl Godwin. We like your orchestra very much." He held out his hand.

Coolly, she shook his hand. *It's not my orchestra, and I wonder what you want?* Ana thought.

"You don't know us," he said, "but we're just harmless music lovers like yourself." His voice was slightly accented, and she tried to place it. German? Austrian? Swiss? "We admire your playing, but we also respect your privacy, *ja*? If you say no, then of course it is no. But the truth is, my little *hausfrau* here believes that she makes the best spaghetti in the world." He shrugged, smiling at Ana. "Well, it's not bad, either. Myself, I eat it often. Won't you change your mind and join us?"

She hesitated. The mental image of a large steaming plate of spaghetti coated with grated cheese made her stomach rumble. She had eaten nothing all day except the half doughnut Tommy had given her that morning. She survived each day at the edge of hunger, and there were no groceries left in her apartment except three shriveled onions, from which she had hoped to make soup that evening.

She avoided eye contact with Karl because she felt an instinctive distrust of the man. But perhaps he was harmless and it was his cold personality that repulsed her. *But he's clever,* Ana sensed, *and he wants something from me. I wonder what?*

"Oh, do come," Beth coaxed. "I've made an apple strudel."

Ana couldn't help smiling at her childlike enthusiasm, and Beth grinned widely in return. She was hard to resist. Karl did not smile but watched Ana intently.

She shrugged. What could it hurt? "Okay, I come," she said. "Where is your place, and what time?" Beth handed her a map, already drawn on a scrap of paper.

She turned and walked toward her sagging automobile, hoping that it would start. She had bought it, her first car of her own, after arriving from Texas with only a little bit of money and with her limited wardrobe rolled into a duffel bag. After she had bought the car, she drove slowly after shopping hours to the supermarket parking lot to practice, with trembling hands, the few driving skills Jerry had begun teaching her. Eventually she passed the driving test, barely, and received her license. She was so proud.

She realized later that two hundred dollars was not nearly enough to buy a dependable car, but it was almost every penny she had and Renault was the only name she recognized. This time she was lucky and the motor turned over after only three tries.

As she pulled slowly out of the parking lot, she noticed that the Godwin couple remained seated in their dark blue sedan, but the car was not moving out. She watched them in her rearview mirror and was only slightly surprised to see that they were watching her.

Back at her small apartment over her landlady's garage, she practiced her music for several hours, took a shower, and dressed in the floral miniskirt and yellow knit shirt that Jerry had bought for her in Frankfurt before their flight to the States.

The Godwin apartment was located over a dress shop that closed at six in the evening. Stairs at the back of the building led to a door painted bright blue and surrounded by pots of scarlet impatiens swinging slowly in a light, salty breeze floating in from the bay. The door flew open before she could knock.

"I can always hear footsteps coming up," Beth said, laughing. "Come in, come in!"

She hugged Ana quickly and impulsively before drawing back and folding her arms across the chest, as though she needed to restrain her enthusiasm. *She's lonely,* Ana guessed.

Karl rose from his chair by the large front window with a fine view of the bay and all the fishing boats coming in before darkness fell. "Hello, again," he greeted Ana. "Welcome! What may I get for you? Wine? Beer? Iced tea?"

She chose red wine, as did Beth, but Karl drank dark frothy beer from a German-style pewter tankard with colorful pictures and a hinged lid on it. "Our violist is on his way," he said. "Name of Martin Hammett. He's a good musician, and we feel lucky when he will play with us. He played with the Boston Symphony before he retired out here."

Ana raised respectful eyebrows. "But that's very fine!"

On the heels of this accolade, Martin arrived. He was an older man with pale skin, silky silver hair, and gentle blue eyes. He wore a white shirt and tie with a brown corduroy vest buttoned under his tweed jacket. They talked about his years with the Boston Symphony while Beth made trips to the kitchen and finished laying the small table in the alcove. After a while, Karl stood abruptly and said, "Perhaps she needs my help." He disappeared into the kitchen, and then his angry voice reverberated clearly through the swinging door.

"This is mush! I told you *al dente!* Is there nothing you can do correctly?"

The sound of the garbage disposal being turned on didn't cover Beth's wail of distress. "Karl, no, no, no! There's no more pasta left to cook!"

"Hopeless! You are hopeless!" he said angrily. "And you never learn!"

Martin and Ana exchanged embarrassed smiles. She thought that this spaghetti might be more trouble than it was worth, but she was not a gourmet cook and food was food, especially if it filled all the empty corners. She had certainly eaten many worse meals at her Aunt Marie's flat in that socialist state under such a ruthless dictator, where food supplies were tightly controlled.

Karl returned with a cold smile and hard eyes. "Just a few minutes more," he said. He began sorting the sheet music that was laid out on a small table, handing some sheets to Martin and some to Ana, to whom he said, "You, of course, must play the first part, and I'll play second with Beth on her cello."

Beth looked flushed and nervous when she bustled into the room with four plates of green salad and again with rolls and butter. She set the bottle of chianti Martin had brought on a hammered aluminum trivet at Karl's place. They moved to the table.

Ana thought that the spaghetti was delicious and she ate a generous second helping, which pleased Beth. If the pasta was a bit overcooked, no matter, because the sauce was rich with the color and flavor of fresh tomatoes, mushrooms, and herbs. Karl picked at his serving and pushed the plate aside while ignoring Beth and talking only to Martin and Ana, who decided that he was insufferable and a total boor.

Dinner finished with the apple strudel that was dark and fragrant with cinnamon and nutmeg and covered with real cream that Ana savored. She resisted the impulse to lick the excess from her lips instead of using her napkin. She helped

Beth clear up and tried to ignore the tears in the girl's eyes. She touched Beth's shoulder lightly in passing.

When the kitchen was tidy, they joined the men. Ana and Martin took their instruments from their cases and began to tune, while Karl went to a closet between the dining alcove and the bedroom. He pulled the alcove door nearly shut behind him, but the breeze coming in through the large front window blew it slowly open again. He had drawn a chain and key from his pocket to open the closet door. Along the wall was a rack of suspended bows with the tension of their horsehair carefully released.

Karl returned to the living room, carrying a violin case and two bows. He sat down and began tightening one of the bows. Ana was fascinated. Her mother had taught her many fine points about music-making. She leaned toward Karl and asked, "Isn't that a Tourte bow?" She bent forward to look at it closely and decided that it must surely be one made by Francis Tourte, the early nineteenth-century designer of the modern bow.

But as she put out her hand for it, he withdrew it quickly and stood up. "Sorry! I shouldn't have brought it out," he said. "It belongs to my uncle, and I must be very careful with it." He returned it to its place in the closet and closed the door.

He began tightening his second bow. "Shall we begin with Beethoven?"

The music went well, and the four of them enjoyed playing together because they were well-matched. Ana was surprised to discover that both Karl and Beth were accomplished musicians.

At 10:30 P.M., Martin looked at his watch and said, "Time for me to go. Sorry."

Ana also packed up and followed Martin outside to the landing at the top of the stairs. As Martin descended ahead of her, Karl came up closely behind her and grasped her upper arm, stopping her where she was. Martin moved on down and got into his car.

"Ana, wait a moment, please," Karl said. "I want to talk to you. You will play with us again tomorrow night, *ja*?"

She had already made up her mind against that. A free dinner couldn't compensate for his behavior, and she was not comfortable around him. She didn't like his type. "Sorry," she said, "I will be busy."

But he tightened his grip on her arm and bent closer to watch her face intently. His eyes had the strange appearance of having light behind them, and for a moment, she was afraid of him. It seemed as if his eyes were impaling her to the wall. She pulled her arm free.

"No, no," he said. "You *must* come. There is something very interesting we will talk about." He moved toward her and again took her arm, holding it firmly so she couldn't get away. "This is a great opportunity I'm talking about. A way to make our lives better. You will see. We musicians have to watch for such opportunities. Is this not so?"

"Some other time. Please excuse me," she said. "I must go now."

His face was inches from hers. His voice grew soft. "Look," he said. "I know the life of a musician. It is not an easy one. And I know a bit about you and your poor little car that won't start and your one-room apartment over a garage." He shook her arm a bit. "Can we not consider a good investment now and then? Shall I call you?"

She was alarmed that he knew so much about her. "How do you know where I live? And my telephone number?" She pulled her arm free and stared at him.

The moving light from Martin's car flashed briefly over the lenses of Karl's gold-rimmed glasses so that his eyes glittered.

He laughed and said, "Oh, I asked Tommy Barger for a list of musicians who might like to play quartets with us, and he gave me the orchestra roster from the bulletin board backstage." He smiled slyly. "Nice fellow, that Barger."

"Goodnight," she said. "Thanks for the spaghetti." She hurried down the steps to her car.

Chapter Three

THE NEXT MORNING, a Saturday, Noelle Wright awakened early and crawled out of bed with reluctance. How she dreaded the chore that she knew she had to accomplish before another day passed. There were several reasons that she couldn't pass it off to anyone else, principally because the matter was all her own doing, and now she had to see it through to its unfortunate ending.

She showered and finished off with an icy-cold rinse to wake up fully and to build her moral fortitude, in the event that might work. Noelle dressed carefully, as she always did, choosing an avocado-green silk dress with a matching jacket. She brushed her short, dark hair until it settled down in soft waves around her head and would cause her no more trouble for the rest of the day.

She ate quickly in her sunny kitchen, enjoying half of an ice-cold cantaloupe, followed by hot tea and toast. Then she was out of the house and on her way with the wrapped parcel on the car seat beside her like a softly ticking time bomb. She put her handbag on top of it so it wouldn't lurk in her line of vision and let her car coast down the long curve of her driveway. At the bottom, she pressed the brake, as she always did, to look up the hill at her home of white bricks, Spanish hacienda-style, with a red tile roof and a crimson door half hidden behind the lush greenery she loved. Overhead, the sky was so bright and clear that it looked like a watercolorist with a wide brush had begun the day with a generous wash of pure cobalt blue from horizon to horizon and hadn't disturbed it with even a whisper of a cloud.

She followed her usual route into San Sebastian, driving about a mile out of her way to travel along gracefully winding lanes of the university campus with its stately buildings, also mostly white with red tile roofs. Water sprinklers swished softly to and fro at that hour to refresh acres of dark green lawn and symmetric beds of red and blue salvia, marigolds, white daisies, and roses of every variation of color. The campus was like a second home to her because she had spent some of the most satisfying years of her life there, first as an eager undergraduate from Seattle, then as a graduate student, a doctoral candidate in music, and, finally, an associate professor on the music faculty.

She had taught Music Appreciation and Introduction to Music Composition to first- and second-year students year after year. But a full professorship still tantalized, out of reach it seemed, for the foreseeable future. After five years of teaching the basic structure of symphony, opera, and chamber music—and the meaning of such terms as tonality, augmentation, suspension, and harmonic change—she came to realize that beyond hoping to give her students a lifelong appreciation of classical music, nothing much else ever came of her efforts. From having been exhilarated by the challenge of her work, she found herself becoming depressed by the recurring thought, *Is this all there is?*

Soft and fragrant morning air drifted across her open car

windows as she drove slowly past the Music and Arts Complex. She could identify several cars already in the parking lot. They belonged to special friends who had urged her to reject the initial offer when she had received it from Hammersmith Music Publishers in London and New York. After hours of internal debate and no little trepidation, she had gone against all their advice and had accepted the offer. She had not regretted it, but she sensed that her former colleagues had not really forgiven her for jumping ship.

The fact was, for the past decade the university's elite music faculty had attracted an important and rapidly developing cadre of active composers—young and old, European, Asian, and American—who were drawn to each other and to the university's reputation for encouraging new composers. Because compositions of merit were forthcoming at an astonishing rate and fledgling composers fed on the rich mutual creativity in the area, Hammersmith had decided to open a satellite office in San Sebastian. They wanted someone to head this office who could keep in personal touch with the evolving talents of these brilliant young composers, keep watch for promising new works, negotiate contracts, and promote premiere performances of these works. The publishers felt that they had been too much at a distance, with no sensitive finger on the area's creative pulse, and that they were missing out on too much new composition of consequence, including a modern opera about the fall of the U.S.S.R., ready for its premiere in London under the auspices of a rival publishing house.

When Noelle had decided to accept Hammersmith's offer, she requested and was granted an indefinite leave of absence from the university to begin another career. Almost from the beginning, she experienced intense gratification. She was stimulated to find herself taking part in the discovery process, helping it move along, and being genuinely on the "cutting edge," where what she did and said made a real difference. When the process reached its ultimate goal and there was actually a premiere performance, she knew that she had played an integral part in much of the success, and she felt a profound sense of pride and accomplishment. She wondered how she could ever relinquish that work. An unexpected bonus of her new career had been meeting Avery and falling in love for the first time in her life.

All of her pleasant nostalgia came to an abrupt end at the southern perimeter of the campus, where peace and quiet underwent an instant change into four congested lanes of fast-moving and aggressive traffic. As she waited at the signal for streams of students to make their way across the crosswalk, she glanced again at the parcel on the seat beside her, and her spirits took a rapid drop into negative territory.

Since she had resolved to bring closure to the matter at hand, she hoped that Ryan Marshall, General Manager of the San Sebastian Symphony and novice composer, hadn't forgotten their meeting scheduled for 9:00 A.M.

In fact, Ryan waited in his office, feeling both resentful and frustrated. Because none of his small staff worked on Saturdays, he felt free to open the top button of his shirt and tug at a beige silk tie patterned with tiny black treble clefs, loosening its knot so it tumbled free over the vest of a beige suit. Being properly dressed at all times was a rule he seldom violated, because he saw his appearance as an important part of a professional image that the musicians would respect. A tacky blue jeans-and-sweatshirt wardrobe and yesterday's unshaved whiskers were not for him.

He ran his hand through sandy hair that was rumpled from its usual controlled and parted style until it fell across his forehead, covering a ferocious frown. The totals he pulled up on his computer frightened him. He *must* have made a mistake somewhere. He pressed Delete and fed the figures in again, but the totals appeared exactly as they had before. He squinted at the screen, blinked several times, and ran his hand across his closed eyes, fighting to maintain composure. He knew it wasn't too smart to keep this disk in his office, but it was marked, clearly and in red, "personal and confidential." He felt sure that no one on his loyal staff would touch it.

He had added these new figures to an already-negative balance: Vegas, -$12,542; South Lake Tahoe, -$5,500; Golden Gate Fields, -$4,367. He closed his eyes and mentally recited every good-luck mantra that came to mind before he pressed the Final Total button. He flinched in pain at what he saw. He felt sick.

He pressed the Print button for four copies and sat with his eyes closed as they emerged from the printer. For the first time, he began to experience cold fear in his belly. How had he let it get away from him to this extent? Why hadn't he had the self-discipline to stop when he was winning and was even a little bit ahead? But that was it, you never stopped when you were winning. Any gambling fool knew that, because there was sure to be an even bigger win hovering in wait out there if he only kept pushing ahead.

The clock showed four minutes before nine. He devoutly wished that he hadn't made an appointment to meet with Noelle Wright. On top of everything else, he had received another letter the day before from his mother, laying on the guilt trip. His father wasn't well. The burden of the factory was becoming too much for him. Was Ryan thinking of coming home any time soon, where he belonged? He was needed at home.

Why, why couldn't they understand?

He stared glumly out the window at the nearly empty parking lot just as Noelle's pale blue Mercedes turned the corner, right on time, as she always was. Too late now to call and put her off.

Tightening the knot of his tie and brushing his hair back, he made a bet with himself that she would park exactly between two white lines, although his car was the only one in the parking lot and she could park any crooked way she darn well pleased. He won his bet, but the victory offered no consolation because there was no money in it.

Brooding, he watched her get out of her car and pick up the parcel from the car seat. From its size, he guessed that it contained his manuscript. Was the fact that she was returning it a good or bad sign? He heard the confident click of her heels on the polished ceramic tiles of the hallway, and then the outer door of the office complex opened and closed quietly. She tapped lightly and put her head around his door.

"Ryan?" she called.

He kept his head down as if he was absorbed in the paperwork in front of him, and after a moment, he looked up as if surprised. "Oh, good morning! Come in, come in."

He couldn't have explained why he made her wait, even for a brief moment, because he liked her. She was unfailingly considerate and patient, willing to hear his side of any controversy, and there always seemed to be enough of those. He was convinced that artistic people functioned with short fuses. Still, making her wait in person or on the telephone gave him the feeling of being in control, and he needed that. She never seemed to notice this quirk of his. Or if she did, she forgave him without comment.

"So what shall we do first?" he asked. "The financial statement or the checks?" Without looking directly at it, he noticed the parcel where she had placed it on the corner of the desk.

"Oh, let's do the checks first." She took a tiny gold pen

from her bag and set to work, countersigning his checks after carefully studying each attached check request and turning the signed checks face down in a neat stack. "Now," she said and smiled at him. "How about the financial statement? Are we doing as well as you hoped, Ryan?"

He picked up the folder marked "financial statements," took one copy for himself, and handed the folder to her.

She studied it with a small frown, tapping her pen lightly on the desk. "Well," she said, smiling again to soften the criticism. "It's better, but the gap is still there, isn't it? We're still fighting that big, ugly deficit."

He leaned forward earnestly and placed his hands flat on the desk in front of him. "But the Daniel Lessing concert is going to solve all that! With higher prices and a full house, we can turn this around, and we're almost there! Audiences are truly eager to hear him, and we were darned lucky to get him on his way up, because we won't be able to afford him next season."

She looked thoughtful but said nothing, and they reviewed the remainder of the line items, including membership contributions, which were also well below his optimistic projection. She bit her lower lip at that but again said nothing more than "hmmm."

He decided it was a good time to change the subject. "Is that my manuscript? I'm sure you can guess that I'm on pins and needles . . ."

She drew a deep breath that became a long sigh. She reached for the parcel, placed it in front of her, and crossed her hands over it. "Ryan," she began, "first of all, I realize that it was my idea that you submit now and not work on it any longer. I felt that five years was sufficient for you to realize your vision of it, and working it over and over would only destroy its freshness and spontaneity. I still feel that this was the right decision." She paused and tapped her fingers on the parcel.

His high hopes began to spiral downward because she had not said, "Congratulations!" That was the word he had been waiting to hear.

"I want you to know," she continued, "that I pressed very hard on your behalf, and the five of us spent a good deal of time evaluating your work. We found much to admire, Ryan, truly. It's a nice concerto. Nicely developed. Unfortunately, however," she broke eye contact to glance down at her folded hands on the parcel, "it isn't *exactly* what Hammersmith is looking for right now." She raised her eyes again to meet his stricken gaze. "They suggest that you offer it to other publishers, and I can certainly help you there. I'll write you another cover letter . . ."

He was no longer listening. What a bitter disappointment! Slowly, she pushed the manuscript toward him. He couldn't bring himself to say anything over the tightness in his throat. He had worked so incredibly hard on it for years, and he felt it was the best he had to offer. He had truly believed that it had promise. What was wrong? Had they thought it should be shorter? Longer? Was the cadenza for solo violin too difficult? Not difficult enough? Would they talk to him about it? Was that done?

With a numb, dreamlike feeling, he removed the parcel from its Hammersmith wrapping and stared down at it, as if he was seeing it for the first time. Before submitting it, in pride of authorship, he'd had it bound in calfskin with its title—*Concerto No. 1 for Violin and Orchestra*—imprinted in gold letters above his name in italic caps. Now he knew that all that expense had been foolish and extravagant. It was only the composition they were interested in, and the gold imprint indicated nothing but vanity.

"Ryan," she said gently, "you mustn't be discouraged," but she soon realized that he was too depressed to listen to reason. She rose, came around the desk, pressed his shoulder with warmth, and left his office, closing the door softly behind her.

His shoulders drooped, and he dropped his head forward into his hands. The telephone began to ring, and he let it go over to the answering machine. Without opening his eyes or caring very much, he heard Emily's voice say, "I want to talk to you, Ryan. This is Emily. May I come to your apartment after rehearsal? Please call me." The line went dead.

He groaned inwardly. *Ah, Emily, my orchestra spy and informer!* he thought. Why had he ever begun this with her? Once, over cups of coffee she had urged him to share with her, he had asked her a few questions about other orchestra members that were—to be honest—improper and prying. He'd heard a rumor about a principal wind player who was planning to audition for another orchestra, and he needed to know if it was true so he could sidetrack that with a little personal talk, an offer of a bit more salary over scale, or whatever it took to hold onto him. There was nothing illegal about any of this, and it was done all the time. Union rules prevented paying a player under the contracted pay scale, but there was no restriction on paying above that amount if the musician was valuable enough and could negotiate it. But it was unethical to pump Emily for information on her colleagues. However, she had taken on this role with enthusiasm, hoping to please him, and she gave him reports on a regular basis.

He didn't really care who was romancing whom, or if some of them were smoking a little pot on their own time. That was none of his affair. The entire matter left a bad taste in his mouth, plus a guilty conscience that made him dislike Emily. Anyway, she wasn't his type. He admired sleek, delicate blondes with long legs and a certain insouciance and *joie de vivre.* Emily seemed so solemn and earnest, and she wore blouses with fluffy ruffles and gathered skirts with gaudy flowers that made her appear round, pudgy, and sexless.

Ryan knew he would have to be a fool not to recognize that Emily was attracted to him. Every time he turned around, there she was. Well, that was her problem. His head was beginning to throb, and he still had the afternoon rehearsal to get through. He didn't return Emily's call, but he knew that she would be after him at rehearsal like a mosquito on a sultry night.

The rehearsal went smoothly and well. At the break, Ana went outside hoping that Tommy would come by with his cigarettes, but he didn't appear. When she returned to the backstage area, she heard his voice in the cubbyhole office set aside for the stagehands' use. The door was nearly closed, and Ana couldn't see who else was in the office, but the two of them were laughing together.

At the end of the rehearsal, exiting the stage, she nearly ran into Tommy, who was waiting for her, smelling of beer and stale sweat. "Annie," he whispered, grasping her arm, "your friend Karl has been looking for you. He's waiting in our office. What a great guy he is! He's real interested in how us guys work back here, and he brought us a six-pack of cold beer."

Annoyed, she pulled her arm free and stopped in her tracks, so the other musicians, eyeing her curiously, had to detour around her. *How stupid Tommy is,* she thought indignantly. *That Karl is no friend of mine! Why does he keep bothering me?*

The door to the stagehands' office flew open, and Karl appeared. With a quick smile, he said, "Hello there, Ana! How good to see you!" He moved toward her with an outstretched hand, but she nodded and brushed past him, hurrying through the exit and outside. He followed closely behind her.

"Ana," he said, "please wait a moment. We want you to come tonight for dinner and more quartets. How about it? Beth says it's tenderloin of beef, new baby potatoes, and fresh corn. What do you think? Are you feeling hungry?"

She opened the door to her car and put her violin in its case on the back seat, maneuvering herself into the driver's seat after smoothing down the patch in the ragged upholstery. Karl leaned closer, his head almost through the window by her side. "Ana, what do you say, eh?"

"Sorry, no. I'm busy tonight."

He put both hands on the open window. "But you can change that, right? Beth says it's Bavarian chocolate torte for dessert. My favorite!"

If he wouldn't back off, she thought, she would simply drive away and leave him standing there. She pressed on the starter. Nothing. She pressed again. Not the slightest buzz. "Oh . . . " she moaned. "Oh, no. It won't work."

Was he smiling slyly at this? She was filled with frustration and anger. He opened her door, looking sorry about the car. "Well," he said, "imagine that! So now you must come with me because your poor little car won't go."

She didn't move but sat glaring at him. He reached into the back and picked up her violin. "Don't be so angry, Ana. I can help you. I know a good deal about cars. Lock it up and leave it here. I'll come back tomorrow, and perhaps I can fix it. Come, now, and have a nice dinner with us."

She was trapped and she knew it. What choice did she have? Reluctantly, she did as he suggested, and they drove off in silence toward the Godwin apartment.

Dinner was a delight to the last bite. Beth was a fine cook, Ana decided, and she wondered how she could return to her own sparse meals. Karl paid his wife no compliments, and his only comment was that the tenderloin of beef could have used more herbs.

Afterward, they played some Beethoven quartets. They were always among the most difficult to play but also the most satisfying for accomplished musicians. This was music that reached their deepest emotions, and to those who could conquer the quartets, they were the greatest of instrumental works. All four of them were uplifted by their own playing, enriched by it, and made happier for an hour or so.

When they had finished, they smiled at each other, still under the spell of the music. As they gathered up their things, Martin said, "I'll drive Ana home. It's on my way."

Karl was taken aback. "No, no," he said. "I will drive her. We have some things to discuss."

She looked from one man to the other, confused by this exchange.

Martin took Ana's arm—his first personal contact with her. "No," he said quietly. "*I* will take her."

Ana smiled at Beth as she found Martin propelling her toward the door. "Thank you for another wonderful meal!" she said.

They moved down the steps, and Martin opened his car door for her. As she moved into his car, she glanced upward to the landing of the Godwins' apartment where Karl still stood, frowning. He held his arms crossed in front of him and his head down. Every inch of his body indicated suppressed fury. They drove off.

After some small talk, Martin said, "I've really enjoyed making music with you, Ana. You've been well-trained. You know, I must tell you that you remind me very much of my wife." He laughed slightly, an embarrassed sound. "My first wife. I've had two, both musicians. Helena was about your age when we met. A fine cellist."

Ana didn't know how to reply, so she remained silent. After a few more blocks, Martin asked, "Do you like to go to the movies, Ana?"

"Oh, yes, I adore American movies, but I don't go to very many because I don't spend the money for that."

He nodded. After a long pause, he said, "Would you care to go see a movie with me sometime?"

She was startled. *But he's so much older!* Then she realized he was another lonely person, like herself. *There are so many of us in the world, just trudging through our lives, trying to make some sense of it all. All we want, all of us, is to make a close, personal connection with another human being. Just one is all we need.*

Movies with Martin? Well, why not? "That would be very nice," she said. But she had waited just a few moments too long, and she sensed his withdrawal back into himself. Stopped at a signal, he tapped the steering wheel with his forefinger, lost in thought. Finally he said, "Well, we'll do that sometime. I'll call you." But she knew that he never would.

Chapter Four

BACKSTAGE, THE LAST of the musicians had packed up and cleared out quickly. Only Emily remained in the shadows to watch and wait for Ryan, but he saw her first and took a quick detour through the Green Room and into the backstage area. There the stagehands were already disassembling the acoustic shell to clear the stage for a Sunday ballet performance. He watched as they maneuvered the enormous sections on their giant casters so that what had been a solid enclosure on stage was separated into component parts for easier storage. Each section was approximately thirty feet in height and eight feet across. To improve their acoustic properties, they had been designed with irregularly placed baffles like oversized shelves arranged randomly across their faces, which gave them the appearance of enormous window boxes.

Once, listening to a lagging rehearsal, Ryan had idly amused himself by imagining that he had the power of a mighty giant and therefore could deposit certain difficult individuals like rag dolls, with their feet swinging in the air, into whatever boxes he chose, giving them the order to "just stay there until I tell you to come down." This delighted him and he laughed out loud, but it wasn't a vision he dared share with anyone.

A hydraulic lift raised and lowered the huge roof of the shell, and it required four stagehands to maneuver it into place or to lift it. In back, a ladder provided access to the outside roof of the shell. There the stagehands scrambled up and down with what seemed to be utter recklessness while they held the railing with one hand and carried tools and equipment with the other.

From the corner of his eye, Ryan spotted Emily approaching. "Ryan?" she called.

He moved instantly toward her and on past, saying, "Not here. I'll call you."

But when he finally reached his apartment, she was there ahead of him, leaning against his door with her viola case at her feet. Her eyes brightened. She smiled sweetly.

He felt a moment of intense, heated irritation. *Would she never give up?* "Oh, hi, Emily," he said, forcing cordiality. "Come on in."

It was a first visit for her, and she looked quickly around the room at the cocoa-brown sofa, the small grand piano by the window with a violin case resting there on top of a stack of music, and built-in bookcases that were filled to overflowing. In the kitchen sink, there was a sizeable stack of unwashed dishes that she was tempted to tidy up for him, but since he seemed so brusque that day, she resisted the temptation.

"Have a seat," he said. "Can I get you a beer? Glass of wine? Coffee?"

She sat on the sofa with her viola case at her feet. "Do you have any sherry?"

He didn't and he wasn't likely to, but there were a couple of drinks left in a bottle of chenin blanc left over from his Wednesday night date with Daphne, the tall, sexy blonde who worked in the box office. As he poured Emily her drink, he could see the message light of his answering machine blinking furiously, as if it had been going for a long time and was growing angry about it. He supposed that it might soon blow a gasket or something. There was nothing to do at the moment but ignore it, because he knew all too well what the message would be.

He opened a cold bottle of beer for himself and returned to the living room. "I have only a few minutes to talk," he lied. "So what did you want to tell me?"

She took a small sip of wine, put her head on one side, took another small sip, and wrinkled her nose. She set the glass down on the table with what looked to him like finality. Chagrined, he decided that she knew a bit about wine. This was definitely a bargain brand. She had discerned it immediately and rejected it.

Blushing slightly she said, "Oh, this is a personal matter. I want your advice because you know the music world, and I respect your opinion very much."

He sipped his cold beer and felt flattered, but only slightly. "Advice about . . . ?"

"My . . . artistic future." She found sudden courage and looked at him squarely with a mischievous grin he had never seen before. "The thing is," she said impishly, like a child with a secret she was about to reveal, "I've come into some money that my uncle left in trust for me." She leaned forward. "All of my life I've wanted to study at Juilliard or Eastman, but my mother wouldn't hear of it. She thought I had only limited talent, and why waste good money? But now . . .," Suddenly she was triumphant and more sure of herself. Her smile grew smug, and she continued, "I have this money and I can do as I please, right? My question is, will they take me, do you think? Am I too old to begin over again? I'm not afraid to work hard at it."

He was nonplussed. How bizarre! What could he tell her? Of course she was probably too old to start over. She was a good, solid musician but not a great one, and it was unlikely that she would improve much from that point. He was fairly certain that any responsible music school would consider her too set in her technique to change much. What they wanted were young, still-malleable talents who were flexible enough to be guided into shape or turned politely aside. He mentally scanned his personnel records. How old was Emily? Twenty-five? Twenty-six?

"Well," he said, clearing his throat," there may be some alternatives you'll want to consider, too. Can you tell me how much of an inheritance we're talking about?"

Her glance slid away from his, and he guessed that she was debating the wisdom of giving him this information. Finally she said, "It's been in investments for ages, so I think it's now somewhere around . . . four-fifty."

Was she kidding? "Four hundred and fifty dollars?" He wanted to smile, but didn't.

She blinked twice. "Thousands," she said.

After a stunned reaction, he remembered to congratulate her. He held out his hand. "But that's wonderful, Emily!" He felt envy and avarice all at once, and a greedy thought flashed across his mind. Perhaps she could get him out of the mess he was in? He knew she was attracted to him. Would she make him some kind of a loan? Purely business, of course.

"Do you have a financial advisor to guide you?" he asked, trying to show just friendly concern.

"Just my mother's lawyer, Horace Walker. I think he sleeps with his ledger under his pillow so he'll dream of rising interest rates and not touching the principal. Stuff like that." She giggled. "Musicians aren't high on his food chain, either. Too frivolous. No use asking him."

Ryan's mind raced. He had to be very careful here. Just because he was under extreme pressure, he couldn't lose all sense of decency. But then, there was nothing wrong with talking to her, finding out what possibilities there might be. He could certainly give her better advice than a lot of other people could. He wasn't attracted to her, but that didn't mean he couldn't be kind to her. Mentally, he checked his lean bank balance. "Emily, let's talk about this further. How about dinner some evening?" He hesitated and then took the plunge. "Have you been up to the Hillside Winery for dinner? Are you free on Friday night?"

Her brown eyes lit up and widened in surprise. He felt ashamed at the intense pleasure she showed. "Oh, yes!" she said. "I'm free, and no, I haven't been there, but I've wanted to go for ages."

"Well, then, let's do it. Shall I pick you about at about 6:30?"

Her smile grew wider so it lit up her entire face. She was obviously thrilled at the way this was all turning out. "Yes, fine. Good," she said. "You know my address? Crescent Circle, top of the hill?" Her warm smile held. She was not trying to be coy in the least.

"I'll find it. Friday, then," Ryan said. Because he felt a twinge of guilt at his somewhat shabby tactics, he bent and gave her a light kiss on her cheek. She turned back at the corner of the hall with shining eyes and a continuing smile that was sweet and trusting. She gave him a tiny wave of her fingers.

He closed his door and leaned against it with eyes shut. *What am I doing?*

After a few minutes, he went to his answering machine

and pressed Play. A familiar voice that he had grown to dread came on in flat monotone. "Okay, fella. Your time was up today, and we haven't had a damn peep outta you. What gives? Don't play any cute games because we've already seen them all. I'll be coming by, very soon. Be there and be ready." The line went dead.

It was after seven that evening when Noelle, relaxing at home, decided to take another look at Ryan's financial statements. She wasn't in the mood to tackle the project because it had been a busy and trying day and she was tired. With the unopened folder in her lap as she relaxed by the big front window to watch the sun sink into the bay, she tried to remember exactly what year she had come onto the board of directors for the symphony association. It had begun while she was still on the music faculty at the university and was asked to serve as a judge for the annual Young Artists' Competition. She had loved doing that, and when nominations for the symphony's board came up, she was invited to serve there also. She accepted.

At first she was assigned to the Benefit Events Committee, which was hard and sometimes physical work. The following year she was appointed to the Fund Development Committee, which she didn't enjoy because she hated asking people for money. After that, it was the Music and Artists Committee, her favorite. She suspected that she was still on the board because she had no family commitments and she was willing to work a lot of volunteer hours. For the past two years, she had been a vice president, and this year, because no one else was very eager to take on the job, she was nominated for president. As is the case with most nonprofit organizations, nomination is a pretty good guarantee of election. Almost before she was prepared for it, she found the full responsibility in her lap.

She sighed and thought, *Well, let's get on with it.* She opened the folder. After she had studied the disappointing figures again, she was surprised to notice that there was a third, unexplained sheet face down beneath the two copies of the statement Ryan had given her. Was this something he had meant for her, or had she picked up the sheet from his desk by mistake? She turned it over and was astonished to read a list that was headed, "Ryan Marshall—Statement of Accounts." Under the heading was a list of casinos and racetracks with negative balances opposite each item. Below the double line at the bottom was a negative total that took her breath away: -$284,638.00.

THAT SAME EVENING, Ryan had left the office early in order to go back to his apartment and change for dinner with Emily. He was still nervous from that last telephone call, and he had taken the precaution of moving his car from its designated covered parking space to the rear parking lot, where there was a small back entry that was almost covered by overgrown laurel shrubbery.

He had copied Emily's address from her personnel records, and as he drove, he wondered if 458 Crescent Circle was anywhere near that impressive white home in a gated estate that he had often admired from Bayview Boulevard below. As the car shifted automatically into low gear for the climb and he passed number 450, he was stunned to realize that Emily didn't live near the big house but in it.

He stopped his car at the double gates that were open for him and stared up at the impressive home. Slowly he turned up the winding drive, passing two lily ponds, a long swimming pool that had been drained, and a five-car garage that stood empty except for Emily's small blue compact. To his left, a path led toward stables that now appeared neglected and unused, with the door hanging half open.

Driveway lights at ground level now became larger coach lights in front of the home itself, a three-story structure with six white pillars across a wide porch that held a wicker table and five or six matching chairs that looked dusty in the waning light. He climbed wide, shallow steps toward handsome double doors of leaded glass, through which he caught a flicker of movement.

He had no sooner lifted and dropped the heavy brass knocker a single time than a beaming Emily threw the door open. "Marshall! Hi! My mother is in San Francisco on business, so I can't introduce you just yet. Shall we go?" She was bright with expectation.

He was greatly disappointed that she wasn't going to invite him to come inside to see her home. She pulled the door shut behind her and started down the steps. He was astonished by the change in her appearance. Gone was the ruffled peasant blouse and gathered skirt she often wore. In their place was a simple linen sheath of a warm, copper shade and beige linen sandals with high, tapered heels. She wore oversized earrings of unburnished gold whose design he recognized as the Oriental symbol for happiness. Her auburn hair shone, newly styled, sleek, pulled up from her neck and bound with a wide brown velvet ribbon.

For a moment he couldn't move down the steps to follow her because he was nearly overcome by the sensation that she was an entirely different person than he had expected to meet and someone he didn't know. Perhaps he had come to the wrong house? He felt disconcerted, disoriented, and not at all in control of the situation. What an uncommon evening it was becoming. He had no idea how it might end.

Chapter Five

THE DRIVE UP into the foothills, however, was not uncomfortable but only rather quiet and relaxed. He was lost in thought about this new person beside him, and Emily was simply contented to find herself exactly where she was, riding through such beautiful country with the one person she admired above anyone else. The evening was soft and warm with light and sweet gusts of ocean breeze reaching even that far inland.

The Winery was about twelve miles into the foothills. It looked very old, built of gray stone and covered with dark green, thick vines with tiny white flowers. The dining area was an outdoor courtyard formed on three sides by the tasting room, the kitchen, and the offices. The fourth side faced west. It opened to a stunning view of the valley below, and on a night as clear as this one was, to the distant sparkle of the ocean and the flickering of city lights.

The courtyard contained about twenty tables where hurricane lamps were lit beside small floral bouquets in crystal bud vases. Ryan and Emily were seated at a wrought-iron table and padded bench that put them not across from each other but side by side, so both could enjoy the view and watch the arriving diners if they wished.

They both decided on the fresh salmon in lemon and dill sauce, with baby asparagus and cous cous. Ryan ordered a bottle of fairly expensive fume blanc to make amends for the cheap wine he had served her at his apartment. After her first taste of it, she licked her lips delicately and grinned at him. He felt duly rewarded for his choice.

By the time their salads arrived—tiny shrimp and black olives over baby spinach dressed in balsamic vinegar, olive oil, and tarragon—the courtyard was filling up with diners. With their salads, they were each served miniature loaves of bread, still warm from the oven, and a small tub of fresh butter. The bread was impaled with a toothpick bearing a tiny flag that identified it as a Winery product, this one containing nuts and feta cheese.

Ryan's fork stopped halfway to his mouth as a striking blonde in a full-length gown of silk chiffon in soft shades of blue and lavender entered the courtyard, followed by a slender young man in a creamy white suit and bright blue tie. Ryan stared at the girl because she was exactly the type who attracted him, but he became aware of Emily watching him as he watched the blonde. His slight embarrassment turned to surprise as the couple neared their table and the blonde smiled warmly and wiggled her fingers at Emily. Emily wiggled her fingers in return as they passed, and there was just a hint of that mischievous smile that had so surprised Ryan before.

A silence fell on their table until Emily said, "She's very attractive, don't you think?"

Ryan finished the last few bites of his salad before replying innocently, "Who?"

Emily smiled her secret smile and said, "Her name is Celia Warren. New in town."

"You know her, then?"

"I met her at the gym, and now we go running on the beach, mornings."

"At the gym? Do you go to the gym, Emily?"

"Oh, just for the last two months. But I think I'll keep at it because I like it. Celia has a boutique in town. Girl stuff. Dresses, sports things, tapestry handbags—all kinds of artsy stuff that I never knew I wanted until I spotted them in her shop."

With a pleased expression, she fingered the six tiny gold buttons on the front of her dress, and Ryan instantly guessed the origin of Emily's new look. He decided it was none too soon to get off the subject of the attractive Celia, although Emily didn't seem to mind talking about her new friend and all of her talents.

He cleared his throat and sipped the excellent wine. "Listen, Emily. About this idea you have regarding Juilliard or Eastman."

Her head came up. "Oh, yes! Right! What do you think?"

The hope in her eyes was difficult to look at squarely, and he concentrated on the lights beginning to come on in the panorama below. "Emily, I had that same desire myself for a long time—years—I guess, so I know firsthand that it's very tough getting into those schools. Lots of stiff competition and plenty of hard work if you do get there." He paused. "And Emily, you know what? We aren't all meant to be soloists."

Her smile that had been full of hope slowly faded. "But Ryan, I'm not afraid of working at it. This is what I want to do with my life, more than anything. I practice hours a day as it is, and that's the most important part of my day." She waited for his reaction.

He didn't have the courage to tell her that this was part of the problem. She had already been playing for about fifteen years, and her technique was now so firmly established that it would be difficult if not impossible to go back to the basics and perhaps change her playing profoundly. She was a good, solid musician and a valuable member of the orchestra, but the spark of genius was missing and that's why she played in second chair instead of first. She likely always would until her skills began to fade and she found herself moving back in the section, seat by seat, if she was still playing at all.

"I know you work at it, Emily, and you're a fine musician." Impulsively, he reached for her hand where it rested on the table between them. "But think about this. Do you really want to go back to square one in your playing and push yourself very hard for another four years or more? Have you thought about just having some fun in your young life? Ever been to Europe, or played the festivals there—Salzburg, Edinburgh, Vienna, Bayreuth? Hey, you could do the full summer, free as a bluebird, and you would have enough money that you would never have to worry about missing meals or sleeping in hostels like most young musicians do. Ever think about doing that?"

She was pensive. "No, I haven't been to any of those places and I've always wanted to. My dad talked often about the two of us and his colleague Andrew spending a summer that way." She sighed. "Well, we never got around to doing it. After he died, my mother wouldn't hear of my going alone, and she wasn't the least bit interested in going with me. So I forgot about it. It sounds wonderfully exciting—and why couldn't I? Have you?"

"Ah, yes, and I would do it again tomorrow and every summer if I didn't have to earn a living," Ryan said. "I loved every minute of it. It's a really fun time and a chance to see a little of the world out there. It's just infinitely rich and fulfilling. I met some of my best friends in the festival circuit, and we still keep in close touch—kindred souls that we are."

Her eyes began to glow. She said firmly, "I'm going to talk to my mother about it."

He was still holding her hand lightly, and he added a little pressure, so she turned her attention to him directly with a question in her eyes. "Let's see now, Emily," he said, "you'll soon turn twenty-one, right?"

Her chin came up. He had access to her personnel records, and he knew that wasn't true, so she deduced that he must be needling her. "I'm twenty-six," she said, "and you know it. I do get your point, however. You're saying I should make up my own mind and go if I want to."

"Now don't get your back up," he teased. He held her hand a little more firmly, turned it over and pressed a light kiss in her palm. "Good girl! It's entirely up to you, of course, but a little freedom wouldn't be all that bad, would it? Something tells me that you've always behaved yourself and never sassed your elders or broken any stupid rules or done anything wicked in your whole, entire life. Is that a fair profile of Emily?"

She couldn't help smiling. He had hit the mark exactly, but what a wimp she sounded like. "Well, you're not entirely off the mark," she said ruefully. "But then you don't know my mother. Nobody ever defies her will of iron, and don't try because you'll lose."

No, he thought, *and I'm hardly yearning for the doubtful pleasure of making her acquaintance.* He was watching the changing expressions on Emily's face and was disconcerted by the last glow of sunset reflected on her skin, giving it the warm color of ripe apricots and bringing out a touch of red in her hair. He had never thought of her as a beautiful woman, and he was startled to discover that, at that moment, she was. He stared at her without realizing that he was doing so. She was abashed at this sudden change in his attitude. With her free hand, she fiddled with her silverware and felt a flush climbing her cheeks.

The dessert arrived—a fresh blackberry pudding with a tiny mound of rum-flavored cream balanced delicately on top. Ryan brought himself back to reality. "I was surprised to see where you live, Emily," he said. "I've often admired that estate from the boulevard below. Have you always lived there?"

"Oh, no, just since I was twelve. It was my Uncle Edward's home, and we used to visit him there often when I was growing up. It was so lovely then—a magical place, like one of those estates you saw in movies of the twenties and thirties. Maybe *The Great Gatsby.* It's not kept up now like it was because we don't have that kind of money. Have you ever heard of my uncle, Edward Masefield Murphy?"

"The name is familiar," Ryan said. "Have I seen it on some buildings downtown?"

"How observant you are! Yes, he was quite a famous architect in his time, mostly around San Francisco and the peninsula, Atherton, Menlo Park, and Palo Alto, where there was a lot of big money floating around. After he had made all the money he thought he wanted, he retired here to be near my dad, who was his younger brother. We were his only family."

Coffee arrived with a small silver tray of chocolate mints. "San Sebastian was a pokey little town then—quiet, sleeping away in the sun, flowers everywhere, and surrounded by orchards," she continued. "Nothing unpleasant ever happened, as I remember."

He savored his fresh-ground coffee. "That's a lifestyle that has vanished like a wisp of smoke in the wind, which is a pity. Did your uncle design his own home?"

"Oh, no. Some early railroad baron built it, I think,"

Emily said. "My uncle began buying up real estate here because it was cheap at the time and this home was part of it. We always came there for the holidays, and he had crowds of incredibly interesting people around—writers, artists, actresses, lots of activity, and usually small classical concerts on the grass by torchlight. I adored this. He had some spirited riding horses and four or five expensive cars. The pool was always filled and heated and the fountains turned on, with gorgeous white swans in the ponds instead of the mucky ducks we have now. It was a shame he never married because he adored children. He was always so good to me, obviously." Emily took a single small mint from the silver tray. "When the city council discovered who he was, they commissioned him to design all of those wonderful old administration buildings you've been admiring downtown, with their large courtyards of hand-painted tiles and scarlet bougainvillea growing rampant on the white brick walls. Those buildings look dated now, but they're still lovely, I think."

"Oh, I agree, absolutely. Let's hope they'll never be replaced with sterile boxes of concrete and glass and no character. And your father was on the university's music faculty? Did he enjoy teaching?"

"Oh, my gosh, yes. It was his whole life. He always wanted me to go into teaching too, but I was never dedicated enough to care about how other people made music. I only wanted to make my own."

He shifted slightly on the bench so he faced her more directly and continued to watch her intently.

She became flustered and heard herself chattering but couldn't stop. "When I was just a little girl and only beginning to play the viola, I always practiced before open windows because I thought it would be a shame if no one else could enjoy the beautiful music I thought I was making. If it floated out into the atmosphere, it would somehow stay suspended there forever and it would make the world better, a nicer, kinder, happier place with no more wars, no more cruelty." She laughed. "What a nutty little kid I must have been, but that's how children think."

He shook his head. "No, no, that's a beautiful concept. I like it. Even my job could take credit for millions of glorious notes floating around up there, preventing a war or two."

Emily laughed with delight. "Right! How true! Unfortunately, no one hears my practicing these days, except the mucky ducks in the pond below my windows. But then, who knows. Maybe it makes better ducks out of them?"

He nodded solemnly, considering. "It's possible. The question is, how can we be sure?"

They were still laughing when the waiter arrived with their bill, and that pleased him because he believed that having a good time was an important part of enjoying fine food. Lately, all too many young people were in a snit of one kind or another, moody and dour, and he resented wasting the imaginative cuisine on such boors. He smiled at Emily because she was so pretty. Still, he couldn't follow the jokes he overheard now about some ducks who swam up on shore for Chopin but fled to the other side of the pond from Schoenberg. Oh, well.

On the drive back down the hill, Ryan told her about his family in Wisconsin who was nagging at him to come back and take over their small cheese factory of thirty employees. "Hey," he said, "I eat a lot of cheese, but I don't want to spend my life making it. There are two sons-in-law already working there. Isn't that good enough?"

She was surprised at his vehemence. She said quietly, "Well, I suppose our parents always want us to do whatever they did themselves." He remained silent. "Look," she said on impulse, "How about dinner at my home on Thursday? I'm a pretty fair cook."

He withdrew his attention from the madrone trees outside, and his eyes lit up with surprise. "Love to!" he said.

ON SUNDAY MORNING, Ana slept late but awakened at the sound of footsteps ascending her outside staircase around ten. She pushed her blanket around to find the white chenille robe that Jerry had bought for her in the dusty little Texas town of Bautista. She pushed her hair out of her eyes and waited for the knock, which came immediately. She opened the door a crack to see Karl standing on the landing, and she was instantly wary.

"Ana," he said. "Good morning! I may come in?"

"No," she said. "Sorry, but I'm not dressed." She opened the door a little wider, and he held out his hand with her car keys. "I brought your car for you. It has a new battery, and here's your warranty." In his other hand he held a white card.

"What does that mean . . . a 'warranty?' And how did I get a new . . . battery?"

Gently, he pushed the door open wider, and she backed off slightly. "Ana," he said, smiling broadly, "I have bought it for you! The warranty says you can take it back if it's no good."

She was dismayed. "But I can't pay for this! I have no money until the next payroll, and that is four days from now."

He laughed. "But I trust you, my dear little Ana. You can pay me back a little at a time, you see?" He moved back from the door. "Beth is waiting for me below in our car, so I must go. But I want to talk to you. Perhaps later today? I will call you."

He ran quickly down the stairs and disappeared around the corner of the garage. Ana's heart sank. She definitely did not want to be indebted to Karl, but she realized that she already was. And he would be back.

She dressed slowly in her one pair of blue jeans and a faded T-shirt. After a cup of coffee and a piece of toast, she sat down at her little table by the window and wrote to Jerry. She brought him up to date on what she had been doing and asked him about the ranch and how the cattle were, as if she had been off for a vacation and wanted to touch base. Then, sensing how meaningless all of it was, she wrote, "Jerry, where are we going? Will you come to see me out here or do you want me to come back? Please tell me what you are thinking, because I need to understand. I still love you, whatever happens. —Ana"

Five days later, she got her reply, but not from Jerry. It was written on Lurleen's pale blue stationery with their ranch logo imprinted beside her return address. Jerry had been ready to leave on a cattle-buying trip to Waco, and he had asked her to reply. The family was pleased that she was doing well in California. She and Brandon did not want Ana to be in need of money, and therefore she was enclosing a check for five hundred dollars. Ana was not surprised that the check had been signed not by Jerry's mother, but by his father, Brandon, in his large, authoritative handwriting. Ana would hear further from them within a very short time. It is signed, "With every good wish, Lurleen."

Ana, still reeling from Karl's second visit on the previous Sunday, was more confused than ever. What would happen to her?

Chapter Six

IT HAD BEEN nearly five years since the young Noelle Campbell faced her first real controversy in her work with Hammersmith Music Publishers, but it had become a very public one among music lovers.

Her most recent talent acquisition had been the young Japanese composer from San Francisco, Masako Natsume. Strictly speaking, she couldn't claim to have discovered him because he had created excitement three years before with his first work, *Concerto No. 1 for Piano and Orchestra.* The San Francisco Symphony had premiered it. Already exhibiting a dramatic skill in using the media to his advantage, he had retreated into the solitude of a spectacular home of glass and redwood at Sea Ranch on the north coast, where he had been accessible to no one.

When he was ready and not a moment before, he emerged in a blaze of publicity to announce the completion of his second concerto, this one for violin and orchestra. Noelle, who had been watching and waiting, was first on the spot with an offer from Hammersmith to publish with a worldwide pre-

miere and all the glory that went with it. After a suitable peri-
od of suspense, he signed her contract.

However, he wanted a *double premiere,* first with the Los
Angeles Philharmonic and a week later with the San Francisco
Symphony. Technically, this was an impossibility, because
word "premiere" indicates a first performance, and there
couldn't be two. Somehow, they had to resolve the issue.

The frosting on the cake for the event was the signing by
the two orchestras of *Vasily Ehrenberg,* the great Russian violin
virtuoso who hadn't appeared in either city for more than five
years because of his high fees and the worldwide demand for
his services. Noelle exulted in the growing excitement. All was
under control until Ehrenberg, who also knew his way around
the media world, gave an interview in which he referred to the
Japanese composer as "a developing talent." He also stated
that, as always, he would play his own cadenza and not the
one the composer had written.

Natsume considered Ehrenberg's demand "out of the
question." He always wrote the cadenzas to his works, he said
flatly, and unless this was guaranteed, his work would not be
performed. Naturally, this was not negotiable.

Noelle did some frantic research in the university's music
library on the subject of cadenzas. She well knew how audiences loved the aspect of a concerto performance when the
orchestra falls momentarily silent near the end of the concerto and the soloist has the full attention of the audience. It is
the soloist's chance to display individual virtuosity and bril-
liance, dazzling listeners with variations based on the themes
of the concerto itself until, having brought them to the apogee
of admiration for his skills, the performer signals the orchestra
to return for the triumphant ending, to the delight and
intense satisfaction of everyone concerned.

Ah, but the music library also had references to composers

who didn't trust the skills of the soloists and who insisted on writing the cadenzas for their concertos. Among composers who did this were such musical giants as Bach, Mozart, and Beethoven. *Hmm . . .*

Noelle was on the transatlantic line to London early the next morning, but with their usual reticence, Hammersmith was not alarmed.

"Not to worry," Trevor Holmes-Owen said. "We have just the person to take care of this. He's Avery Wright, our legal counsel for the States. He's in San Francisco at the moment. We'll have him pop right over."

He arrived the next morning, and Noelle felt reassured the moment she met him. He was soft-spoken and courteous, and he deferred to her judgment whenever possible, but he knew the music world and its applicable law. In his dark gray vested suit with a tiny white pinstripe, his dark hair neatly trimmed with a touch of gray at the temples, he was the perfect image of a person in control.

Fortunately, both of the artists in question were accessible at that time. Ehrenberg was visiting a longtime friend who was retiring as professor of composition with the music faculty at the university, while Natsume had just been appointed to fill that position. Avery called them both from Noelle's office and set up an immediate meeting for the following day.

Natsume arrived first, looking very young and unexpectedly tall and slender, with his glossy black hair trimmed short and parted on the side. He wore a black silk suit with a crisp white shirt and a black string tie. He was solemn and did not engage in banter.

Ehrenberg arrived moments later. He handed his ebony walking stick and wide-brimmed white straw hat to Noelle's secretary, Amanda, with a tiny bow. He wore a blue velvet jacket, a wide red silk ascot, and a navy blue knitted vest over a white shirt with a high collar. Unusual as his apparel was, Noelle thought that it suited him.

Avery introduced composer and soloist and talked a bit about Ehrenberg's long and brilliant career and then about the excitement aroused by Natsume's first concerto performance. Then he listened courteously as each man stated his case, after which he had a suggestion. "I've given this considerable thought, and I've made some arrangements at the university," he said. "Now I want to ask each of you to do a simple thing for me. Will you go over there and listen to informal recordings of both cadenzas and compare the two? Because you are both at the top of your game, I have a feeling that each will find some aspects to admire in the other's work. Then we will sit down again and talk. Will you do that? Shall we meet back here at the same time tomorrow?"

Ehrenberg brooded for five minutes or so with his head down and his eyes closed. Natsume sat erect and motionless, his dark eyes unblinking and fixed on a spot over Ehrenberg's head. Reluctantly, both agreed to Avery's suggestion.

The following day, the two of them arrived together, and their voices preceded them down the hallway outside Noelle's office. As they came through the outer door, Natsume was saying, ". . . Yes, yes, I understand. But I will need at least three years. I do not like being *pushed.*"

"Of course, of course," Ehrenberg said, waving his walking stick in circles ahead of him. "I'm a patient man. I will not push you. No, no. Not at all."

Waiting in Noelle's office, Avery winked at her and said softly, "Imagine that! A new artistic collaboration in the making."

They shook hands all around, but Ehrenberg was eager to tell his news. "I'm most pleased to announce that Mr. Natsume has greatly honored me with a promise of a new work," he said. He glanced quickly at the composer. "In a few years, when he's ready. The concerto will be dedicated to me, and I will play its premiere performance."

Avery and Noelle applauded. "Wonderful news," Noelle said. "Congratulations!"

"And the cadenza for this one?" Avery asked. "You've resolved that issue?"

Ehrenberg gestured broadly, brushing aside any thought of controversy. "There is much to be admired in each version. We will defer to your decision, Mr. Wright," he said.

"Splendid!" Avery said. "How about this? One cadenza for the Los Angeles performance and the other for the San Francisco performance? What an excitement *that* would be!"

The two artists raised eyebrows and exchanged surprised glances. Yes, indeed, they agreed, this would create excitement of the first order. The four of them then went out to lunch, and Hammersmith picked up the tab.

The next morning, Noelle had an early appointment at the printer's lab, and she was about an hour later than usual arriving at her office. Amanda, her usual cool, blond, mischievous self, grinned and wiggled her forefinger at the open door between their offices, leaving Noelle to guess at who might be waiting for her.

It was Avery, dressed casually in an open-necked sport shirt, khaki trousers, and brown loafers. It was the first time Noelle had seen him dressed in anything but a suit and tie. She liked the change.

"Morning," he said. "How about if we play hooky and you show me your town? Have you had breakfast?"

"Yes, I've had breakfast and no, I can't take off this morning," Noelle said. "I have another appointment with a printer about some Renaissance artwork we're using on a music cover.

But I'd love to show you my town, to which I'm definitely partial."

"How about lunch, around one?"

They agreed on that and for the remainder of the morning, she looked forward to it and had some trouble keeping her mind on her work. At one, they left the office after confusing Amanda.

"Will you be back?" she asked Noelle.

"Oh, certainly," Noelle replied.

"Probably not," Avery said.

Over lunch in the fuchsia garden of a hillside restaurant, Avery confided that he was close to retirement and had pretty well decided that he would settle in San Sebastian. They began an apartment search during the next two weeks between bike rides, picnics, long walks on the beach, and three foreign movies in a row. They were together every evening and all day on the weekends. On the third Sunday of his visit, Avery rented a small sloop, and they left shore on a clear and bright morning when the rising sun was still creating tiny golden sprites that danced across the water.

Noelle had packed a lunch with everything tasty she could find in her kitchen. Her housekeeper, Esperanza, had baked blueberry croissants the day before, to go with a giant thermos of coffee.

Around eleven, they were becalmed. Avery looped a short length of rope around the tiller so the boat would drift in the right direction while they enjoyed lunch.

Afterward, he said, "Noelle, we have to talk. I haven't been forthcoming about myself, and I'm not comfortable about that."

Her heart did a quick flip. What could he mean? She tried to read his expression, but the wide lenses of his sunglasses only reflected her own face back to her.

He dropped his usual bantering tone. "I'm taking early retirement," he said. "My doctor advises it. I've had a small health problem for a long time—most of my life, actually. I nearly bought the farm when I was ten because of a faulty heart valve. I spent about a year in bed missing school, base-ball, riding bikes, climbing trees—all that good stuff that gets little boys out of bed every morning." He looked out over the water. "I have a good doctor and he makes me take care of myself, so I'm fine." He smiled at her, but she felt stricken and could find no words to address what he had just said.

"I'm telling you this," he continued gently, "because I've grown so very fond of you in this short time. I don't regret that, not for a second, but I don't know how you feel. I don't want you to expect something I can't give you. Do you under-stand what I'm saying? My lifespan is uncertain and precari-ous. The most we two can be is very dear friends. I can't . . . and don't plan to marry, ever."

The remainder of the afternoon was a blur at the time and remained so. She could never recall afterward anything they had talked about. The following day, he had to return to San Francisco for a few weeks. He called her nightly but things weren't the same. It seemed to her that he had warned her off, told her to keep a distance, and to withhold any genuine emo-tion she might be concealing. It was as if she had been offered a fine, impressive gift box to open with high expectations, only to find it empty.

She was grateful for her work and the need to keep busy, but evenings were difficult. She spent some sleepless nights when racing thoughts chased each other in circles. Was their relationship over without them being ready to admit it, and now they were just going through the motions?

On Friday evening, she sat down and wrote him a letter. "You are the first person," she wrote, "that I've ever wanted to spend the rest of my life with. If we all knew ahead of time what the future held, would we ever do anything? If it's many years or only a few, I want to share them with you. I want us to marry. Will you?"

He answered by telegram, "My joyous and grateful heart says yes. Is next week too soon?"

They married within ten days, barely giving her widowed mother time to make the trip down from Seattle. They left on an extended honeymoon trip, touring Europe, laughing over their college French and their complete lack of Italian, gorging on magnificent food and fine wines, and seeing tiny villages, great cities, sapphire lakes, green valleys, and mountains tipped with snow. They bought silks and leather jackets, some Impressionist art by an unknown painter in Montmartre, and some bulky wool sweaters in Scotland that would be much too warm to wear in southern California.

Back home again, they bought a boat and he began teaching her to sail. They bought a lot near the top of a hill and began looking at building plans. They planted a garden on the hill even before the foundation was poured for the house, which was to be white, Spanish-style, with a red tile roof. They never considered any other plan.

She continued her work with Hammersmith, and Avery, retired, did pro bono legal work whenever he heard of a need.

In early April of their second year together, Avery decided to test his growing strength and self-confidence by walking his favorite golf course instead of riding a cart, as he usually did. It was a hilly course, and Noelle was apprehensive.

"Darling," she said, "are you *sure?*"

"Yes, love. I'm sure. I want to do this. I'm making progress, and I want to keep it up. I want to live a normal life and not be constantly on guard. Please don't worry. I feel great." A car horn beeped outside, and he picked up his clubs. "There's

Gordon. Gotta run. Let's have dinner on the wharf tonight. Don't cook anything." He kissed her quickly and was gone.

His foursome had reached the twelfth fairway before Avery had to admit that he had been wrong. A severe chest pain brought him to his knees. An anxious Gordon called for help on his cell phone, and the pro arrived with a doctor who had been waiting to tee off, but there was little that he could do. The damage was massive and irrevocable, and it was already too late.

The golf pro called Noelle to tell her only that Avery was ill and she should meet them at the hospital, but she knew from his shaken voice that it was much more serious than that.

The happy times, the wonderful times, the best years of her life had come to a sudden and shocking end and were no more.

Chapter Seven

NOELLE'S HOUSEKEEPER, ESPERANZA, liked for everyone to be happy. She worried about Noelle because Avery's death left her alone so much of the time in that big house. She was delighted when Noelle became active with the symphony. Still, it wasn't enough. One day, between running the vacuum cleaner and polishing the dining room table, she brought up the subject of her two nephews and a niece.

"They've just come up here," she said, "and they can speak no English. So sad because they don't go to school."

Noelle had been balancing her checkbook and only half listening. "Umm. Where do they live, Esperanza?"

"Out in the valley. With their mama and papa, but all so poor. I help how I can, but mostly they need to learn the good English, and I'm not so good at that," Esperanza said.

Noelle looked up, her interest piqued. "Are they illegals?"

Esperanza crossed her hands over her breast, looking shocked. "Oh, I'm sure they have their papers!" she said.

Noelle wasn't so sure. She went back to her bank account. "Well, maybe we can help them. I'll think about it."

IN HER SMALL apartment across town, Ana had been getting telephone calls from Beth. Just morning chats, at first. Then Beth suggested that they meet for a hike on the beach and a cup of coffee afterward. Ana agreed because it was a chance to get out of the apartment. Beth brought her sketch pad, and they stopped many times when something interesting caught her eye, like a flight of gulls coming in low over the water, or a dune with a small patch of the succulent called pigeons' beak, brilliant with spikey little orange flowers.

They trudged up the highest dune and perched at the top, where they watched a gaggle of terns on the beach below, fighting over the carcass of a crab that had washed ashore. Ana loved the ocean because her own country was inland and land-locked.

After a companionable silence, she asked, "Where is Karl from, Beth?"

"He's German, from Darmstadt, but his family came to the States when he was fourteen. He goes back about every year or so, when we go to the music festivals."

"Where did you meet him?"

"We were both students at UCLA, where I was studying music and art and he was supposed to be an engineering student, but he liked music the best. We began going to concerts together." She held out her hands, palms up. "And it went on from there," she sighed.

The sigh gave Ana the courage to ask, "And do you get on well together, you two?"

Beth was silent, staring at the incoming tide. She sighed again and reached for a small branch of greenery that poked up through the sand. She broke it off and began shredding its leaves, one by one. Finally she said, very softly, "No, not really. He has such a strong will, and no matter what I think, he always gets his way." She turned to look squarely at Ana, "I do love him. I know I do. But sometimes . . ." she broke off.

"Where is he when you come out here with me? What does he do with himself all day?"

Beth shrugged, "He never tells me where he goes, even when I ask."

They clambered down and went for coffee. When Ana returned to her apartment, she parked under the acacia tree that dropped little yellow balls of fluff on her car, but at least it provided shade. When she slammed the car door shut, Karl came around the back of the building.

"I've been waiting a long time for you," he said. "You should stay at home more."

IN THE BIG white house at the top of Crescent Circle, Emily woke very early on the morning after her dinner at the Winery with Ryan. She felt an overwhelming surge of happiness even before she was fully awake enough to understand it. When she did, she giggled and wrapped the sheet around her shoulders, hugging herself with both arms. Oh, it had been so perfect! Ryan was as sweet, gentle, and understanding as she had always known he would be, if she could only break through that professional reserve he hid behind, revealing the true Ryan. How easy he was to talk to now, even when she couldn't always find the right words, or very clever ones, but it didn't matter. It was as if they had known each other for a long time.

She sat up abruptly in her rumpled bed and put her hands between her knees, concentrating. Dinner! She'd invited him to dinner. He had accepted, and it didn't seem like just politeness. From the way his eyes lit up, she could sense that he really wanted to come and wanted to spend more time with her. Oh, happiness!

But what to serve? It had to be something that would be a real treat for him. Not like the things in sauces that her mother loved and that she often fixed for her but didn't really enjoy herself.

Emily rolled out of bed and rummaged through the top drawer of her cabinet for underclothes. She pulled on the blue jeans she'd worn the day before and one of the oversized white T-shirts she loved to wear around the house—her favorite that had five measures of Mozart's *Eine Kleine Nachtmusik* printed across her bosom.

In her bare feet, she dashed down two flights of carpeted stairs to collect her cookbooks and bring them back to her room. Her mother hated it when she went around the house without shoes. She thought it was common and ill-bred because, after all, who might come to the house at any time and see her that way? Fortunately, her mother was in San Francisco, and Emily could act as ill-bred as she wished.

She turned the pages quickly until she found one of her favorites that sounded about right. Grilled beef tenderloin with Roquefort cheese and red pepper butter. Yum. She would need to call her mother's butcher ahead of time to have him save a good cut of tenderloin. She'd need fresh tarragon and a delicate Roquefort, not too strong, because Ryan knew a lot about cheese. And what else? New baby asparagus and potato balls in butter and parsley. To complement it, a good pinot noir. She had discovered that he seldom ate dessert, so she decided on fresh-ground coffee followed by a small brandy in the tiny crystal beakers that her parents had bought years earlier in Czechoslovakia. So far, it sounded good.

Was it too early to head for the market? She glanced at the little gold clock her father had given her so long ago to time her practices. It was not quite 6:30, and she should practice first anyway. She seldom broke that rule that she'd set for herself years before, and having Ryan in her life was no reason to go completely bonkers. She giggled again. Or was it, all things being relative?

She set the cookbooks aside and took out her viola case. As she usually did, she stood by the wide-screened windows for a moment or two, putting her thoughts in place and clearing her mind of everything except the music she was going to make. It was no good going through the motions mechanically. One must feel the music with every fiber of one's being. She heard the chatter of the ducks in the pond below and remembered her duck jokes with Ryan. *Okay, ducks,* she thought, *here goes! This is going to be special!*

She stood there a little longer, totally content. She loved the big, high-ceilinged room at the back of the house because it was completely hers. Fine old hardwood floors were bare because carpets muffle musical sound. She kept the windows open most of the year, and though she closed them on the coldest days in winter, there weren't many of those. Her mother rarely climbed the second flight of stairs, and Emily felt certain that she didn't much care about what her only daughter did or didn't do in her own room. The music was certainly no attraction to the older woman. Emily sometimes thought that her mother was hostile to it, and that was a strange attitude for a woman who had married a music teacher. She recalled her mother's behavior a few days earlier and wrinkled her nose.

She had climbed out of bed and began practicing while she was still in her long cotton nightshirt. She played without interruption for almost two hours—Brahms, Mozart, Fauré—until hunger pangs got their way. She stuck her head quietly outside her door and heard no sound from below. She hoped that her mother was either still sleeping or had left the house very early. Emily went down the stairs barefooted, on tiptoe, to the deserted kitchen.

She found the pitcher of orange juice in the refrigerator and poured herself a large glass of it. The Pyrex Mr. Coffee was still plugged in and hot, so she set out a cup and saucer and put a slice of wheat bread in the toaster.

"Good grief, but you have a hard head!" her mother's voice came from behind her.

"Meaning what?" Emily asked.

"It must be at least fifty times I've asked you not to walk around our home in your undergarments! It's like talking to the wall!"

"Why is it a problem? I'm covered to my ankles, for gosh sakes."

"You know perfectly well that Celinda is due any minute, and she'll likely bring that lazy Juan with her to do the garden." Her eyes narrowed, and her mouth pressed itself into thin, hard line. "But maybe you want him to see you in your nightclothes? Is that it? Emily, I won't have that kind of behavior in my home!"

Emily took her orange juice and left the kitchen without a word. She began practicing her music again and kept at it for another hour until she finally dressed and went to the kitchen to finish her breakfast. She realized at once that her mother had vengefully dumped the coffee, washed out the coffeemaker, and returned her cup and saucer to the cabinet.

Celinda and Juan arrived arm-in-arm, laughing, a full hour late. Emily gave up the idea of breakfast and returned to her room with a small knot in her stomach. As usual, she felt like an outcast in her own home. For as long as she could remember, there had been very little warmth between her mother and herself, for reasons that she could never fathom. She had always tried not to offend her mother and to be what she thought was a good daughter, but her mother's cool distance and disapproval never softened. It seemed to Emily that there was no love for her there, and perhaps there never had been. But why? She had once asked her father, but his answer was no answer at all. "Sweetheart, you'll understand when you're older."

By Thursday, she'd completed her shopping and the house was spotless. She had washed and polished enough of her mother's china and crystal, including her mother's pride and joy—the large fluted crystal bowl from Austria. Emily filled it early in the morning with white lilacs and white roses, cut just past dawn when they were at their pristine perfection. She placed the bowl in the center of the mahogany table on the linen cloth with handwork insets that her mother had bought in Greece. On either side of the flowers were matching crystal candelabras with six small, white candlesticks.

The table looked lovely, and she was proud of it. Why didn't they enjoy these fine things more often? Yes, she was using all of her mother's most treasured items without permission. But what good were they, sitting unused in the buffet? Besides, her mother would never know. She would be very careful about that.

She spent most of the day cooking, took a shower, shampooed her hair, and did her nails in a pastel rose polish. Dressed, she stood before her full-length bedroom mirror for inspection. Rose velvet trousers and a sleeveless overblouse of rose and violet chiffon from Celia's shop made her look a bit mysterious and charming. Her eyes sparkled, and her cheeks had fresh color of their own. *Well, okay!* she thought.

By seven, everything was ready, and her Chopin compact disc played softly from the living room. If only he was right on time, everything would be perfection.

In his apartment, as Ryan dressed, he thought about the first time he had visited Las Vegas, which was also the first time he'd ever been inside a gambling casino. After he had entered through the huge, double-glass doors at the front of the building, he had stopped short, transfixed by the scene in front of him. The room was immense and as brightly lit as a stage, with action, movement, noise, and smoke everywhere. At first glance, it seemed to him like chaos, but he soon realized that the patrons there knew exactly what they were doing and went about their business with an intensity and determination that was reflected on their faces. Ryan felt himself being drawn into the excitement around him, and he knew he wanted to be a part of it.

Bells rang on slot machines and huge amounts of coins dropped from them into waiting hands or hats. At intervals, beautiful young women in scanty outfits ran over with their heavy bags of money and paid the winners of larger amounts. The women who won emitted shrill squeals of emotion. At the blackjack and roulette tables, the faces were studies in concentration, with all eyes locked on the cards or the wheel or the dice. That was where Ryan headed.

At that time, his bank account was reasonably flush, and he felt no reluctance in spending some of it. Gambling was all just for fun, wasn't it? Just for the pleasure of the game? He found himself placing rather large bets, and for a novice he was quite lucky. He won often. He didn't find his victories at all unusual, and he decided he was just a lucky kind of a guy.

After some five or six visits to that same casino, he was treated as a special and valued guest. With that treatment came some nice perks—a free suite, complimentary meals, and wine with dinner. Some of the dealers began to call him by name, and he liked that. They treated him like he was one of the legendary "high rollers," though he knew he was far from that. Still, he began to head for Vegas on every free weekend.

Of course, there were bad weekends when he lost several

thousand dollars. After one particularly disastrous weekend, he signed over his entire payroll check that the bookkeeper had just given him the day before.

He began to pay his gambling debts with credit cards but soon they were maxed out, so it was necessary to take out additional cards. He asked for and was given a line of credit at the casinos. He began to feel uncomfortable at the ones that pressed him to pay up on his growing debts, so he moved to other casinos and signed for a line of credit whenever they would give him one.

He realized that he was in trouble, but he believed that his lucky streak would return and he would make that big win and pay everything off. Wasn't that the way it worked?

From his apartment window where he stood with a towel wrapped around his waist and his hair still wet from his shower, he quickly spotted the long, black Chrysler sedan with its Nevada license plates. Although it was hard to see from his angle of vision, he was fairly certain that someone was sitting in the car, watching and waiting. He had not answered his telephone all day, nor had he responded to the four message-waiting signals.

As he watched, the passenger door of the black car opened and a heavyset man in a dark suit crossed the parking lot to enter the lobby below. He didn't dare call Emily, because the clerk would know he was still in his room, and so would the man watching for him.

He continued dressing. With only a few minutes to spare, he went carefully toward the back exit he'd been using, checking the parking lot first from a hall window. His heart stopped. The long, black car had moved to the back of the building and was parked directly opposite his own car. There was no way he could escape unnoticed, and no way he could escape at all unless he called a cab. In a panic, he rushed back to his room and locked the door. He had to think of a way to call Emily and make some excuse for being late, but how? One thing was certain—he had to find a way to get access to some money, and quickly!

Every half an hour he checked the back parking lot, going up and down the rear staircase until the muscles of his legs began to ache. Finally, at 8:45 P.M., he was vastly relieved to see that the black car had gone. Ryan rushed down the stairs and out to his car, driving off so frantically that he had gone six blocks or so before he realized that he couldn't remember whether or not he had locked the door of his apartment. It was too late to go back. And what if the black car was following him?

At Emily's, the wrought-iron gates were open, and he drove up the hill quickly, hoping for the best. But when his car entered the brick parking area in front of the house, his hopes faded. All of the parking lights had been turned off, as well as the veranda lights. He rushed up the steps and rang the bell once, twice, three times. Inside, the house looked dark, although he thought he could see a rosy glow in the foyer opposite the leaded glass doors. But the rosy glow did not move. He paced the veranda for several minutes and rang again. And again. There was no answer.

He stood at the top of the veranda stairs and groaned softly. *She will never forgive me for this,* he agonized. Now that he knew her better, this bothered him a great deal. *Just when we were getting on so well,* he thought. He was ashamed of himself and disheartened. Couldn't anything go right? Ryan finally gave up and returned to his car. He slowly exited through the iron gates that closed silently behind him.

Inside her home, Emily sat motionless in the foyer. With some light at his back, she had seen Ryan clearly through the glass doors but had made no move to open the door. When she pressed the wall button to close the gates behind him, tears began to run down her cheeks, ruining the expensive new makeup from Celia. So, after all, her great romance was an illusion that had just vanished like a wisp of smoke from a late summer bonfire.

On the following day, he sent her two dozen yellow roses and an abject apology, pleading a personal emergency. He asked her to call him, but he had no way of knowing if Emily accepted his apology because she did not respond.

AS THE NEXT Saturday morning rehearsal wound down, Ryan waited in the dark backstage area, determined to catch Emily. Idly, he watched two stagehands in the far corner near the storage area for the Steinway piano. From the tone of their voices, he knew that they were arguing, and angrily, and he kept his distance. Their disagreements were not his problem.

There was enough light to see them, however, and he couldn't help noticing how different they were. Ken Christopher was head stagehand, and he looked the part. He wore his dark hair in a short brush cut, and in his usual black trousers and spotless white knitted shirt, he could have gone almost anywhere and not have been criticized. Soft-spoken but uncompromising, he always insisted that the work be done right and without any loafing into overtime. When he had a choice, he never selected Tommy Barger for his team, and Ryan had noticed that there was not a good working relationship between the two men. They barely spoke and ignored one another whenever possible.

That day, however, Tommy was working backstage. Unkempt as always, his jeans had visible oil spots on them, and his shirt was shrunken too much to cover his puffy belly. Ken spoke briefly to him, but Tommy turned his back and walked off. Ken followed. The argument became heated but in undertones, because the orchestra was still in rehearsal. As Ryan watched, Ken pointed at some music stands that needed moving. As he walked off, Tommy raised a finger in a vulgar gesture behind Ken's back. Ryan turned away in disgust just as the music came to an end and the musicians began pouring out of the acoustical shell and into the backstage area.

Emily emerged, walking quickly, and Ryan fell into step with her.

"Emily, wait a sec," he called. "We need to talk."

"Hello, Ryan." She kept walking.

"Emily, please. You must listen to me. Do you have a minute?"

"No," she said. "I have shopping to do. Errands."

He took her arm, drew her into the Green Room, and pleaded, "Emily, I must explain. Please."

She stopped, put her viola case on one of the green plush chairs beside her, and crossed her arms, looking adversarial. "What is it you want, Ryan? I can't imagine that we have a thing to say to each other. I got your message the other night, loud and clear." He flinched and shut his eyes for a moment. "Emily, I'm more sorry than I can say. You'll never know." He chewed on his lower lip. "I'll be honest. I got myself into a little personal trouble and it wasn't . . . safe to come earlier. Will you let me explain?"

She looked at him directly, frowning. "What kind of trouble? What do you mean?"

He looked behind him as the last of the musicians streamed by with their instruments in their hands or under one arm. Several people looked curiously in their direction.

"Not here, Emily. I will tell you, I promise. Can we have lunch or dinner later?"

She dropped her head again and stared at the carpet. "Why?"

"Because I want to explain things to you. Will you give me a chance to do that? Please?" He reached for her hand, but she pulled away. He grasped her arm just above her elbow, and his grip tightened. He appeared tense. "Emily?"

Finally she said, "Well, okay. Dinner, then. Sometime soon, but not tonight. I'm busy." She wasn't.

"All right. Could I pick you up on Sunday, about seven?"

"Sunday will be okay." She withdrew her arm and reclaimed her viola, walking off without a farewell.

When he picked her up on Sunday evening, he expected to meet her mother who had returned from San Francisco, but she didn't appear. Ryan had made dinner reservations at a small inn ten miles outside of San Sebastian, where it sat on a hillside of huge boulders overlooking the ocean. It was called simply Halcyon—calm and peaceful—although breakers crashed against the rocks night and day and sent giant plumes of spray licking up at the expanse of glass on two sides of the building.

The dining room was all cedar with open beams and a small fire glowing in a rough, stone fireplace. There were only about a dozen candlelit tables, and only a few diners were seated when they arrived. In the background, an excellent sound system softly played a cello concerto that she recognized immediately. She had a copy of it herself and knew that the soloist was her idol, Yo Yo Ma.

They were seated at a corner with a clear view of the ocean for as far as they could see. They both decided on a Spanish *paella* of shellfish, meat, and saffron-seasoned rice. Ryan ordered an expensive bottle of merlot that arrived immediately. The waiter uncorked it, poured, and departed.

Ryan held his glass in her direction. "To Emily," he said. "And to forgiveness, however undeserved." His eyes moved to the riotous breakers outside the window wall, and he was silent for an interval while he gathered his thoughts. "I want to be honest with you," he began. "painful as it may be. The thing is, I've been an irresponsible idiot and have only myself to blame. I'm afraid you'll agree when you hear about the mess I've trapped myself into. It was the stupidest thing I've ever done, but I loved it while I was doing it." He looked directly at her. "Too many trips to Vegas, I'm afraid. I'm not going to go into the gruesome details, but there is a problem I've got to take care of, and I will. I just need a bit of time. These people, these debt collectors . . . don't want to give me that, and I'm afraid they play rough. I have to admit that I didn't want them to find me that evening and I was evading them, until I can work this out."

"Ryan!" She was horrified. "Are you saying they would physically hurt you, beat you up or something?"

His smile was grim. "Well, I'm not a big enough fish for anything mortal. At least I hope not. But I think they wouldn't hesitate to mash my face in a bit, or break a couple of fingers."

"Oh, Ryan, that's frightening! Can't you call the police?" Emily asked.

"Well, I do owe them the money."

She bit her lower lip, debated with herself, and plunged ahead. "Maybe I could . . . help you?"

He knew she meant the money, but he had definitely changed his mind about that. He reached for her hand and said, "Thank you, dear Emily, but no. I got myself into this, and I will find a way to get out. Now that you know, I don't want to talk about it any more. It's been a hard lesson for me, but obviously one that I needed." He refilled her glass, which was down only a little. "How was your mother's trip? Did she go shopping?"

Emily was glad enough to change the unpleasant subject.

"No," she said. "Strictly business. She was an accountant, you know, before she retired, and she has quite a few investments to take care of. I don't know much about it because she doesn't confide in a weak-brained, empty-headed musician." Her tone had a bitter edge to it, and Ryan watched her intently. There was something between these two women that he would like to understand, but couldn't. At least, not yet.

"Tell me more about your father," he said. "He sounds like a guy I would have enjoyed knowing."

"Yes, he was a fine man. I loved him so much and admired him, and I still miss him. Always will, especially when I hear one of his favorite pieces of music."

"Did he take you to concerts and recitals, that kind of thing?"

"Oh, yes, all the time, almost every weekend. Andrew Ashton went with us, usually. He was a colleague of Dad's. He taught wind instruments at the university, and they had been great friends for years, even before my parents married. My mother did Dad's taxes for a few years, and it went on from there. The funny thing was, my mother never cared much about going to concerts, and it was a mystery to me why someone who didn't love music would marry a musician. They took some trips to Europe in the beginning, but that ended when I was born. It seemed to me that they never had much in common. They seldom went anywhere together. Not that I can remember, anyway. It was always me, Dad, and Andrew."

Ryan was thoughtful. "And did your mother mind that— the three of you always going off without her?"

Emily raised her eyebrows, "Oh, I suppose she did mind. She was grumpy about it, but that's just the way she was, always in a negative mood. We never cared if she didn't come with us. For some reason, she never warmed up to Andrew, and it made us all uncomfortable the way she constantly sniped at him. Sarcasm, that kind of thing. He didn't deserve that. He was a nice guy."

The *paella* arrived on bright red platters, steaming and fragrant with herbs and spices. The waiter served them in matching red bowls with a basket of crisp hot rolls on the side. They ate in contented silence because they both appreciated fine food.

Ryan had finished the last spicy bit of seafood and sat sipping his wine. "Tell me. How did your father die? He was rather young, and you were only about thirteen?"

"Yes, a bad time to lose one's father, if there is such a thing as a good time for that kind of loss," Emily said. "They were off at a music conference at San Luis Obispo, he and Andrew. They always went to these week-long events together because they had all the same interests and they had such a good time together laughing, joking, and teasing one another." Her eyes misted. "I was totally crushed, as you can imagine. We were so close, since I was a little girl. He was the center of my life, my guiding light. What's it called, a lodestar? I don't think I'll ever get over it, really." She scrambled in her bag for her handkerchief. "My mother said it was a heart attack, but I've always sort of wondered. He had no record of heart trouble, and he was only forty-eight. Why would he have a heart attack just sitting around in auditoriums?"

"Did you ever try to get more of an explanation from your mother, or see any medical records?"

"Oh, she never wanted to talk about it and always cut me off when I asked," Emily said. "No one else would tell me anything, either. Adults seem convinced that young people have no need to know these things." Bitterness had crept into her voice again.

"And Andrew? What happened to him?".

"Oh, Andrew left the university immediately afterward

and moved back east. I was terribly hurt by that, because I believed he was fond of me and I liked him a lot, like another favorite uncle. Oh, he sent a few cards from time to time, but I never hear from him now, so I lost two people I cared about at the same time."

Ryan nodded his head as if something had just been confirmed, but he remained silent and pensive, staring out the window. Emily frowned, watching him.

"Ryan, why did you nod your head just now? What are you thinking?"

"Oh, did I?" He smiled at her. "Nothing much. Just a thought I had."

"Like what?"

He tapped his fingers on the table and watched her as if he was making up his mind. He took another sip of wine and twisted the stem around and around.

"Ryan? Are you going to tell me?"

"You don't give up, do you?" he said. He drew a deep breath and let it out slowly. "Emily, that was all a long time ago. Are you sure you want to dredge it up again? Why not just let it go?"

"No. I don't want to just let it go. There's something here that I don't understand but I think you do. What is it? Please tell me."

He shook his head. "Emily, I didn't know your father or Andrew, and I have no right in the world to make wild guesses about what might have happened. It would be nothing but conjecture, and that's always dangerous. Let's forget it."

"But what do you think? I've been left in the dark all these years, and I don't have a clue."

He bent his head, closed his eyes, and rubbed a little circle on his forehead. Finally he said, "Look. It's only a guess on my part, connecting the dots on what you've told me. You might not really want to hear it."

"Go on."

He frowned, concentrating. "Okay, then. Here's my thought. You've said that your father and mother were unhappy. There was a lot of hostility between them, and they didn't care about the same things or share much of anything. She very much resented his close friendship with Andrew, right?" He paused and waited until she nodded.

"Do you think he and Andrew were more than friends? Could your father have been so unhappy in these complex relationships that he just couldn't . . . go on?"

She stared at him, eyes wide and unblinking. He watched her face sympathetically, and he could pinpoint the exact moment when she comprehended his meaning. Her head dropped forward into her hands. "I've wondered," she said in a muffled voice. "And you're saying he might have taken his own life?"

"Of course I can't know that." He gave her a little time before he spoke again. "Emily, in the middle of the night, in fits of depression, people do things that they wouldn't have done the following morning. I think that's the reason we ask 'why,' when these things happen. Even those closest to the people rarely know for sure, ever."

She wiped her eyes and blew her nose, "I can deal with the part about Andrew, but not the rest of it. I thought he loved me. Why would he want to hurt me like that and just disappear from my life?" Her eyes glittered with more unshed tears.

He kept her hand firmly in his. He said softly, "If he hadn't loved you very much, he would likely have left home years ago."

They were quiet for a while. Coffee arrived, and they

drank it in silence. The waiter came with their bill and Emily turned her face away, hiding her despair.

Ryan said, "Remember, Emily, I'm only guessing, but it would explain a lot of things. I can't know these things for sure, but your mother does. Try to talk to her, now that you have an idea about what might have been. Ask her about Andrew. I do think that needs to happen between you two."

She gave him a tremulous smile. "Yes, of course you're right. I must try."

The next morning, Emily was an hour into her practice when she spotted her mother sitting on the bench by the smaller pond wearing one of her flowered cotton wrap-around aprons with huge front pockets bulging with bread scraps that she was feeding to the ducks. She wore the wide-brimmed straw garden hat that Emily remembered from forever, and her muddy green garden gloves lay beside her on the tile bench. From Emily's view, her posture, as always, was erect. Her spine was stiff, her body tense and under control. Her mother wasn't someone a daughter would be tempted to rush up to with a spontaneous hug. Irene Murphy didn't invite affection and might even push it away, so Emily had learned years before not to offer any.

But now, everything had changed. Emily put her viola in its open case and headed down the staircase before she lost courage and changed her mind. As she approached the bench, Irene glanced curiously at her and turned back to the ducks. She said nothing but scattered some bread crusts between them for Emily to toss.

Emily could take the ducks or leave them. To her, they were extremely messy, smelly, and noisy, but she knew that her mother was fond of them so she dutifully tossed a few crusts. In a little while, she said, "Mother, I need to talk to you."

"Well, here I am."

Ana's Dream

"I've been thinking a lot about Dad, and what might have happened. I think I understand about all that now. I guess I'm a few years late on the uptake."

Irene's raised hand stopped in mid-flight. "I thought you would figure it out eventually. You're a bright girl." She tossed the bread.

Emily hesitated, unsure of how to proceed. The ducks grew more aggressive and came up on the bank, splashing fresh mud on their shoes. The soft white fluff under their wings had become a muddy brown with their scuffling.

Emily said, "I didn't understand about Andrew, but now I think I do." She kicked a little trench in the mud with her heel of her shoe. "I didn't understand any of those things. I'm . . . sorry if I've judged you unfairly all these years."

"No reason for you to be sorry. You had nothing to do with it." Irene drew the remaining bread crusts from her pocket and tossed them as far from the bank as she could. "Well, actually, I suppose you did, in a way." She brushed off her hands and smoothed the front of her apron. "Let me tell you how it was, Emily. Your dad was the first man I'd ever been involved with. I rarely dated in high school or college. I was very shy around the male species, and I didn't know how to attract them, so I was thrilled when we began dating, years after we had graduated. Eventually, he asked me to marry him. I thought that our early years together were happy, but what did I know? When I became pregnant with you, he left me alone, but I thought he was being careful. When we brought you home from the hospital, I discovered that he had moved all of his things into the spare bedroom, and that's where he stayed."

She closed her eyes briefly and Emily held her breath. Her mother continued. "He told me that he loved me and our baby, but the intimacy of marriage was distasteful to him. I

92

was shocked and stupefied. My womanhood, such as it was, had been demolished. I felt worthless. More than that, I felt cheated. My life seemed to be over when it should have been just beginning." Irene drew a deep breath. "Things were very different in those days. The university wanted its staff to be 'family-oriented.' He was concerned about his place on the faculty because he loved his work and he wanted to stay there. I guess I was a convenient prop. He was always very happy about having had a child, and he told me that he would never leave as long as I wanted him to stay. It would be my decision. He wasn't proud of himself, but that's the way it was."

Emily said softly, "We don't really know the people we live with day after day."

"No, we don't. But the sad part is that we often don't know ourselves very well, either." She recalled looking at herself in the mirror the night her husband had dropped this bombshell on her. She still looked young, with short auburn hair and soft brown eyes, her body still trim, her skin fine and flawless. She had stared at herself and thought, *Now, who am I?*

Emily said, "And we made it all worse, Dad and I and Andrew, always going off together and leaving you behind."

"Oh, yes, you did, and those were lonely times for me. But it wasn't your fault. You were only a child. You did what they did, which was to shut me out." She gave Emily a sly, slanting glance. "I always thought Andrew should have been your mother because you liked him so much better than you liked me."

Emily was ashamed. "Mother, I never thought you loved me. You never showed me that you did."

"I guess I didn't feel very lovable, so how could I love anyone else? I suppose I got tired of competing for everyone's love. It was always the three of you and the music, and I was out of that charmed circle. After awhile, I didn't care any longer. I concentrated on my work and loved you from a distance, as well as I could."

Emily's throat felt tight as she held back tears. "But why didn't you leave and build a new life with someone else?" Hesitantly, she put her hand over her mother's on the bench between them. For once, Irene didn't withdraw her hand but turned it over and took Emily's in hers.

"There was no one else," Irene said. "We lived a kind of isolated life, and as I said, I felt unworthy of being loved. Your dad was a good man, but he carried around a heavy load of guilt. Human nature being what it is, he blamed me for making him feel guilty. It works that way sometimes. Most of all, he hated the duplicity of his double life, pretending to be in a marriage that didn't exist. Our dishonesty was a mistake. It usually is. It hurt all of us."

Emily felt the need to comfort her. "Well, I didn't know that, and I was happy."

"We didn't want to hurt you, and it would have hurt you if he left. There would have been a lot of questions that he didn't want to answer. It just seemed easier to go on the way we were." She clutched Emily's hand tighter. "It worked in its fashion for a long time, but finally he was too unhappy to go on. He couldn't face being two people for the rest of his life." She smiled a little sadly. "These things are much better now. People value their individuality and aren't so willing to waste their lives the way we did."

Emily's mother raised her head and breathed deeply, looking around her garden and at the ducks in the little pool, the trees, the bright sky, and the puffy white clouds drifting eastward. "I'm glad we've talked."

Emily imagined that she could actually see tension slipping away from Irene's body as her mother moved her shoulders and rotated her head from side to side. Her mouth softened into a tiny smile. "Well, my dear," she said. "Shall we go inside before the ducks eat our shoes?"

AFTER A VERY quiet dinner together, Emily returned to her studio. It was growing dark, but she turned on no lights because the music she wanted to play was something she knew by heart—the viola part to a Fauré string quartet. While she played, the years of regrets slowly began to ease, and the sorrow softened a bit.

When she finished, the room was quite dark. She sensed a small movement near the doorway and her mother's voice said, "That was lovely, Emily. I liked that and you played it very well."

Irene was leaning against the doorframe with her hands clasped together in front of her. "Em, I've baked those walnut and applesauce cookies you used to love when you were a little girl. Remember?" Her voice had changed, the hard edge gone. "I got out some of our good china with those little eggshell-thin cups that you always loved. We should use them more, don't you think? Would you like to come down and share a cup of jasmine tea with me? It's ready."

"Yes," Emily said, wrapping her arm around her mother. "So am I."

Chapter Eight

NOELLE SAT AT her desk in the spare bedroom at the back of the house where she didn't have a view of the bay but of the hillside garden she and Avery had planted. Native ceanothus with its coppery foliage and small white clusters of flowers provided a dramatic contrast to the gray needles and tiny blue flowers of rosemary, both doing a fine job of holding the steep bank in its place. The view of the garden filled the window and climbed beyond and out of her sight.

She had her favorite breakfast on the desk beside her, prepared early before Esperanza could arrive with her usual urging of the nice, hot bowl of oatmeal she had insisted that her own daughters eat every morning. Now grown, her daughters had escaped to clerical jobs in Los Angeles, where they gleefully ate cold pizza and Pepsi for breakfast.

Noelle admired her own colorful arrangement of fruit and avocado slices on one of the platters she and Avery had found on their trip to Italy. In Umbria, the town of Deruta was known for its manufacturing of *majolica* ceramics, and rows of shops displayed wares that ranged from tacky to exquisite. They had roamed through several shops and found nothing.

On a narrow side street, they spotted a shop that was so small and dark that it seemed unlikely to support much of anyone. Because they wanted the old and not the new, they entered the shop, passing the elderly woman in black with red plaid slippers who sat sleepily at the entrance on a straight-backed chair with a yellow cat snuggled in her lap. She nodded to them but did not get up, having little expectation of selling anything to the hordes of tourists who usually looked and left without buying anything.

In the semidarkness of the cluttered shop, it was difficult to see what was available and Noelle had nearly passed the four platters stacked on a dusty shelf by themselves when a brilliant patch of blue caught her eye. She took a tissue from her handbag and wiped the dust from the top platter. She was elated to recognize a traditional regional design of the brightest combinations of jade green and a clear, bright blue. She wasn't concerned if one of more of the platters with their unique shape might be chipped. She wanted them.

Avery had glanced at her. Without a word, her expression signaled pure delight. He smiled at her and moved to help carry the platters to the battered counter, where the old woman, reluctantly leaving her sunny space, came into the shop to wrap the platters in yellowed newspaper and tie them with a knotted length of string. Noelle could scarcely wait to get back to her hotel room to immerse the platters in hot, soapy water. They did not disappoint and were lovelier than she could have hoped. Even now, they continued to evoke her most treasured memories of Italy and the Italians—their relaxed ways of dining, their pure enjoyment of good food, and their outdoor living—which reminded her so much of southern California.

She ate an icy slice of pear, then one of peach, then some fat, purple grapes. How fortunate they were to be here, so close to the Imperial Valley where much of the fruit was grown that all the states enjoyed. Next, a fat slice of avocado. Why not?

Reluctantly, with the platter emptied, she turned her attention to the latest reports Ryan had given her at the meeting the day before. Contrary to his expectations, ticket sales for the upcoming season were relatively flat after an initial surge of interest with the new brochure. They had a way to go yet. She turned to the membership category, which actually meant contributions. Memberships were definitely well below what Ryan had projected. She made a note to call the board chairman for membership and urge a harder push, but she well knew that most of the board hated asking for money, as she did, too. Well, it had to be done. There was a big gap between what funds were secure and what money was only wishful thinking. She wished that her position wasn't principally one of pushing everyone for just a little more effort— only one more push, but endlessly.

She heard the Dutch door of the kitchen open and close, and she knew that Esperanza had arrived. Within a few minutes, with her white apron fastened around her waist, the little Latino woman tapped on Noelle's open door and bent forward, putting just her sleek, dark head into the room.

"Good morning," Esperanza said. "Can I show some pictures for you? These I took with your fine camera you gave me."

Noelle had indeed given her housekeeper her expensive camera the summer before, but it was not nearly as valuable as the one Avery had left. She certainly didn't need two cameras because she seldom took pictures unless she traveled.

"Of course, of course. Come in," she said, moving Ryan's reports to one side to make room for Esperanza's photos, which she was already drawing proudly from her apron pocket. They were, of course, pictures of the small children of her niece and newly arrived from Mexico. Two boys and a girl, they sat at a decrepit picnic table under a meager tree with drooping branches and few leaves. In the background, there was nothing but dry grass to the edge of the photo. On the right side of one photo, a slight and slender woman with long dark hair was half in and half out of the picture, turning away from the photographer, but not soon enough to conceal the fact that she was expecting another child.

The little housekeeper pointed and said, "This is Luis, the oldest. Then Maria, then the baby, Miguel. Look how bright they are! Always so happy!"

It was true. In spite of their barren surroundings, each child wore a bright grin, and dark eyes danced with expectations of great things to come. She studied the photos, wondering what the future actually held for them. When she turned around, she realized that Esperanza had slipped out the room, leaving her with plenty of time to admire Luis, Maria, and Miguel.

Of course she knew that anyone with any heart would want to help them but she thought of her father and she felt the same hopelessness that his good works had always given her. Of course she had been too well-brought-up to put her doubts into words but her thoughts and resentment had been strong enough. *Yes, but if we help ten who need it, fifty more will take their place.*

Her father had been raised as a Quaker—or more properly, a member of the Society of Friends—but as a young man he moved to Philadelphia to train as a dentist. Eventually, he moved to Washington State, where he met and married a woman who, although she wasn't a Quaker, totally supported him in its philosophy. Noelle, an only child, grew to resent the fact that her father spent almost every weekend doing dental work for the poor and indigent, without charge. She could still hear his gentle voice saying, "If we find someone in need and we can help, we must do so."

Growing up, she had hated the fact that they were never free to do family things on weekends. Sometimes she went with her father and helped him, but usually it was her mother who helped him. Noelle could recall, with some bitterness, how pleased her parents had seemed with their weekend's work, while she had spent the weekend alone, studying, puttering in the garden, and doing homework. If she grew frustrated enough to voice the mildest complaint at their weekend arrangements, her father would give her such a look of reproach that she immediately fell silent. She was especially disdainful of the complacent looks her parents exchanged when they reviewed their weekend's accomplishments, so obviously proud of themselves.

Still studying the pictures of the three little children under the sparse tree, she began to wonder if her parents had found something that she hadn't, at least so far. Before she met Avery, she had felt herself to be always in a waiting mode, unfinished and incomplete, without a strong purpose in her life. He had changed all of that, but for such a tragically short time. She felt she was again adrift and just going through the motions of living a full life. Surely there was something more.

Another credo her father had embraced came back to her. "Noelle, don't build your life around yourself. Don't be selfish. There are so many others out there needing a little help. Just look around." At the time, she had kept her eyes downcast, rejecting this thought as hopelessly naïve and futile. Now, she wondered if she should try.

She finished the last of her cup of tea and picked up the photos that she returned to Esperanza in the kitchen. "Will you draw me a map of how to find these children and your niece . . . is it Angelina? Ask her if I may come to visit early Thursday morning."

She left the house and drove to the campus bookstore, where she bought three books in the children's section entitled *Beginning English for the Young Spanish Speaker.*

She also bought fat tablets, a box of pencils, coloring books, large boxes of crayons, and three small rulers.

Driving home, she began to laugh at herself. *Oh no! I've become my father!*

THE SPECIAL CONCERT was only two weeks ahead. Anticipation and anxiety were in about a fifty-fifty mix, and Noelle met almost daily with Ryan to maintain promotional efforts at a high pitch. She was concerned that Ryan seemed more stressed than usual, at times nervous and impatient. She suspected what was bothering him. She had done nothing about his personal financial statement, which she read by mistake. What could she do about it? After all, it wasn't as if he had confided in her. At a Monday morning meeting, they finished going over the ticket reports, and he leaned back in his chair and passed his hand over his eyes. He seemed to be already exhausted, but it was only ten in the morning. Perhaps he realized that she had seen his disastrous personal report and wondered how far it had gone.

"Seems as if there was something else . . . " he said, ruffling through the papers in front of him. Then he reached into his "In" basket and found a rather scruffy envelope bearing numerous postmarks and forwarding addresses. He handed it to her. "I don't know what to make of this. You might want to take a look. Someone is asking for information about one of our musicians—that young violinist, Ana Breckenridge. I'm not sure what we should do about it. Maybe she doesn't want to be found."

Noelle studied the envelope with curiosity. The handwriting was definitely European, with crossed number sevens. The return address listed an unfamiliar name and a street address in Salzburg, Osterreich. The letter was addressed to J. Breckenridge at a place in Texas that neither Noelle nor Ryan had ever heard of. The envelope showed several other addresses, marked out, and then the address of the San Sebastian Symphony Association.

"Want to read it?" Ryan asked. "The English is a bit garbled, but someone is definitely trying to trace her."

Noelle opened and read the letter that was short and definitely garbled but intelligible. Its intent was clear. Where is Ana Iliescu Breckenridge?

Noelle was thoughtful. "Well, we don't want to get her into any trouble, because we don't know why she left Europe and we don't want to help anyone find her if she doesn't want to be found. Do you want me to take it? I'll be discreet until we know what this is all about."

"Oh, fine." Ryan said. "Please do."

ORCHESTRA MEMBERS DRIFTED onstage for the regular Saturday rehearsal, all rather quiet and withdrawn. Good musicians will testify that some nervous tension is always present before every performance, or else there is something lacking in the performer's attitude. Perhaps the musician doesn't really care enough and might want to consider another profession.

Emily was already in her chair as co-principal violist, number two in the section. In the first chair, Phil Mathiesen had already warmed up and now he held his instrument across his lap with his legs extended in front of him and ankles crossed. He stared across the row of music stands and the podium between his section and that of the first and second violins, where Ana was repeating one troublesome phrase over and over. She felt his eyes on her and looked up coldly and blankly at him but then returned to her music.

Phil brooded for a moment or two with his lower lip extended in a pout. Then he leaned toward Emily, who was still warming up, nudging her foot with his. She stopped playing but kept her instrument in position under her chin and her bow arm extended.

"What?" she asked.

He kept his voice low. "You know something? I think that little foreigner should be dumped from the orchestra. There's something about her that I don't like and don't trust. Auditions are coming up and there are plenty of good American musicians available."

Emily wanted to ignore his malicious comments. Since Ryan had admitted that it wasn't appropriate for him ever to have asked her any questions about the other musicians, she was relieved and happy to be free of that sticky task. She had hated it even as she did it because she thought she was helping Ryan, but it had made her feel somehow diminished and degraded. She no longer needed to listen to Phil's gossip. She had known him for a long time and disliked his crude jokes and insinuations and she didn't agree with his low opinion of nearly everyone.

"What I think," she said, "is that we won't be auditioning anyone for her social life, Phil. She's okay. Why don't you just leave her alone?" She was annoyed that he had distracted her. She turned a page of her music and studied it. "She always shows up, and she's dependable enough in the section. She seems like a pretty good string player to me, even if she's always late. Aren't you just peeved because she brushes you off?" She raised her viola and began playing again, loud enough to drown out Phil's nettled reply. He gave a snort of derision and with the tip of his bow flipped the page of the music they shared, so she lost her place and had to stop. She glared at him.

Ryan walked onstage and placed a memo on the podium for the music director, Lucas Richter. As he walked off again, he glanced at Ana—the little temptress with the provocative eyes—but that day her eyes were totally on her music. She didn't glance up. Offstage, he lingered by the stage door to be available if any problem arose that was not an artistic one. Everything else was his problem.

Across the stage, he spotted Tommy Barger peering around the open door of the acoustic stage. Since the setup for the rehearsal was still in place from the night before, Ryan was puzzled about Tommy's need to prowl around, moving a few stands an inch or two in different directions. Then he crossed the stage front to pass near Ana, bending slightly toward her to speak softly. She shook her head negatively but didn't look at him or stop playing.

Tommy left the stage near where Ryan stood and slouched off toward the alcove where a small red light on a huge urn indicated that the coffee was ready. Coffee was meant to be paid for by those who drank it, and nobody ever saw Tommy contribute anything. But Ryan noticed that he usually helped himself liberally, as he did now.

Lucas Richter strode onstage briskly to the podium, arranging his music and watching the clock for the moment they could begin. His eyes swept the orchestra. He tapped his baton on the edge of his stand, and the orchestra fell silent. "We'll begin with Rimsky-Korsakov," he said. "This will be the last run-through on this, because we've played it before. We'll spend the rest of our time on the concerto, and I want to ask all of you to put in some extra time on this work during the week. It is difficult, and we need to be letter-perfect by

Friday, when our soloist will be here to join us. This is an important concert."

The musicians listened in silence. "Our concertmaster is going to play the soloist's part for this rehearsal." The string players were impressed, and they tapped their instruments with the sides of their bows, a sign of approbation for one of their own.

Richter glanced at the clock and tapped his baton again. The instruments came up. As the seductive sounds of *Shéhérazade* filled the hall, Ryan left the backstage area to go sit in the auditorium and enjoy listening. His thoughts strayed to the programming for the special concert, and he wondered, as always, how the audience would respond. Richter had programmed an overture, then the soloist playing the concerto, then intermission, and completing the program, the orchestra work *Shéhérazade*. Ryan knew that programming was the music director's eternal dilemma and how difficult it was to please everyone—management with an eye on ticket sales, patrons, critics, musicians, and the board. It was entirely the responsibility of the music director to program. Although Lucas listened patiently to any suggestions or complaints, he usually proceeded to plan his season pretty much as he had intended to do in the first place. He believed strongly that a good conductor must maintain his independence and not allow his board to dictate his programs. If, however, he dissatisfied enough people, the board would replace him, and he knew it. He walked a careful line and kept his own counsel. For that reason, too many interviews were a danger. It pinned him down and limited his options.

From the beginning of his tenure at San Sebastian, board members and patrons had grumbled about the fact that Richter almost always programmed the soloist during the first half of the concert, just before intermission. By the time the concert ended and the fans swarmed backstage to fawn over the exhausted soloist, he had often escaped to the peace and quiet of his hotel room for a quick shower, a change of clothing, and a brief rest before the required socializing at a reception or dinner hosted by a member of the board. That meant that his day finally ended at one or two in the morning. It was a demanding life, and he did not dare show his boredom or the fact that he was weary to the bone.

When the local arts critic complained to Ryan that he could never chat with the artist after a performance, Ryan had talked to Richter about it.

"Look at it this way," the music director had said. He brushed thick, blond hair from his forehead, and it fell back as it had been. His blue eyes, fixed intently on Ryan's, were penetrating and serious. "Look," he said, "the soloist will go on to another city, and more applause and adulation and all that, but the orchestra stays here. Surely we don't want to build our success on the soloists we engage? I want the concerts to end with applause for our musicians. Aren't they what this is all about? I want the patrons to go home with the orchestral sound in their heads. That's what will keep them supportive, don't you agree?"

He had a strong point, and Ryan did agree. They dropped the subject, but it came up again from time to time, and Richter ignored it as before. He gambled that at the end of each season, the patrons would have more to savor than to criticize.

The rich mosaic of the symphonic suite about the *Arabian Nights* storyteller always pleased and excited the audiences, and Ryan knew that it would do so again on the coming weekend. It reached its climax and ended as Richter signaled for the break. Still keyed up, the musicians streamed out from the acoustic shell and toward the coffee pot.

Ryan waited at the end of the line for his coffee because he had time. He filled a plastic cup and turned toward the outside area of lawn and trees and the parking lot. As he passed the door of the stagehands' small office with a sign on the door reading "I.A.T.S.E., Kenneth Christopher, Head Stagehand," he waved at Ken who was signing payroll records at his battered desk. He spotted Ryan and raised his hand.

"Ryan? Got a minute?"

Ryan changed course and walked into the office. Ken came around his desk, closed the door, and asked, "How's it going? Everything okay?"

Ryan nodded, "Okay, so far." He drank some of his coffee, hot as it was.

"Look," Ken said. "We've got a little problem here. Maybe you can help me out."

Ryan was wary. "What kind of a problem?"

"It's Barger. The guys don't like working with that guy. They say he's lazy and a slacker, always goofing off, letting the other guys do his share of the work. He usually needs a shave, a good shower, and some clean clothes at least once a week. But the real problem is, he sneaks a beer while on the job, every chance he gets. That's against regs, even if he goes outside and lurks behind the garbage bin. It increases the danger for the guys who have to depend on him."

Ryan sipped his coffee and nodded, but said nothing. This was not his problem.

Ken picked up a pencil, tapped a little rhythm on the desk, and tossed it down. Ryan knew him well enough to realize that he was uncomfortable with what he was going to do. "Are you satisfied with his work?" Ken asked. "Sloppy setups? Equipment out of place? Any rudeness, lack of cooperation, anything like that?"

Ryan shook his head. "Not that I know of, but he's not my favorite guy."

The head stagehand ran his hand through his short hair. "Ryan, some of the union rules protect the goof-offs as well as the good workers, and it's hard as the devil to get rid of a bad apple who can file a grievance, claim unfair termination, and fight it for months on end. Nevertheless, I've decided to write this Barger guy up to the union. I don't like the man, to be honest, and I can't trust him. I want to get rid of him."

Ryan, on guard, said nothing. He was aware that no one liked Tommy Barger very much, and he didn't either, but this was coming at a bad time. The lights flickered off briefly and on again, signaling that the break time was nearly over.

Ken came quickly to the point. "Would you consider also filing a complaint against the guy? It would bolster my report quite a bit, to be honest."

Ryan hesitated. He knew that Tommy would put up a nasty fight for his job. All kinds of ugly things could ricochet off of that, such as a stagehands' strike if they felt personally threatened. It could certainly complicate things. He believed that Tommy was the kind of guy who, if he was in trouble and forced into a corner, wouldn't hesitate to take others down with him. Ryan flicked his empty coffee cup into the waste basket. "Let me think about it," he said, walking out of the office.

AS HE RETURNED to the darkened interior of the back-stage area, Ryan spotted Tommy and Ana in the far corner in close conversation, their heads bent, inches apart. Tommy was holding Ana's right arm above the elbow, but Ana pulled her arm free and stalked off. Ryan frowned in the darkness. What was it with those two?

He returned to the auditorium and chose a seat in the

middle of a row near the back. He slumped down in the seat and tried to shut out the unpleasant memories of his early morning hours but couldn't.

After his last dinner with Emily, he had resolved to quit running and hiding out and to come to some accommodation with the people to whom he owed so much money. He had made some bad mistakes, and now he had to show them that he was going to pay up. He returned one of the repeated calls and asked for a morning meeting. At six in the morning, Frank Werner tapped twice on the door of Ryan's apartment. Ryan admitted him quickly. Frank was a big man—muscular, good-looking in an earthy way, and neatly dressed in gray trousers and a blue knitted shirt. He could have been an innocuous anyone, but Ryan knew that he wasn't.

Ryan told Frank that he wanted to come to some agreement and to settle his debts. "Look," he said. "I'm in a very visible position here. Lots of people know me. I'm not going anywhere. I do have a plan and I will pay up, but I need some time."

"You've had time. It's been weeks."

"I know, but I don't have that kind of money. I can get it if they'll give me a little wiggle room. What can we work out?"

Frank Werner lit a cigarette and gave Ryan a hard stare, and Ryan made a strong effort not to break eye contact. After a few moments, Frank said, "Lemme use your phone." He dialed, spoke softly, and listened. "Yeah," he said. "Gotcha." He hung up.

"Okay," he said to Ryan. "They'll go along with this, up to a point, but they want security. What d'ya have—property, bank accounts, stock, insurance?"

Ryan had little in the bank, no property, and no stock. He hesitated and then took the plunge. "I've got a life insurance policy . . . for a quarter million. Double for accidental death." Just putting it in words made his blood run cold.

Frank nodded, "Okay, that'll do. You'll have to sign it over."

Ryan did so with a cold fear in the pit of his stomach. The thought of double indemnity in case of accidental death and the possibilities it opened up made the hair bristle on the back of his neck. He wondered if his nightmare would ever end.

He noticed someone seated in the last row of the auditorium, and he glanced over his shoulder to recognize the couple who had been showing up for almost every rehearsal—the tall blond man in gold-rimmed glasses and his little companion with all the freckles and the baseball cap. He frowned. Why were they always hanging around? He thought about intercepting them and asking a few questions, but about five minutes before the rehearsal came to a close, they left their seats and exited to the perimeter hallway that sloped upward to the front lobby and down to the backstage area. He got up abruptly to follow them.

As the musicians left the stage, Ryan saw the woman in the baseball cap approach Ana and try to delay her by grasping her arm. But again, Ana pulled free and walked quickly to the backstage area where the musicians left their cases.

Ryan was puzzled. What was Ana's connection with these people? Did it matter? He wished he knew. Things were definitely piling up.

WITH THAT PAIR of concerts successfully completed, the musicians had a few days to relax before they began more rehearsals for the special concert with Daniel Lessing. Ana had begun marking off the calendar days until he would arrive.

On Tuesday, she had her payroll check, and she decided to cash it at the farmers' market while she bought some fresh fruit and vegetables. She chose a small chicken that she planned to cut up and bake in olive oil and herbs. She decided on fresh green beans and a small eggplant, skipping the tempting asparagus—which was too expensive—and some peaches and figs. Driving home, her spirits lifted at thought of the dinner she would cook in the evening. She wished that she had someone to share it with, but her only friend was Beth, and she had no intention of sharing anything with Karl.

She parked under the acacia tree and climbed the stairs with her packages, holding the rusted screen door open with her foot while she unlocked her door. The apartment smelled musty and stale from Ana's cigarettes from the night before because she hadn't emptied the chipped saucer she used as an ashtray. She put her packages down and struggled to open the window that had been badly painted apple-green over the previous gray paint so it stuck shut each time she closed it.

There remained a bit of coffee from the night before, and she put the pot on the burner to heat while she unpacked her groceries. The small apartment had a chipped kitchen sink, a tiny refrigerator, a three-burner gas plate for cooking, a small table with two chairs, a wall bed that she let down at night, and a miniscule bath in one corner.

She sat at the table and drank the coffee that was as bitter as she knew it would be. From the opened window, she could see the back of Mrs. Janner's house. Before long, the back door opened and her landlady emerged and marched toward the garage apartment, dressed as usual in a flamboyant Hawaiian shirt over baggy khaki trousers with sandals and white athletic socks. Her wispy grey hair was in a knot of sorts on top of her head and over that was perched the favorite straw gardener's hat with a mass of dusty white and yellow cotton daisies falling over the brim. Ana wondered if Mrs. Janner had taken a good look at that hat at any time over the past ten years or so. Her landlady crossed the gravel driveway and stumped up the stairs, knocking loudly on the door.

Ana opened the door only a bit. "What is it, Mrs. Janner?"

The older woman reached into the pocket of her khaki trousers and pulled out a long, rumpled white envelope that she held out to Ana. "This came for you, while ago. Registered. Had to sign for it. Looks like some sort of legal stuff." She peered at Ana and tried to push the door open wider, but Ana held it in place with her foot. "Not in any trouble, are you?" Mrs. Janner asked.

"No, no," Ana said. "Thank you for bringing me the letter." She took the envelope and tried to push the door shut as Mrs. Janner peered through the opening with suspicion.

Ana closed her eyes for a stressed moment before glancing at the return address on the long, white envelope. It read, "Woodings and Wilmot, Attorneys at Law, 101 Bexar Building, San Antonio, Texas, 78205." She stared at it for a few moments before turning it face down on the table and pacing the apartment with her hands covering her face. She was frightened. Legal things always frightened her. What could it be but trouble?

Finally, she pulled out the chair and sat down, slitting the envelope with her dinner knife and spreading out the small stack of legal-sized paper in front of her. She began to frown before she had read a word, and nothing improved from that point.

She struggled over the legal terms and wished she had a dictionary. By page three, it was clear to her than Jerry had filed for an annulment of their marriage. His grounds were desertion. Hers. That came as a shock because this possibility had never occurred to her. Could they do that? No one had warned her. She had never felt more alone.

She counted the weeks that had passed without even a

postcard from Jerry and that should have been a signal that trouble was coming, but she had always hoped that he would eventually ask her to come back. She tried to recall only their happier times together and to skip over the quarrels. Wasn't a little separation supposed to make his heart grow fonder, and to make things right between them again? Surely that was what Lurleen had promised. But why had Ana trusted her, when her first interest had to be the happiness and the future of her son?

Was it really over? Was her dream of a new life in the States going down, a failure already? How could this be? Did Jerry really no longer love her? Or had he, ever? She sat with her hands covering her face, numb with shock. What was love, anyway? She remembered reading some borrowed paperback novels that always ended with one of the leading characters giving up everything to make the other one happy. Was that it? She knew that this had not been any part of her plan, and it wasn't now.

What would happen to her? Her position in the symphony was not secure because she had been filling a temporary vacancy. If another vacancy opened up, could she pass another audition? She had no friends and no support among the other musicians because she had made no effort to develop any. She had almost no money and no prospects.

Anxiety began to build in her mind. If she failed an audition and found herself without a job, would the immigration people cancel her visa and her work permit? Then where could she go? She wished she had someone to talk to. She thought of Beth and checked her watch. No, it was nearly five in the evening and too late for Beth to come to the apartment. Maybe the next day she would talk to her, but in strict confidence.

She read the last page of the legal papers again. There was no question of any alimony, it said, because the marriage had been of such short duration. However, Mr. and Mrs. Brandon Breckenridge had generously offered a small, one-time settlement for Ana, and this would be forwarded to her when she had signed and returned the enclosed agreement of annulment.

What was the use? She knew that she had very little choice. How could she fight this when she knew it was what the influential Breckenridge family had decided was best, and they had plenty of money while she had none?

Her shoulders slumped. She didn't bother to wipe away the slow, hot tears that ran down her cheeks and fell on the papers in front of her. She picked up the last sheet where her name appeared below a dotted line. Biting her lip, her throat tight, she signed with a trembling hand. Her marriage was over.

Chapter Nine

ONE OF ANA'S earliest memories of the city she grew up in was of a Sunday walk with her mother, Lucienne, through the splendid symmetry of downtown Palace Square. She had stared with wide eyes at the gigantic buildings surrounding it, none of which she had ever seen before. She was too small to understand that these handsome structures were the heart of this socialist country's administrative, political, and cultural life, and that the city was so old that it was first written about in 1459. Her mother explained this long history to her throughout their walk, but it was mostly just words to Ana. Her mind fixated on the imposing buildings around her and she could only wonder how any person could be so brave as to go to the top of one of these mammoth structures that seemed to her to soar straight into the clouds.

Even the ugly communist headquarters building seemed beautiful to her because she understood nothing of her country's agony under the ruthless dictator and his iron-willed wife, both of whom everyone feared. Her mother held her hand as they climbed wide stone steps to enter the vast, dark cathedral.

The heavy door creaked from disuse. No one was in the church and the cold air smelled musty and stale.

Ana worried that there might be mice running between the pews, and she thought she could hear their little feet scuffling on the marble floor. She didn't like mice. Lucienne pointed out the ancient brass marker that told them that the church had been built in the year 1772, but that meant little to Ana because it was difficult for her to remember further back than a month or so.

They knelt in one of the back pews, and her mother looked over her shoulder before bending her head and closing her eyes for a whispered prayer. Ana had never seen her mother pray before, and she watched her curiously. Lucienne knew it was dangerous to do this, because their country had been officially an atheistic and communist society since the Second World War. No masses had been said in this church for a very long time, although most citizens of the country still secretly considered themselves Orthodox.

After a few more minutes, Lucienne gripped Ana's hand as they walked quickly up the nave and past the transepts, to pause in front of the high altar that was empty of religious symbols and looked dusty and neglected. Without releasing her daughter's hand, Lucienne hesitated with the urge to genuflect before the altar but decided against it because there was nothing there but cobwebs. It felt very wrong to her to walk on past, but they scuttled down the opposite side of the cathedral and out the heavy doors again, where Lucienne hesitated in the shelter of large pillars and looked in all directions before continuing down the marble steps to the sidewalk.

"Who are you looking for, Mama?" Ana asked in a whisper.

"No one. It's all right, darling, but remember what I told you. This visit is our little secret, and you mustn't talk about it. Some bad people might not understand."

"Then why did we come here?" Ana asked. "The church is dark, and it scared me."

"Because I wanted you to see it. It's part of our history, part of who we are. Someday it will be beautiful again and we will all dress up and go there together to sing lovely songs about God and faith and loving each other. But for now, we must be patient and say nothing. Do you understand, Ana?"

Uncertain, Ana nodded.

She remembered that day as one of the good times with her mother. It wasn't always good, and she sometimes didn't see Lucienne for days on end. Ana loved her mother with all her heart, and she thought of her as being exactly like the princess in her storybook, with her lovely green eyes and long blond hair that shone like silver in the sunlight. She was tiny, with graceful hands and tapered fingers. She could play any instrument that she wanted to. Or so it seemed to Ana. Lucienne gave music lessons when she wasn't busy playing in the violin section of the philharmonic or for the opera or ballet companies. Comprehensive violin lessons for Ana had begun from the time she could hold a miniature instrument in her chubby hands.

They lived with Lucienne's sister Marie in a fourth-floor walk-up flat. Life had been unkind to Marie. Although she had the same dreamy green eyes as her sister and her niece, Marie's hair was a limp, nondescript brown, and she had not been considered tiny since she was eleven years old when food became her daily consolation. Marie had been born with a cleft lip and palate from her mother's bout with German measles during pregnancy. She was filled with anger and resentment about it. Why should her sister have everything—beauty, talent, men, and a darling child—while she herself had nothing?

Although Lucienne told friends that she was separated

from her husband, she never worried about it and Marie knew she could have another husband if she wanted one. Every man Lucienne knew was attracted to her, while no man was attracted to Marie.

Ana always remembered that Marie had been very sweet to her when she was small, holding her on her lap every evening and reading the stories from the little book she had bought Ana from her meager earnings. Every morning, she brushed Ana's hair to make it shine and tied it with one of the ribbons she saved from many sources. She put Ana to bed when Lucienne was out, which was most of the time.

Marie had a part-time job at the end of the block as an assistant to the muscular butcher, Miklos. Because it was difficult to understand Marie until one knew her well, she was not permitted to work in the front of the shop or meet the customers but was relegated to the back to stuff sausages when there was any kind of meat available.

On the days when Lucienne was not home, Marie took Ana with her to her job at the butcher shop, where the little girl sat in the corner on a small stool and read her storybook or else sat on the floor with the few stubby crayons that she treasured and carefully colored the newspaper pictures that Marie saved for her.

At the butcher's, Ana watched with distaste each time Marie took her big apron from the nail in the closet and put it on. It wasn't laundered often enough, and it was stiff with dried animal blood and smelled terrible. Ana hated it when Marie tried to hug her when she was wearing the smelly apron, but if she pulled away, Marie would grasp her arm and pinch, hard, frowning at her. Ana learned not to draw a deep breath at such times and to stand very quietly until Marie released her.

Back in the flat, Marie would examine the scraps of meat that Miklos had made available to the workers, because it was at the point of becoming spoiled and rancid and he no longer dared sell it. Although Marie accepted any meat that was offered and cooked it with whatever wilted vegetables she could find at the market, the smell and taste of the meals nauseated Ana, and she often preferred to eat two slices of bread and homemade jam for dinner. That infuriated Marie.

In the evenings, Marie would stretch out on their ancient and lumpy blue plush sofa and fall asleep. She was usually in her favorite dress, a gaudy one of purple rayon that she had found at the flea market. It was too tight around the hips, with a sagging hemline and mismatched buttons in front. She often slept with her arms thrown over her head, and the underarm areas of her dress were ringed with stale sweat. Ana hated that dress.

When she was about five, Ana asked Lucienne about her father. "Where does he live? Why doesn't he come to see us?"

Lucienne took her on her lap and hugged her. "Darling, he can't come to see us right now. He lives in Russia. He's a very, very important man with the army, maybe a general by now. He drives a big black car and wears a handsome uniform with many golden medals. He's a brave soldier, and you can always be proud of him."

"What's his name, Mama?"

Lucienne hesitated. "Sergei," she said. "Someday he will come to see us, and he'll bring you many expensive presents. You'll see." She kissed the tip of Ana's nose.

Ana loved this story and often asked Lucienne to tell her more about her father. But once, when her mother was tired and cross, she told the story differently and referred to him as "Anton."

"But Mama . . ." Ana had begun.

"Oh, do go to bed, Ana, and don't be tiresome."

Later, when the Russians began pressuring their country to

conform more closely to communist doctrine and the dictator showed his independence by refusing, things became tight in their economy. Lucienne and Marie raged about the current urbanization of the small farms, the destruction of the farmers' villages, and the continued rationing of bread, sugar, and flour, all under tight government control. But it was really the constant pressure from the Russians, Marie said. Why couldn't they leave this poor little country alone? There was almost nothing left of it.

"Yes! Down with the Russians!" cried Lucienne, waving her nearly empty wine glass in the air. "Shoot them all!"

Ana was shocked. "But not my father!"

Lucienne's green eyes narrowed as she studied Ana's face. "My darling," she said, "he was not Russian! No, never! He was Austrian, and he came here to play the piano with the philharmonic. Oh, Ana, such a handsome man, so tall, with curls of black hair all over his head and warm, brown eyes. He was called Friedrich."

Ana was puzzled into silence, and sometime later, when they were alone, she asked her Aunt Marie if she had known Ana's father.

Marie hugged her close. "Yes, yes, my little darling," she said. "You have a very fine father. I met him once when he came to get your mother in his big car. He is from London, and he sang with the opera here. A beautiful voice, like an angel! Oh, your Mama was so taken with him. His name was Trevor."

Again, Ana remained silent. It was all beyond her understanding, and she suspected that a wise child never believed anything an adult told her. It was the beginning of disillusion and cynicism and a belief that there was truly nothing she might believe without any doubt, but she kept these thoughts to herself.

Ana was thirteen when Lucienne left the flat and never came back. Her scrawled note to Ana explained that she loved her new friend, the French organist Marcel, too much to live without him. They were going away together to be married. They would send for her soon. Ana should continue with her music, practice every day, be a good girl, help Marie, and remember everything that Lucienne had taught her. "Above all," she wrote, "be happy for me!"

It wasn't long after that that Ana began to sense Marie's growing resentment. The older woman had been stunned to find herself with the full responsibility for her niece and very little income to meet it. At first, Lucienne sent checks and loving letters, but on no particular schedule. One was from the Salzburg Festival, and another came from Geneva. She sent touristy colored photos of these areas, and she always promised that they would be together soon. But after a while, the letters and checks stopped coming, and they heard nothing more for many months. Ana tried to forget that she had ever had a beautiful mother that she so loved and told herself that she would never see her mother again.

As soon as she could get a temporary work permit, Ana began taking any music work she could find, substituting (illegally at her age) with the ballet and opera orchestras and playing with pickup groups for weddings or parties. She was only fourteen when she began doing this, but she lied easily about her age. Her solemn demeanor made her seem older than she was. She always gave most of the money she earned to Marie and kept only enough to buy the long black dress her work required and to keep heels on her run-over shoes.

When she was fifteen, she met up with three other young musicians and they instantly joined forces. They were Heidi from Vienna, Ian from Bristol, and Mikhail from the Ukraine—a truly international troupe. Ana, Heidi, and

Mikhail had made it a rule to speak nothing but English among themselves, because English was gradually becoming the international language, replacing French. They felt that they could go anywhere if they spoke it well enough. They were improving, although they had acquired some of Ian's Bristol pronunciations.

They eked out a precarious living with their music. They had a large jar where they saved small amounts of their earnings in the hope of buying a used bus so they could hit the road. But first they had some gigs to play. The next one pending was a wedding between a beautiful young local girl and a wealthy Italian, crowded with relatives from both countries, with all the beer and excellent wine anyone cared to drink.

It was 3:00 A.M. when the party finally broke up, and outside, a warm drizzle had begun to fall. It was too late for a bus, and taxis in the area were rare, so they decided to walk home. Ian, who played cello, drove a decrepit Fiat. His instrument was too large to carry very far, but the car was too small for the rest of them. With a lot of raucous laughter, they managed to cram their instrument cases into small corners of his car and wave him off. They were carefree.

Ana and Heidi took off their shoes, waded happily in every puddle they passed, and kicked water on each other. Because their long dresses impeded their fun, they tucked their skirts into the lower edges of their underwear so they looked like they were wearing fat black bloomers.

After their many glasses of beer, everything seemed hilarious to them. They laughed, sang, and made a detour to pass by the river, a tributary of the Danube. At that early morning hour, it ran gray and sluggish in its banks. A few fishing boats drifted and waited for dawn. Ana, Heidi, and Mikhail leaned on the railing and told each other stories of their economically deprived early lives. They rejoiced with the optimism of youth because they were confident that poverty had ended for them.

By the time Ana reached her Aunt Marie's flat, it had begun to grow light on the eastern horizon. Her long hair was dripping wet, and it hung in sodden strings around her face and down her back. Her feet and legs were wet and muddy, but she didn't care. She felt happy and so hopeful for the future. She sang her favorite old song, still around since World War II, of the German streetwalker *Lili Marlene* standing under the lamplight. She climbed four flights of stairs with her muddy shoes in hand.

She tried to be quiet when she unlocked the door to the flat, but it was wasted effort because her aunt was not sleeping. Ana opened the door to face Marie, who was barefoot in her faded bathrobe, her skimpy hair sticking up in spikes on top of her head.

She sat facing the door with her arms folded across her chest, and her face darkened in an ugly scowl. Ana knew her aunt's temper, and she guessed that her fury had been building for hours and was now likely out of control. Her cheeks were a mottled purple, her eyes narrow and full of malice, her mouth tight. Two large paper shopping bags sat in front of her, stuffed and spilling over. In a quick glance, Ana recognized her own meager belongings, including a treasured pair of green suede shoes with silver buckles, left behind by her mother but now too small for Ana to wear.

"Tramp! Tramp!" Marie's scream was shrill. "Out all night! No good, just like your mother. Always the men! Always the good time!" She reached into the paper bag nearest her and began throwing items at Ana—some shoes, a sweater, a knitted hat from the past winter, a tattered book, and some ancient phonograph records. "Get out! I don't want you here anymore! This is a decent house. Get out of my sight!"

Sobbing, Marie ran into the tiny bathroom and locked the door, but Ana could still hear her outraged wails. Ana was numb with shock, and she stood with her hands hanging limply at her sides, at a loss as to what she should do. She was stunned at the depth of Marie's anger, but, young as she was, she had guessed that this was coming. For weeks, Marie had been growing colder and more suspicious toward her, doubting every explanation of where she had been, even when it was true, as it usually was. Whatever closeness had existed between them was gone.

Ana looked around the depressing and cramped apartment that lacked a bright spot of color anywhere. It had been this way for as long as she could remember. Of course, she knew that her aunt was under no obligation to provide a home for her. She had little enough for herself and had been kind in years past. But Ana was shocked and frightened to realize that time and Marie's patience had run out and were not likely to revive.

Slowly, she picked up the thrown items and stuffed them back in the paper bags. Her carefree feeling had evaporated. She resolved that she could make it on her own, and she didn't need anyone. Still, she was only sixteen years old. Now, who would know or care what happened to her?

As she stumbled down the staircase that was still dark, she felt a rush of gratitude that if she had no family, at least she had one friend. When she went to her small flat, Heidi readily took her in. She was glad for some extra income to help with expenses. But her third-floor flat was small and cramped, and the two of them had to share a narrow and lumpy pull-down bed. They didn't mind because they knew it wouldn't be forever. Neither of them was much of a cook, but they managed. They traded clothes, shared secrets and whatever money they could earn, and they giggled a lot. Heidi was Ana's first real friend.

Plans moved ahead. Ian had located a used bus, an oxidized dark blue that had turned to a flaking purple. He found it at a price they thought they would be able to afford in the near future. There remained one problem—Heidi, Mikhail, and Ian had visas to travel freely, but Ana had no identification papers whatever. That was a lapse on Lucienne's part. In her country, emigration was nearly impossible, and civil rights were only in the memories of the older generation.

But Ian had an idea. He told Ana, "You look so much like my sister Penny that you could be sisters yourselves. Same size, same hair, same eyes, except for the color. A black-and-white ID won't show that her blue eyes aren't your green ones. I'll write and ask her to send her visa so we can get you across the border."

"Will she do it? She could get in trouble . . . " Ana said.

"So could all of us, but we'll be careful. Anyway, she's getting married soon, and she'll need a new visa anyway. Besides that, she never goes anywhere to use it."

By September, they were ready. Penny did send her visa and wished them luck. Ana was fascinated at how much she resembled Ian's sister.

"She didn't mind sending it, not a bit," he said. "She's a little nester who wants to build her nest and hatch lots of baby birds. The two of us got shifted among the relatives after Mum died, and all she wants now is to get married and make a little place of their own where they will stay put for the rest of their lives."

"And does your father still work off of his fishing boat for months at a time?"

"Aye, what else? It's the only life he knows."

They removed four of the back seats of the bus to make

room for fold-up camp cots that they could assemble each night. With a camp stove, a large water jug, and some canned groceries, they were ready to roll. As young as they were, it seemed all a game to them, and they were not afraid in the least.

As they neared the border, Ana's spirits began to lift in anticipation. With a little luck, she would soon escape the reign of terror, and she promised herself that she would never again live under the iron hand of the despot whom most of the citizens called "the madman."

In the bus, the other three coached Ana while she clutched her borrowed visa for good luck and set up her cot in the back of the bus.

"Now remember," Mikhail said, "stay under the blanket at all costs and cover your face. Cough as much as you can. Say nothing! Your accent is a dead giveaway."

"And also," Heidi said, "pinch your cheeks so you look like fever."

"And remember," Ian reminded her, "you are Penny from Bristol."

"Yes! Yes! Stop! I will remember it all," Ana cried. "You are making me nervous!" She knew they were jumpy because she wouldn't be the only one in trouble if they got caught.

When they were within five hundred yards of the border, Heidi poured the fetid medicine they had been saving on Ana's clothes, her hands, and even her hair. She began her vigorous coughing, and by the time they reached the guard gate, she was growing hoarse. Because the old wool blanket was hot, her face was red enough without Heidi's pinching.

Ian, in the driver's seat, produced their visas and explained that they had a sick person on the bus. They were taking her home to her family. The guard then came on board the bus to look at Ana, who coughed and moaned. Holding Penny's visa for comparison, he stared at her with distaste but finally shrugged, returned their visas to them, and waved them and their noxious germs on their way. As soon as they were out of sight of the guard shack, they howled with delight and stamped their feet.

"You were great!" Heidi screamed. "A real Greta Garbo!"

But when Ana threw off her stuffy blanket and came to the front of the bus, they held their noses. "Whew!" Mikhail said. "She smells! Find a creek and we dump her in!"

They did find a small pond, where Ana submerged herself, feeling refreshed and happy. Then they drove on into Hungary, stopping at small inns or hotels where they might get a night's work in exchange for meals and two rooms. They reached the capital, the twin cities of Buda and Pest, which straddle the Danube. They were able to find plenty of work there in the many restaurants but also as substitutes at the Opera House and the many concert halls of the beautiful old city. During the days, they explored such historic places as the thirteenth century's Matthias Church and the ancient Buda Castle. They held impromptu concerts under the green canopy of City Park and collected contributions in Mikhail's red cap.

From there, they drove into Czechoslovakia and its capital, which the citizens called "Praha," on the Vltava River, which cuts a north-south route, dividing the lovely old city into gardens and park on its west side and twelfth-century Old Town to the east, where small restaurants and taverns lined narrow streets, a target area for every itinerant musician. Prague was a center of culture and had a rich tradition in music and literature. Ana knew and had often played the works of the famous Czech composers Dvôrāk, Smetana, and Janacek, who are celebrated there annually in a spring festival. She discovered that she wanted to learn more about them. For the first time, she ventured into a library and began to borrow books and read about these men of genius and also of the Czech writers Franz Kafka and Rainer Maria Rilke, of whom she knew nothing.

The more the four of them traveled, the more she became aware of the large gaps in her education. Marie had never cared whether she skipped school or not, as she herself hadn't gone far. Lucienne was interested only in a music education for her, so she could earn a living. Ana often felt ignorant around the more worldly Heidi, Mikhail, and Ian, and she kept quiet but listened closely when they discussed and debated world affairs.

They had been in Prague for two months when Ana met a young Israeli violinist while the two of them played as one-time substitutes in the back row of the second violins for the fabulous Czech Philharmonic. They became instant soulmates, spending each day together, inseparable. Their close friendship came to an abrupt halt with Daniel's forced return to Israel. Ana was bereft and brokenhearted. Her friends decided that it was time to move on to Germany. There was always tomorrow.

Chapter Ten

THE FOUR YOUNG musicians settled on Frankfurt
because there was an American military base nearby and they
had the idea that all Americans had money and were eager to
spend it. Ana, especially, wanted to meet Americans.

When Daniel had to make his hurried departure for Israel,
he gave Ana as many gifts as his limited budget would allow—
a white cashmere sweater, a beaded handbag, a tiny bottle of
genuine French perfume, and a large basket of fresh fruit. This
was the first time that Ana had thought of men as a source of
gifts, and the thought never would have occurred to her when
she considered Ian or Mikhail. They were like brothers, and
the four of them shared everything equally. But Daniel's gifts
were a different idea entirely. The gifts were for her, and
although she shared the fruit with her friends, she hid everything else away in her knapsack and kept it secret as much as
possible in such tight living quarters as folding cots on a bus.

Her first new friend in Frankfurt was Emil, and he was not
an American but an apprentice cook at Hermann's *Hofbrau*,
where they found their first job of any duration. Hermann
served traditional German dinners, and he loved chamber

music, so they worked every night but Mondays. Although they were thrilled with their job, it had its drawbacks. Hermann paid them real money and included their dinner each night, but long periods of musical silence while there were diners in the restaurant upset him, so he had established the rule that they had to play without interruption and drink only water until ten in the evening, when most of the diners were finished. Then they could take a half-hour break for dinner. After that, they played on until one in the morning. It made for a long day.

Emil was attracted to Ana from his first sight of her. Her friends had noticed that when Emil served them, her dinner was always more generous than theirs, with little extra treats such as a half of a canned peach, a tiny bite of strudel, or some cream on her rice pudding while theirs was bare. They teased her, but not too much because she usually shared her treats with them.

She flirted mildly with Emil, who had a thatch of blond hair and bright blue eyes and was rather shy. Egged on by Heidi, she began meeting Emil during the day, and it soon became a clandestine affair. They met in the afternoons near the financial center where the annual trade fairs were held, for trips to the movies or walks along the river bank. The lovesick Emil had chosen this location for its anonymity, but he had a suspicious wife, and she began following him.

It was a lovely spring day with early blossoms popping out on the trees when Ana and Emil went window-shopping and she spotted some leather boots and skirt in a shop window. Because he was in love with Ana, he weakened to her entreaties and bought them for her, though he couldn't afford them and would have a hard time hiding the expense from Gerta.

He was right to have been worried. The next afternoon,

when Ana arrived at their usual corner bench meeting place in her new leather skirt and boots with a delicate gold chain borrowed from Heidi around her neck, she found Gerta waiting for her. Gerta slapped at her face and screeched, a shocked Ana screamed, and Emil, a late arrival to the scene, covered his ears. It was the last time Ana saw dear Emil alone, but at least she was able to keep the skirt and boots. They were much too small for pudgy Gerta.

It was only a few weeks later that three Americans came to the *hofbrau* for dinner. Ana's glance was drawn to the taller one, who seemed, in the dim light, to be all of one color—a tawny gold, from his clipped hair to the tan of his face and the khaki of his short-sleeved summer uniform with gold insignia that Ana couldn't decipher. They were speaking English and when the tall one threw his head back with a burst of laughter that drew smiles from surrounding tables, she caught a glimpse of even, white teeth. After dinner the three men moved closer to where the musicians were playing and ordered another round of beer in Hermann's pewter steins with hinged tops and pictures on all sides. The tall one sat directly in front of Ana. She stole a glance at his shoes. *Ah, good leather. No holes in the soles, surely!* she thought. She let her gaze climb and was startled to meet his eyes watching her. Her heart contracted and she glanced quickly at her music, but not before he had grinned at her and she had allowed herself the hint of a smile in return. She and Heidi had talked about Americans before and had decided that American men didn't like aggressive women. When the three men left just after midnight, laughing and joking, Ana's spirits drooped, and she wondered if she would ever see them again.

Two nights later, however, the taller one returned alone. Ana wasn't sure at first, because he wore a navy blue knitted shirt and dark blue trousers instead of a uniform. But he took the same table again, directly in front of her. This time, she took a chance and gave him a warm smile. He grinned back, and he stayed. At their dinner break, he ambled back to the table near the kitchen where they were seated and already cutting their meat.

"*Sehr schon!*" he said. ("Very beautiful!")

"*Danke,*" said Mikhail.

"*Wie geht?*" ("How are things?")

"*Gut, danke,*" Mikhail replied. He pointed his knife toward an empty chair. "Please, sit down. American, no? We can all speak some English."

"Oh, good. My German is pretty weak." He held out his hand and introduced himself. "Jerry Breckenridge, U.S. Air Force, from Texas."

The men shook hands, exchanging names, and Ian pointed his knife at the women. "Heidi, from Vienna, and Ana, from hell country."

The four of them laughed and began eating their *fleisch und gemuse* with enthusiasm because it was their first meal of the day, except for coffee and rolls. The men talked freely and laughed, but Ana and Heidi were silent except to answer the American's questions with soft smiles. Under the table, Heidi nudged Ana's foot, and in reply, Ana stepped on Heidi's toe.

The tall Texan stared at Ana with a faintly dazed expression, his mouth just slightly ajar, as though something had surprised him or caught him unaware. The other three exchanged amused glances and covert nudges. He stayed until they had finished playing and he was waiting by the exit when they came out of the building. Ana hesitated, and the other three moved on without her.

"Walk you home?" he asked, reaching for her violin. They moved off slowly after the others, and by the time they reached the row of flats where they had rented rooms, Ana knew that he was a helicopter pilot attached to the Rhine-Main Air Base.

"We fly recon," he said, "and sometimes rescue, when it's needed. And we fly the brass to meetings and for inspections—that kind of stuff." Although he spoke in a slow drawl, most of it was incomprehensible to Ana, who knew nothing about the military.

"I'm almost finished with my tour," he said, "and then I'll be discharged and head for the States."

Ana's hopes took a blow. "But not soon, no?"

He laughed down at her. "Three months. That's not very soon, is it?"

He began coming to see her whenever he had time off, and she felt confident that he was attracted to her. He brought her little gifts from the base exchange—a jade bracelet, some good Swiss chocolate, and a silk scarf. But his goodnight kisses seemed brief and diffident to her, and she was puzzled.

"Maybe he's just shy," Heidi said. "Or maybe that's the way they are in Texas. Cattle first, women second."

Ana groaned and said, "I don't understand! I know he feels affection for me and all that, but he always pulls back, too polite. And I don't like it that he talks so much about his family. He tells his father everything, I think, and he thinks his father knows all."

One day he showed her a picture of his mother that had just come in his mail. She was in a parade, riding a palomino mare at the head of a mounted group of women on matched palominos. They were all dressed alike in white, except for narrow, blue silk scarves knotted at their throats, with white gloves and big white Stetson hats worn low on their brows. His mother had long, blond hair down her back. She wore some kind of leather belt around her waist that held a pole standard in place, topped with a Lone Star flag whipping in the wind. Ana thought she was the most beautiful person she had ever seen. *Imagine, leading a parade, and on that big horse!* she thought. Ana was afraid of horses.

He talked a lot about Texas. His family bred Hereford cattle on eight hundred acres, and he wanted a herd of his own, just as both of his brothers had. "It's not like it used to be," he said. "The money isn't nearly as good, but it's what we do, all the same. My dad is keeping his eyes open for me at the cattle auctions, and we think the helicopter will revitalize the big spreads, make it easy to get around for things like checking fences, locating lost animals, and bringing in emergency feed. All those things can be done in hours now, when it used to take days in the saddle or riding in a pickup truck. Now we have to find a 'copter my dad can afford, next year for sure."

"But all that land!" she said. "That must be as large as a city?" No one that Ana knew owned any land at all.

"That's how much it takes, because so much of it is not good range land. Too dry, too full of mesquite and scrub oak. But you have to take the bad with the good."

Ana tried to imagine all these lives concentrated on cattle, but she couldn't because she had never been around animals. She was a city girl.

In August, Hermann decided to paint the entire *hofbrau* inside and out. He had hired an artist to do a new mural where one entire wall was covered with a painting of the Black Forest and some rampaging wild boars. His new design was for another of the Black Forest, this time with a hunter and his bow and arrow. Hermann was very excited about the new mural.

Meanwhile, the four musicians had two weeks free. Heidi decided to go visit her uncle, and Mikhail would join Ian on a visit to Bristol to see Penny's new baby, so Ana had the flat to herself before her Saturday night date with Jerry. She shampooed her hair and dressed in the leather skirt and boots, her one good white silk blouse, and, of course, Jerry's jade bracelet. She rummaged around in Heidi's things, hoping that her friend had forgotten her green eye shadow—good American Revlon. She found it and helped herself to it before returning it to its hiding place in Heidi's rolled-up stocking.

She and Jerry ate dinner near the river and then walked to a nearby park that had a gaudy carousel and a small but perfect lake with white swans and water lilies. Vendors in clown costumes prowled the lanes selling ice cream and balloons, so Jerry bought her a dachshund made of pink balloons with a purple polka-dot bow around its neck. They found a bench where they could watch the swans and she wrapped the balloon dog's ribbon loosely around the top rung of the bench.

He reached for her hand, enfolding it in both of his. "Ana," he said. "I don't know if you're counting, but I'll be leaving in two weeks, and I guess you know that I'm really going to miss you."

Two weeks! So soon? No, she hadn't been counting. She hadn't wanted to think about it because she wasn't making any progress with Jerry and she wondered if he would really mind leaving her. She placed her free hand on top of his and exerted a little pressure. "And I will miss you, Jerry. I can't believe that you are really going off and maybe I'll never see you again." She looked at him with mournful eyes and commented, "You've been wicked to make me fall in love with you, only to leave me behind."

He was taken aback, and he looked at her and then away, at the water and the swans. "I know it isn't fair, and it's been bothering me, too," he said, "but I didn't plan it this way." He wrapped his arm around her shoulders and drew her close, nuzzling her neck and burying his face in her long hair. "Ah, Ana. Why are you so sweet? What shall I do about you?"

She nestled closer, melting against him and hoping that he could detect the last few drops of Daniel's French perfume that she had applied to her throat, wrists, and behind her ears. She could feel the hardness of his body through his shirt, and she felt very small beside him. She pressed her cheek against his. Her eyes were closed. They were motionless and concentrated only on each other.

A handsome blond woman and a small boy in green *lederhosen* came around the shrubbery. The boy held the leash of a white poodle, and the little dog came over to sniff at Ana's boot. Annoyed, she pushed him away with her foot.

"Klaus! Klaus!" the woman called, but the boy ignored her and stared at Jerry.

"*Woher kommen Sie?*" ("Where do you come from?") he asked.

"Outer space," Jerry said.

The blond woman glared at him and grasped the boy's collar to drag him off. Across the lake, an elderly woman scattered bread crusts for some glossy pigeons that were scrambling around her feet. Klaus waited until all the pigeons had landed and then ran through them, wind-milling his arms and screaming, so they all flew off in a flutter of gray. The old woman shook her fist at him.

"What a brat!" Jerry snorted. "I'd like to warm his little butt!"

Now their mood was shattered, and they sat hand-in-hand in thoughtful silence. Before long, Klaus, his mother, and their dog retraced their route to pass in front of Jerry and Ana again. As he approached, Klaus made a quick grab for Ana's balloon dog and ran off with it, screaming with joy. His mother ran after him, crying, "Klaus! Klaus!"

Furious, Jerry also ran after him. To Ana, the scene was hilarious and as mother, boy, dog, and Jerry disappeared around the shrubbery, she laughed until tears welled in her eyes. She hoped Jerry caught the monster-child and beat the devil out of him.

Jerry, still angry, hot, and disheveled, returned without the balloon dog. "A little gangster in training," he said, scowling. "I couldn't catch him!" Ana smothered her giggles and covered her nose and mouth with her handkerchief. She turned away from Jerry, but he misunderstood.

He put his hand on her shoulder. "Ana! Are you crying? Don't do that!" He took her in his arms. "Sweetheart, please don't cry over a silly balloon dog! We'll get you another one." He stroked her hair and then had an inspiration. "Hey, even better, how about if I buy you a real dog, a puppy? Would you like that, Ana? Have you ever had a puppy of your own?"

Ana shuddered inwardly. *Dogs! Spare me!* she thought. Food was scarce enough without having an animal to feed. She shook her head, praying that he would forget, but things were not progressing the way she had planned, and time was growing very short. She felt pressured and decided that after all, she would be the aggressor. She pressed her cheek against his. "Jerry, I want to be with you. Please come back to the flat with me where we can be alone? Please?" she begged.

He stiffened and pulled away, startled, and then took her head between his hands and looked intently into her eyes. He hadn't planned on growing even closer to Ana, but rather in putting more distance between them so he might leave with a clear conscience.

"Please!" she coaxed. She jumped up and took his hand in both of hers, holding tight, drawing him with her. Wrenched in two directions by his very strong emotions and against his better judgment, he bought a small bottle of cognac, and they returned to her flat.

The next morning, she woke early and hurried to tidy the

small room before breakfast. The candles on the small table had burned down the night before, and stale smoke made the room smell stuffy. The two glasses that had held cognac were empty but unwashed, and a small fly had drowned in the sticky residue of one glass. She put them into the tiny sink and ran cold water in them.

Without dressing, she buttoned her coat over her short nightgown and slipped into her shoes after rummaging in several purses for any change she could find. From Heidi's sewing basket, she found her scissors and slipped them into the pocket of her coat.

She ran to the corner market where she bought two eggs, one fresh peach, two cinnamon rolls, and a small bag of fresh-ground coffee. On her return trip, she drew the scissors from her coat pocket and snipped off the best one of Frau Wedekind's yellow roses from some that had grown through her iron fence to the outside sidewalk.

Back in the flat, she cleared the litter from the small kitchen table and searched the closet for the blue-and-white checkered cloth that she and Heidi never bothered to use. She found it, wrinkled but clean, and spread it on the table under a jelly jar filled with water for the yellow rose. After putting the coffee pot on to heat, she dressed in a black miniskirt and a clinging pink blouse and brushed her hair. Jerry still slept. After breakfast, she decided, they would go walking along the river, under the willow trees.

On Monday they went shopping for groceries because there was absolutely no food left in the kitchen. They held hands all the way to the market and all the way back, walking very close together with their hands clasped tightly in the pocket of his coat. She was glowing. At last, Jerry seemed to be falling in love. When they were together, he rarely took his eyes off of her. She knew a few playful tricks and bits of

provocative teasing, along with some jokes she borrowed from
Ian. He was enchanted with her. They laughed a lot, telling
each other funny stories about their families and childhoods,
although her stories were carefully edited. On Sunday afternoon, he fell asleep on the sofa, and she puttered about in the
tiny kitchen, fixing him a mug of coffee. He woke, missed her,
and called, "Ana, where are you?"

She sensed that spending so much time with a woman he
was attracted to was a new experience for him, but she knew
that he had grown up with only brothers around him. Ana felt
tender toward him because he seemed so young and unworldly in so many ways, and so different from the young European
men she knew.

By Tuesday, he was very depressed at the thought of leaving her, to return to the States. There had to be a way for her
to go with him, but time was so very short. Everything about
his departure was already scheduled and the paperwork almost
complete. He made an urgent trip to see the base chaplain,
who was not encouraging. It didn't help that Jerry was nervous
and tense.

The chaplain was a dedicated young man who took his job
seriously. He reviewed the hurriedly written application in
front of him on his desk, shaking his head. "Now,
Lieutenant," he said. "you know the regs. There just isn't time
to get this done. You should remember that these rules are
made to protect you fellows. This is a serious step you're considering. How well do you know the girl? Someone who seems
wonderful when you're over here doesn't always turn out that
way in the States, but then it's too late. Why don't you go on
home, talk to your parents, and think about it? If you still
want to do it in a few months, you can start on the paperwork
to bring her over there. Perhaps a proxy marriage?"

The idea of talking it over with his parents was alarming,

because he had little doubt that they would heartily disapprove. But he didn't intend to lose Ana. There had to be some way. He would make some more inquiries.

Jerry took Ana shopping for new clothes on Tuesday afternoon. She chose a pale rose silk dress and jacket with shoes to match. *Italian shoes! Real leather!* He had brought his dress uniform from the base and left it at her apartment.

On Wednesday morning, with Ana clutching her bouquet of tiny white roses and stephanotis, they took a cab to the small Lutheran church Jerry had located in a poor part of town where the pastor, happy with a generous contribution, waited for them.

They were elated and jubilant as they ran up the front steps of the small church, holding each other's hands tightly. Jerry pushed open the heavy oak door, black with age, and they entered the church. Inside, the air was cold, and it was dark, except for two small candles burning on the altar between a small bowl of white lilies. Above the altar, the single round stained-glass window had yet to catch any sun, and its blues, greens, and reds were muted and dull. There was no one there.

A fragment of memory passed through Ana's body. It was so unexpected and sharp that it was painful, and she gasped and stopped still in the middle of the center aisle. She felt cold, and she began to tremble. What was it? Had she been in this church sometime before? Impossible. She hadn't been inside a church since . . ."

Then she had it. Not since that walk with her mother through Palace Square and the clandestine visit to the cathedral when she was so young. She felt a longing for her mother that left her weak in the knees. *I don't even know where she is. What am I doing?* she thought. On this most important day in her life, there was no one here just for her, no one who had loved her all of her life and who cared about what happened to her. To be honest, she and Jerry scarcely knew each other, and she was planning to leave everything familiar and go thousands of miles with him to a strange country and a life among people who were very different than she was. They might love her, or they might not.

On that long past day, hadn't her mother promised that they would all be together some day soon, attending services in the cathedral, loving each other, and singing songs of peace, joy, and freedom? Where had all of that gone? Tears welled up in her eyes.

Beside her, Jerry was startled. "Ana, what's wrong? Are you all right?" He put his hand under her chin and lifted her face to his. "Ana?"

She trembled all over her body, and she felt weak and faint. She grasped the back of the pew at her side and bit her lip. *What am I doing?* she wondered.

Just then, the pastor in his white surplice entered the chapel, and he was followed by two stocky woman who were obviously his frau and his housekeeper. They would be witnesses. Their eyes all turned to Ana and Jerry as they waited for them in front of the altar.

At that moment, the sun moved around the southeast side of the church and climbed its old walls to reach the single stained-glass window over the altar, bringing it to life and advancing its rich colors to the white cloth on the altar and the white surplice the pastor wore. With Jerry's hand gripping hers very firmly, she stared at the scene in front of her. The cold and dark little church now seemed bright and warm, and the three people who waited for them had kindness on their faces, wishing them well. Slowly, the two of them moved forward, and the service began. Tiny as it was, it was sweet and intimate.

When it was over, Jerry's kiss was both gentle and newly passionate. The two women smiled broadly and tossed small handfuls of rice over them, crying, "*Das ist schon!*" ("Beautiful!")

They were blissful, and all their doubts and problems melted away. Or at least they forgot to worry about them any longer. They would depart for Texas in less than a week. Reluctantly, Jerry left her alone in the flat for a couple of days while he returned to his base to take care of final retirement paperwork, clear the base, and file for a change of status now that he had a dependent and Ana was officially qualified to travel with him on a military aircraft.

Ana was euphoric. She waltzed barefoot around the flat, singing to herself as she packed her limited belongings in a duffel bag that she wished were not so tattered. It was still difficult for her to believe that her impossible dream had actually come true.

It seemed heartless to leave without telling Heidi, Ian, and Mikhail goodbye, but she would have to do that in writing. She wondered if she would ever see them again. They were the only true good friends she had ever had. She felt disloyal as she rummaged through Heidi's things, searching for anything she might borrow. She found a locked diary that she forced open with a kitchen knife. Since she had never seen Heidi writing in a diary, there had to be something else in it. She was right. Between the pages, Heidi had squirreled away paper money of the various countries that they had traveled through, in addition to a sizeable amount of U.S. paper bills, which Ana guessed had been tips from American servicemen at the *hofbrau*. Because Heidi spoke and understood more German than the other three, they had let her handle their money. Ana didn't think of it as dishonesty on Heidi's part. One had to do what one had to do, because just surviving in this world was difficult enough.

With only a moment's hesitation, Ana took all of the U.S. currency, which totaled nearly a hundred dollars. She left a note for Heidi.

> *Darling, my dream has come true! Yesterday we were married. We will leave for America in two days. I'm dreadfully sorry not to see you before I go. You and Ian and Mikhail are the only friends I've ever had. Please forgive me that I must borrow a little bit of the money you had hidden in the diary. I am going so far away and I have nothing. I swear I will pay it back as soon as I can and I will send it to your uncle's address in Vienna, as I won't know where you are. Please don't think bad things of me. I am sorry to take your money. Also the Revlon green eye shadow. I will always love you.*
> *Your friend, Ana.*

Chapter Eleven

THEY FLEW ALL night and next morning, and the last leg of their flight was by commercial airline. Jerry and Ana arrived in San Antonio in searing heat that created a wavering pattern above the asphalt and made Ana feel dizzy and disoriented when they stepped outside the air-conditioned terminal. Their plane was nearly half an hour ahead of schedule, and they were already outside the terminal and on the sidewalk with their luggage when Jerry spotted his parents dashing from the parking lot.

Ana's heart flipped over to see that Jerry's mother looked exactly like her picture—tall, a striking silvery blond in a peach silk shirt with matching western-style trousers. A bit taller than Jerry, his father held Lurleen's arm. They both wore western boots and white Stetson hats, as did many of the others that Ana saw rushing in and out of the terminal.

Jerry dropped her arm and rushed up to grasp his mother in both hands and swing her off the ground. He gave his dad a bear hug, and the three of them talked at the same time between gales of laughter. The two men punched each other vigorously on their upper arms.

"Jerry, darlin'," his mother cried, "you're lookin' good!"

Ana had stopped in her tracks to watch them shyly until Jerry remembered to go to her. She was wearing the second outfit Jerry had bought her—a flowered skirt of burnt orange, brown, and gold, with a matching knit shirt of gold. More new shoes, light brown, with heels. She had tied a brown velvet ribbon around her long, straight hair that hung down her back, shining in the sunshine. He put his arm around her waist and drew her toward his parents. She drew a deep breath, for courage.

"Mom, Dad, this is Ana." He pushed her toward them. "Ana, this is my mom, Lurleen, and my dad, Brandon."

They both smiled courteously. Lurleen bent to lightly kiss her cheek, "Ana, dear, so good to meet you!" Her voice was soft, melodic, and gracious.

Brandon also kissed her cheek, staring intently at her. "Ana," he said. "How do?" He looked at Jerry and said, "Well, son, let's get on the road. No use hangin' out here in the heat."

Lurleen took Jerry's arm and laughed up at him, and Jerry reached for Ana with his free arm. Brandon, in the habit of leading the way, did so promptly at five paces ahead of the other three, and carrying the luggage.

The family car was a very long light-blue Lincoln Continental. It was the most elegant car Ana had ever seen. She sank deep into the back seat of dark blue leather and was immediately impressed that the powerful air conditioner was already cooling the interior of the car. Jerry climbed in beside her and closed the heavy door with its tinted glass. Brandon drove, very fast and excellently, passing every car as he came to it. Lurleen sat beside him but twisted herself around so she could chatter away to Jerry.

"Whole gang's waitin' at the house," she said. "All your buddies jes' dyin' to see you again." She reached a slender hand toward Ana and wiggled her fingers because the space between the seats was too large for them to touch one another. "Hope you don't mind, darlin', but all Jer's old girlfriends are comin' out of the woodwork to welcome him home." Jerry beamed in anticipation, and Ana smiled uncertainly and wondered what else might be waiting for her at the Breckenridge home.

The big blue car left San Antonio and headed south while Lurleen and Jerry chattered on about people Ana had never heard of. Her eyes began to droop with fatigue, and Lurleen noticed and signaled to Jerry. He reached over to tousle Ana's hair and draw her head to his shoulder. Amused, they lowered their voices, and Ana was asleep in an instant.

It was more than an hour later when Jerry roused her. "Wake up, sweetheart," he said. "We're comin' up on our lane."

She opened her eyes, still dazed with sleep, and could see nothing but open space, dried grass, mesquite bushes, a few scraggly trees, and most of all, glaring sunshine even through the tinted glass. After one more turn there was a wide metal gate, propped open under a high arch with a brass sign that read "Breckenridge," and in smaller letters, "Registered Herefords."

The lane was long and straight, treeless, and fenced on both sides to keep animals out. It led to a large house of light fieldstone, at least a quarter of a mile distant, glowing golden in the fading sunlight. Although the car windows were closed, Ana could hear the thump of music growing louder and louder. A broad asphalt parking area was crowded with some very big cars, some small cars, and at least six pickup trucks.

Brandon leaned on the car horn as they neared the house, and young people began pouring out of every door. Jerry was out of the car when it had barely stopped. Laughing raucously, the young men pounded him on the back and punched him in his gut while the girls—*all so beautiful,* Ana thought—hugged and kissed him, giggling and screaming. Under a canopy at the side of the house and next to a lighted swimming pool, a heavily amplified Western band of three guitars, a string bass, and an accordion played the fight song of the Texas Aggies at an ear-splitting level. Ana was overwhelmed by the noise level and the chaos around her, but for Jerry, it was a supremely happy time. He loved them, and they loved him.

Everyone was courteous to Ana, although she thought that the women were staring at her covertly and whispering among themselves. She spotted an armchair that looked luxurious and comfortable, and she sank into it. After a while, Jerry brought her a frosted glass of beer and a plate of cold shrimp, potato salad, and rolls and left her to eat while he mingled and laughed with his friends. She talked hesitantly to anyone who came near her, but as they usually came in groups of two or three and talked over one another, she had trouble following their conversations and felt inarticulate and less than brilliant. It didn't help that she still wore clothing rumpled from travel while they all looked fresh and charming in mini-dresses of every hue over long, suntanned legs.

Lurleen came over and beckoned to her and when Ana stood, she linked her arm through Ana's. "Want to see the house, darlin'?"

It was by far the largest home Ana had ever been in, heavily carpeted throughout in a creamy off-white. There were large fireplaces in three rooms and a kitchen elaborately fitted with enough of the latest equipment to cook a meal for a very large crowd. Ana lost track of the number of bedrooms with attached baths. In the room Lurleen called the library, there were few books but a gigantic oil painting of misty foothills, a towering oak, and meadows of wild bluebonnets that covered most of one wall.

In one bedroom, Ana thought that the bed looked especially inviting because of its fluffy floral quilt with matching pillow covers, and she couldn't resist touching it to see if it was as soft as it appeared to be. Lurleen laughed and said, "Poor lil' darlin'. You're still tired, aren't you? That ol' jet lag has got to you." She turned back the quilt and gently pushed Ana down on the bed, pulling off her shoes. "Now, you rest, and we'll wake you in a while."

She turned a bed lamp on low beam, turned out the overhead lighting, and closed the door. Ana was humiliated to be always sleeping around these lively, active people, but it was true, she was exhausted. She moved her head around on the pillow, thinking that it was the nicest, softest . . .

It was hours later when loud honking of horns woke her. Still groggy, she stumbled to the half-open window that faced the front of the house and parted the semi-sheer white drapery to peer through. Ray Don, Jerry's brother, was at the wheel of an older model bright red pickup truck with its radio turned up to full volume. Doors opened, and again young people poured outside. Jerry jumped down the steps, two at a time, and banged his open hand repeatedly on top of the truck over his brother's head. They laughed uproariously.

"Hot damn!" Jerry cried. "My good ol' truck! You've had it painted!" Ray Don slid over. Jerry climbed in, and they went roaring up the lane, racing the engine while the onlookers howled and applauded.

It was after midnight when the party finally broke up with more hugging, kissing, and promises to get together. "Right soon, hear?"

She glanced at herself in the large mirror at the dressing table and tried to smooth her hair and straighten her skirt, but at that point, it wasn't of much use. She found her way to the front of the house as Jerry came bounding in the door. She marveled that he was still so full of energy and showed no signs of weariness.

He put his arms around her, "Hey, sweetheart, guess what? My folks have a surprise for us! Dad bought a spread just down the road with a nice little house, good barns, the whole deal, and Mom has fixed it up with everything we'll need. What do you think of that? We're going to head over there now, okay?" He held her hand tightly in his and pulled her with him to where his parents stood talking to the last few guests to leave. After more hugs and kisses all around, Jerry and Ana went outside, and he helped her up into the seat of the red truck.

When the lights from their lane faded, Ana saw an expanse of ink-blue sky so filled with stars that it took her breath away, extending as it did from horizon to horizon. She had never dreamed that the sky could look like this. In the city, she had paid little attention to the sky and less to the stars because glare from the ground lights wiped out all of that. She stared, transfixed. The stars, some large and bright and some just tiny dots, twinkled and glittered over the entire earth, so she, Jerry, and the red truck seemed just an insignificant spot in the road. She rolled down the window and put her head out a little way. How fresh and good the air smelled! She looked behind them and to both sides. There was no light to be seen anywhere. She had never dreamed of such silence and serenity.

After about four miles, Jerry turned into a dark lane with a barbed wire fence on either side. The lane was not paved but graveled, and the red truck bounced when it hit potholes, shaking Ana so her head bobbed from side to side. A sizeable plume of dust followed them. Ahead, she could see a small house of red brick with a light burning inside a wide screened porch that ran the width of the house. Jerry cut the engine, ran around the truck, and reached in to help her down. "We're home," he said happily. "Isn't this great?"

She followed him up a narrow concrete walk to the screened-in porch and inside, where he pulled a key from his pocket and unlocked the front door. She stared in amazement. The little house had been completely furnished with maple furniture, hooked rugs, checkered curtains, and small vases of flowers on tables where lamps with ruffled shades were lighted. A king-sized bed was made up, fresh towels hung in the small tiled bathroom, and bars of scented soap waited in ceramic dishes with bluebonnets painted on them. A brief glance into the kitchen revealed a stocked refrigerator, colorful dishes in the cabinets; matching, shining pots in all sizes hung from hooks above a stove that looked new and spotless. Ana, stunned, looked at the gleaming appliances lined up along the counter. They had names on them like Microwave Oven, Convection Oven, Blender-Food Processor, Espresso Machine, and Coffee Mill. Ana stared. What were all these things? Jerry laughed and said, "My God. Mama has outdone herself, and didn't she have fun!"

They showered, dried themselves on the oversized towels, and fell into bed, exhausted, without unpacking a thing.

The next morning she woke to find that Jerry was already up and out of the house. A note on the kitchen table said, "We're checking out the barns. Can you make us some coffee? Back soon. Jer."

Also back was the blazing sun. The softness of the night before was impossible to imagine. She walked around the house like a visitor and changed nothing. She made the bed and struggled to pile the decorator pillows exactly as Lurleen had arranged them, but she thought that she hadn't done it quite right. She added a little fresh water to the small vases of flowers and then, hesitantly, opened the kitchen's screened door and went outside.

There was no sound anywhere. A towering oak tree sheltered the back of the house, and she stood in its shade to look around, where open space on either side of the house was filled with dry grass for as far as she could see. Behind the oak tree, there were two very large barns and a smaller one that were whitewashed and enclosed with a fence of barbed wire and a wide gate built with a large X across it to hold its sides in place. A rope was looped over a pole to keep the gate closed. She became aware of insects buzzing. A lonely black crow, screeching, flew out of the oak tree and vanished.

She wondered about going back to the barns to find Jerry, but the thought of discovering some large animal, of whatever kind, kept her from doing so. She circled the house and noticed that the only flowers were on two pink oleander shrubs near the front door.

After a while, she went back inside the house. It was still very quiet all around her. Carefully, struggling with some of the words, she read the directions for the coffee mill and the espresso machine. After a few mistakes, she was able to grind some coffee beans that smelled wonderful and to pour them into the machine, add hot water, and start the coffee brewing. If they didn't return soon—whoever was out there with Jerry—she would drink some coffee by herself. She poured herself some orange juice and wondered what time it was, as her small watch still ran on German time. Besides that, she had forgotten to wind it.

She waited. More time passed. It seemed to her that she had become insignificant and of no real importance to anyone here. But that couldn't be so, she told herself firmly, because she had skills of her own and was a person in her own right. Her mood lifted, and she went into their bedroom to find her violin in its case, as it had accompanied her duffel bag all the way from Germany. She went into the second bedroom, raised the shade a little, took the instrument out, tuned it, and began to play some Mozart from memory. She felt redeemed, as if she was herself again.

After a time, she sensed that someone was standing at the open door behind her, and she stopped playing. She turned to see Ray Don and Brandon at the open door, with Jerry beaming proudly behind them. She could manage only a startled "oh."

"Hear that?" Jerry said. "I told you so!"

Brandon and Ray Don seemed at a loss for words, but the older man finally said, "Right nice, sure enough!"

Ray Don recovered his usual good spirits enough to say, "Adam Tucker should hear that!"

They all laughed, and Jerry told her, "Adam is the bluegrass fiddler with our local band."

She put her violin away and went into the kitchen, where the men had already poured themselves coffee. Ana cut slices of a coffee cake Lurleen had provided, and they sat around the table, eating and talking. The men were full of plans. Two hired hands were to arrive very early the next day. The barns were ready with grain and water waiting. Ana didn't understand any of it. She listened with apprehension, and when she asked a few tentative questions, the men laughed and Jerry said, "Wait and see. You'll find out tomorrow."

She watched Jerry closely and listened to him talk, and she was dismayed to realize that he had already changed from the man she had known in Germany to someone who seemed almost completely different. He was bigger and broader in his working clothes, more relaxed, and more sure of himself. She realized that he was where his roots were and where he belonged. It was already difficult to recall the diffident young man in uniform who had listened so respectfully to their string quartet.

Just past dawn on the following day, the animals arrived in a huge truck and trailer with metal sides and large round openings for circulation. It was not yet fully light when she heard the truck rumbling down their graveled lane in an enveloping cloud of dust where Jerry and the two hands waited. Ana ran to the kitchen window, where she could see the animals climbing wildly over each other and bawling with apprehension. Jerry and the two hands opened the wide gate, and the frightened young steers poured from the open doors on the side of the truck and into the fenced area, scrambling over each other so that a few fell but came quickly to their feet. All of them ran in circles in an ear-splitting cacophony of animal sounds. Jerry had his first cattle delivery, with more to come.

In the days that followed, a certain routine was established. Jerry spent most of his time in the barns, but he also found time to visit with his parents at their place at least once a day, often early in the morning while Ana still slept. He seemed happy and busy, and there was seldom time for the two of them to just sit and talk together.

Although the mornings were fresh if she woke early enough, the heat soon rose, enveloping everything and absorbing every bit of moisture from the atmosphere. The little house was not air-conditioned, but there was a huge ceiling fan in the hallway that moved the air around and helped a little.

Jerry talked about air conditioning. "Maybe later," he said. "It would be a big job here because it should have gone in when the house was built. It would mean tearing up the attic, putting in ducts, all of that."

She didn't know what ducts were. "Maybe your father . . . " she began.

"No! They've done enough for us already. We'll wait until I can afford it," Jerry said. "Plenty of people go through Texas summers with just a fan, and anyway, I want to build in about five years." She tried to keep the house exactly as Lurleen had arranged it, moving nothing and changing nothing. Jerry kept reminding her that it was her house now, and she could fix it any way she pleased, but she never felt that this was true. It was Lurleen's house, Lurleen's decoration, and Lurleen's way of living, generous as it was.

When the little vases of flowers wilted, Jerry brought fresh ones from his mother's garden. Ana thought she might try to plant her own garden because there was nothing outside but the dusty pink oleander bushes. The trouble was, she had never grown a garden and had no idea where to begin.

Jerry discouraged her. "It's too late now in this heat," he said. "Wait until spring when Mama can help you. She can make anything grow." Was there anything Mama couldn't do?

There were two things, however, that she had to learn, Jerry said. First, she must learn to drive the red truck so she could do errands in town. "We'll start in the lane. You can drive up and down until you feel okay with it." The second thing was learning to ride a horse.

A horse! she thought. She couldn't believe what she was hearing.

"You bet!" he said. "We'll get us a nice pair, a gentle mare for you. There's a pretty little creek at the back of this property and some good trails, and you'll need to learn how to ride before our annual trail ride in September."

"Trail ride?" Ana asked.

"All of us," Jerry said. "We go for four days, camping out,

riding over a hundred miles. Ana, you'll love it." Her stomach tightened. She didn't want to even think of such a thing.

They would soon go shopping in Bautista, about eighteen miles south. "Not much of a town," Jerry said, "but we can get what we need. Some better clothes for you, blue jeans, western boots." Her boots were all wrong, he said. "Those are city boots."

Bautista was two dusty blocks long with a market, a garage with two gasoline pumps, a church, and a drugstore. But most prominent of all was a long building with a corrugated metal roof and a loading dock along the entire front, above which a sun-faded sign read, "South Texas Feed and Farm Supply."

Ana was excited because she had a plan. She wanted more than anything to recapture the intimacy she and Jerry had shared in Frankfurt. She wanted him to concentrate his attention on her, as he had then. She suspected that he was slipping away from her. Jerry had told her that a large number of German immigrants had come to Texas for the land grants begun in the nineteenth century and had settled around Fredericksburg and New Braunfels, so she had no trouble finding a German cookbook at the market. She studied the recipes and carefully selected all the items she would need to surprise Jerry with an authentic German dinner like the ones he had so enjoyed in Frankfurt. Afterward, if he wasn't too tired, she would play her violin for him by candlelight. She wanted him back.

When she had finished her grocery shopping, she hadn't spent much of the money Jerry had given her, and he was still not in sight. She looked for a shop that she would have called a "chemist," and she spotted a large one with glass windows across the front and a sign that read "Bautista Drugstore." Close enough. She hurried there and was thrilled to find whole shelves of cosmetics and hair treatments in a bewildering array. She looked for the Revlon section. She chose two eye shadows, one green and one blue, and paid for them. She counted her change. Feeling only slightly guilty, she counted out forty dollars and folded it into a little square so she wouldn't spend it. Soon, she could make a little package for Heidi and send it to her uncle's address. She felt good about that.

The day before she had planned to fix her surprise dinner for Jerry, she learned that another load of young steers was scheduled for the next day. Should she postpone her plans? But by then the food she had already bought would no longer be fresh, so she decided to go ahead.

During the long day, Jerry sent Luis to the kitchen door several times for cold beer and later for sandwiches, but she didn't see Jerry until almost dark. She was ready with her German dinner, but the meat had to be cooked at the last minute. She had decided on *Wiener Schnitzel,* with boiled potatoes, cabbage, onions, and hot rolls from a package called "Brown n' Serve." She had pounded and breaded the veal, and she would brown it quickly and serve it, as Hermann always did, topped with eggs, sunny-side up and moist.

It was nearly dark when Jerry dragged himself into the kitchen with his face burned to a dusky red and his hair and clothes coated with dust. He washed at the kitchen sink and wanted a cold beer, first of all, which he drank in two long gulps. He tilted back on the kitchen chair and rolled his head around, eyes closed, too weary to move. His legs were stretched out in front of him and crossed at his ankles.

Ana knew he must be weak from hunger. She bustled around at the stove to brown the meat and to fill a plate, adding potatoes, cabbage, a whole onion, and a hot buttered roll before placing it in front of him.

Smelling the food, he opened his eyes. "What's this?"

"*Wiener Schnitzel,* Jerry!" Ana said. "Eat! You'll feel better." She was proud of the way it looked on the plate.

He groaned. "Oh, Ana. I'm almost too tired to eat, and it's so blasted hot!" he said. He glanced at her shocked expression and picked up his fork. "What is this, veal?"

"Yes. You loved it at Hermann's, remember?"

He poked at the egg with his fork, "I guess we're more used to beef around here." He cut a bite and chewed on it with a small frown. "Maybe a little barbecue sauce?"

He ate about half of it and pushed the plate away, "Sorry, hon, but I'm beat. Gotta take a hot shower and shuck these clothes."

She went into their bedroom half an hour later to find him showered, his hair still damp, wearing boxers and a T-shirt, spread-eagled across their bed and sound asleep.

DRIVING LESSONS BEGAN the following week, early in the morning. Because Jerry's truck was heavy-duty and large, Ana had to sit on a telephone book and her bedroom pillow to see over the dashboard. He started her in the lane, and with the automatic shift, she caught on quickly enough that he left her alone for several hours to ride up and down the lane at fifteen miles an hour. At the gate, gigantic trucks terrified her by roaring by at an astonishing speed, so she was careful to turn around well before that point and obediently continued back and forth, back and forth.

Around ten, Jerry was waiting by the oak tree where he signaled her to stop and park. She managed to do that and was proud of herself. He opened the door of the truck and lifted her down "Good girl! You're doin' great. Can I send you on some errands now?"

"Of course!" she said happily, "but not past the end of the lane."

That evening he told her that they were giving a barbecue in two weeks. "I want to get my ol' gang together, like we used to do. Everybody brings something, but the host furnishes the meat and the beer." He ordered a long oak picnic table and benches from a carpenter in Bautista, and Luis delivered a big metal drum on a stand, with its outside painted silver, for barbecuing the meat. Jerry put in orders for a smaller version of the western band, plus two kegs of iced beer. The cook from the South Texas Barbecue Café would work his magic with steaks cut an inch thick and mounds of pork ribs.

"Ana, I want all these folks to know you," he said.

But she had an idea of her own. "I want to play for them, Jerry. I want them to see that I can do something good."

He was dubious. "I dunno, Ana. These guys like country and western. They can be a damned noisy bunch when they get tanked up, and they won't appreciate your kind of music."

"They can learn," she said. "I want to do this, Jerry!"

He shrugged. "Just don't get your nose out of joint if they don't listen the way you want them to."

She began seriously rehearsing Pablo de Sarasate's *Gypsy Airs* for its showy virtuoso aspects. She planned to bake her mother's favorite strawberry torte if there were any fresh berries at the market. And she would not wear blue jeans and a plaid shirt. She was not a cowgirl. She would wear her flowered skirt with a long-sleeved white shirt and a velvet ribbon around her hair.

Jerry borrowed about twenty folding chairs from his mother's church, and he set them up in two rows in the living room. The table and benches arrived, the band arrived, the kegs of beer arrived, and shortly after that, with a full moon just peeping over the horizon, Jerry's friends began arriving. Each woman carried a covered dish of potato salad, baked beans, guacamole, tiny tortillas, or an original creation of her own.

The party was a noisy success, and it was nearly nine before Jerry gave the band a break and herded as many people as would cooperate into the living room where, in spite of the ceiling fan, it was still warm and stuffy. The audience was mostly female because the men had eluded Jerry and were smoking cigarettes and telling jokes down by the barns.

Ana began nervously. The palms of her hands were moist, but she soon forgot herself in Sarasate, playing with her eyes closed. The exotic music recalled memories of her mother, their music-making together, her childhood friends, her early years, the flowing river, spring flowers everywhere, and green trees making a canopy over wide streets, their branches moving gently in a fragrant breeze. She increased her tempo as the music moved toward its climax. The women were as motionless as statues, and she was exhilarated because she knew that she was playing very well, better than ever.

Incredibly, the spell was shattered. Ray Don opened the screen door and signaled to Jerry, and everyone turned to look. There was the bawling sound of an animal in pain. Ana's playing faltered, but she was determined not to let her concentration break and she continued.

"It's one of your calves, dad-blast it." Ray Don's whisper was hoarse. "Caught in the bob-wire fence! He's tearin' hisself up!"

With a worried look in Ana's direction, Jerry tiptoed out and within minutes, the few remaining males followed him, one by one. It was no use. Ana's playing slowed, faltered, and finally stopped. Her concentration broken, she suffered a complete memory loss. Looking stunned, she dropped her bow arm to her side and lowered her violin.

The women hesitated and looked at each other uneasily.

Was it appropriate to applaud even if Ana hadn't finished to the end? There was a hesitant smattering of hands touching lightly. Ana bowed her head and quickly left the room with tears in her eyes.

She made a friend of her own a few days later. She was alone when someone knocked on the door of the screened porch at the front of the house. The woman standing there was tall and buxom. She wore an ankle-length dress in bright splashes of yellow and green, and Birkenstock sandals on her feet. She carried a tapestry bag large enough to hold a weekend wardrobe over her arm. A wide-brimmed straw hat covered a mass of long, dark hair pulled into a knot in back but coming undone around her ears.

"Hey!" she said, grinning. "Are you Ana? I'm Harriet Simon. I teach music at Bautista High. I know all about you, and I thought I'd come and say hello."

Ana was amazed and delighted. Harriet spent nearly two hours with her and Ana played Samuel Barber's *Adagio for Strings* for her, and this excited them both—Ana because she was still in trauma from her failed performance at the barbecue, and Harriet because she dreamed of beginning a classical music series in Bautista. Ana provided her with the first sign that it might be more than just a dream. They made plans.

Over dinner that night, Ana told Jerry about her visitor, but she mentioned nothing about their plans because she wanted to surprise him later and she was not altogether sure that he would be pleased. Jerry said he was glad she had found a friend.

After two weeks and a lot of coaxing, Harriet had herself a committee of seven women who thought they might like classical music, and they held an organizational meeting in Ana's living room. She baked another strawberry torte, and they ate it to the last crumb, with coffee.

Harriet talked about the high school auditorium, its excellent acoustics, and its fine piano. "We've got us a nine-foot Steinway concert grand!" she said. "Travis Werner's mother bought it when she thought she could make him into another Van Cliburn, but it didn't take. After she died, he donated the piano to the school so he wouldn't ever have to play it again." She burst into peals of laughter.

Harriet tried to charge her committee up. "Ana has played all over Europe! She was like . . . a child prodigy, and we're so lucky to have her here! Now we have to do our part. I've reserved the auditorium, printed the fliers, and printed the tickets for Ana's recital."

She began passing out bright pink fliers printed in scarlet ink. "Ana will be playing . . . "

"Oh, oh!" said one of Jerry's friends, a slender blonde named Denise, who looked shocked.

"Denise, what's the matter?" Harriet asked.

"Well," Denise drawled, "I don't know what Ana will be playing, but the Aggies will be playing Austin. That's the weekend of the big game!"

"Oh, no!" Harriet moaned. "Oh, no! We're dead!"

Ana looked from one person to another. "What's a big game?"

Now there was no hope of keeping their plans to herself, because the fliers were already circulating and were posted at the drugstore, the gas station, and all over the high school. A few tickets were already sold, ten of those to Harriet.

Ana placed one of the fliers by Jerry's plate when he had finished his breakfast the next morning.

At first he was amazed, then amused. "What the devil are you up to?" he asked. But amusement turned to disbelief when he noticed the date for the performance.

"Oh, oh! No way!" he said. "We'll be in College Station for the big game. You'll have to cancel this, Ana."

"Jerry," she wailed, "I can't! Everything is printed, tickets are already selling, the auditorium is rented, and I promised to play!"

He stared at her in silence, and she could sense his anger building. The tips of his ears reddened. When he spoke, his voice was flat and quiet in a way that she hadn't heard before. "Listen, Ana, and try to understand this," he said. "There are certain things this family does together, and this is one of them. We've gone to the big game every year since I can remember. All of us. The whole family. My daddy reserves an entire floor of the best hotel in town, and he picks up the tab for his relatives from all over the state. We spend the entire weekend there, and it's a very big deal. It's family. Everyone is looking forward to meeting you." He put his hands flat on the table in front of him. "Now I don't care what you do about your . . . concert, but as far as the game, you're going!"

He turned, left the house, and climbed into his red truck. The engine came to life, and he made a wide swing around the graveled area and roared down the lane. He didn't come back for lunch. Ana wept with frustration.

Two days later, Lurleen called and said, "Hey, you two stop your bickerin' and get yourselves over here real early tomorrow. Brandon is all set to teach Ana to ride. Early now, hear?"

Ana barely slept, and she felt nauseated at breakfast. But since she and Jerry were scarcely communicating, she said nothing. She wore the blue jeans, plaid shirt, and western boots that he had selected for her and tried to ignore the knot in her stomach.

At the Breckenridge home, the placid mare Beauty was saddled and waiting in the riding ring. Straddling the surrounding fence, about ten children of the hired hands were waiting for the show.

Lurleen hugged Ana and said, "Don't worry, darlin', you'll do fine. All the lil' kids around here learn to ride on Beauty. She's gentle as can be. Don't you be afraid in the slightest."

Brandon helped her mount and gave her a few instructions before he took the lead rein and walked Beauty and Ana around the ring several times. Her hands trembled so much that the reins shook. Under her, the mare felt round and fat, and the saddle seemed stiff and too large for her. The stirrups were loose on her narrow boots, and she thought surely they would slip out. Beyond the fence, Jerry and his mother watched and talked quietly. Brandon stopped the mare and unhooked the lead rein. "Okay," he said. "Let's go, Ana. You're on your own!"

In a voice that quavered, Ana said, "Okay, horse, go a little." She touched the toe of her boot to Beauty's fat belly, but the mare didn't move.

Brandon whacked the mare across her rump with his folded glove and roared, "Move, Beauty!"

Startled and getting no control from her rider, the mare took three rapid steps and halted abruptly. Ana slid forward in the saddle and then back. She dropped the reins and grabbed desperately for the pommel. The mare was confused and started up again in a rush while Ana slipped sideways and out of the saddle. She landed on her back in the dust.

Jerry, Lurleen, and Brandon stared in disbelief. The children laughed and screamed, and Beauty continued around the track without a rider. Brandon grabbed her reins as she passed, and Jerry ran through the gate to pick Ana up in his arms. She was sobbing from humiliation and pain. The nearest hospital was nearly forty miles away.

Big game weekend came, and the family went off without

Ana. Although her fractured collarbone was still bandaged, she could play her violin without too much discomfort, and she did. Eighty-six people who hated football came to the concert, and they gave Ana a standing ovation. Afterward, they asked for her autograph and took her picture with their Polaroid cameras. Harriet had promoted her well.

Afterward, Ana was elated. At last, she was coming into her own. She and Harriet came back to the house and shared a bottle of red wine in celebration. It was so good to be making music again. She could still hear Mendelssohn in her head, but she had to wait over Sunday for Jerry's return so she could share this with him. Surely he must be proud of her this time.

It was nearly eleven on Sunday evening when Lurleen called. "Sorry to be so late to call," she said. "I hope you weren't worryin'. We just got back, and we're all pretty wiped out. Don't get much sleep over these weekends. Jerry is going to stay here tonight because they've got that auction in Amarillo on Tuesday and they want to get an early start tomorrow. He's in the shower now, but he'll be callin' you soon, hear? Maybe tomorrow, before they leave?"

Ana was stunned. Not to even speak to her, not to ask about her recital! Stressed, she paced the floor of the little house and eventually went outside to sit at the picnic table under the oak tree and smoke a cigarette. Their differences, she knew, were growing serious. She began to be afraid of tomorrow. She was right to worry. Jerry didn't call, and she cried herself to sleep.

On Tuesday, still without a word from Jerry, Ana was drinking coffee at the kitchen table when Lurleen's car pulled into the shade of the oak tree. Warily, Ana watched her gather her things and climb out of the white convertible, wearing a crisp sleeveless dress of lemon-yellow with yellow linen shoes. In one arm she cradled a large album, and in her free

hand she balanced a covered plate. Over her left arm she carried a large handbag of woven raffia, the entire front of which
was stitched with silk flowers of yellow, bright blue, orchid,
and cerise. Ana held the screen door open for her, and she bustled in and put everything she carried on the table.

"Hey, darlin'," she said. "I've brought us some fresh-baked
cinnamon rolls. Is that coffee still hot?"

Ana had nursed her hurt and anger since Sunday evening,
and she felt sullen and defensive. She poured Lurleen a mug
of coffee and sat at the table without saying anything.

"The guys are all gone to Amarillo," Lurleen said, "so I
thought I'd come to visit you. Did your concert go okay?"

Ana nodded solemnly. "It went fine," she said. "A standing ovation. Many people."

Lurleen raised her eyebrows and said, "Is that right? Well,
you know we all missed you. Lots of folks asked for you, and
it was a shame you couldn't be with us. Jerry was so disappointed." She put her coffee mug down and pulled the leather
album toward her. "I thought it might be a good idea if I
brought over some pictures so you could learn a bit about the
Breckenridge family." She smiled at Ana. "They're quite illus-
trious, you know, and known most everywhere in Texas. I tell
you, I was in awe of them when I first met Brandon. They're
a proud bunch, but they're okay once they get to know you."
She wrinkled her nose at Ana. "Of course, you'd best do everything their way."

She began turning the pages of the album. There was a
sepia photo of an older man with a white handlebar mustache
and thick, white hair curling to his shoulders. "This is the first
Judge Breckenridge, 1904," Lurleen explained. "There's been
about six since that time. Judges, I mean." She turned the
pages slowly, revealing college deans, doctors, members of the
Texas legislature, a U.S. Senator, and a Secretary of the navy.

After about twenty pages of photos, Ana stopped listening because she had begun to realize that this was not an idle pastime. Lurleen had a purpose. That became clear at about page number twenty-six. She closed the album.

"Now, Ana, you must tell me more about yourself, your family, all that," Lurleen said. "Seems we hardly know anything about you, and Jerry isn't much help. We know a bit about your talented mother. So now, tell me about your father."

Ana's stomach muscles tightened in panic. She couldn't remember what she had told Jerry about her father—which of the many stories she'd settled on. She concentrated on her hands, folded in front of her on the table. "Well," she began, taking a chance, "he was in the Russian army, a colonel, I think. Right after they were married, he was killed in Afghanistan, so I never knew him."

Lurleen stared at her. "Oh? But Jerry said . . . "

Ana closed her eyes. Wrong guess! It took Lurleen a few moments before it became clear to her. She reached for Ana's folded hands and covered them with her own. "Oh, you poor lil' darlin'," she said gently. "You don't know who he was, do you?"

Ana's numb silence was an answer enough, and she was too ashamed to say anything or to open her eyes. Lurleen was thoughtful, tapping the table with her long frosted nails.

Ana jumped up, excusing herself. She went to the bathroom, where she cried hard, her body shaking, but she knew she couldn't remain there all day. She was certain that Lurleen would be patiently waiting at the table, and she was. If she noticed Ana's tear-streaked face, she didn't mention it.

"Ana," she said gently, "are you happy here? Brandon and I don't think you are."

Fresh tears prickled behind Ana's eyelids. "I . . . don't

know," she said over the lump in her throat. "Jerry and I aren't close now, the way we were before, and I don't know what's gone wrong."

"Most likely, it's because you haven't had time to learn to enjoy all the things he does," Lurleen said. "You know what, Ana? Texas is still macho, pretty much a man's world. Oh, there are some powerful women here and there, but mostly, the men call the shots, and the women just fall into step, all charm and grace, even if they are a couple of steps behind. If you want to have a strong marriage with a Texan, you have to go the way your husband goes."

Ana was silent and sullen. That didn't seem at all fair to her.

"Did you know," Lurleen continued, "that I was a pretty fair golfer when I was young? East Texas junior champion, two years in a row!" Her eyes grew distant as she remembered emerald-green fairways, long power drives off of the tee, gold cups, women who shared her love of the game, the applause of admiring fans, and newspaper interviews.

Ana was amazed. *Golf!* Another skill she knew nothing about. "Do you still play this game?" she asked.

Lurleen drew a deep breath and released a long sigh. "No, not much. Brandon isn't an eager golfer, and there are no good courses here within a hundred miles. Like most sports, you must play regularly to be any good at it." She gave Ana a rueful smile. "Now it's all horses. Haven't you noticed?"

Ana remembered the colored photo of Lurleen leading the parade. She followed Lurleen's thought to a conclusion and was alarmed. "Oh, but I couldn't give up my music! It's the only skill I have. It's what I am!"

"Well . . . " Lurleen looked doubtful as she reached for Ana's hand. "You're a sweet girl, Ana. It wasn't fair of Jerry to bring you here without . . ." She frowned. "Maybe it would have been better if you had just visited us for a while." She thought about that and then shrugged. "Well, the fact is, it's a very different kind of life for you, and it just isn't working out, is it?"

Ana sat in miserable silence. She was failing this test, whatever it was, and she knew it. After a long pause and still holding her hand, Lurleen said, "Look, Ana, Brandon and I have done a good bit of talkin' on this, and he has a little idea that might help. He wanted me to talk to you about it. Do you think that a little break . . . some time apart from each other, would be a good idea? We can call it a trial separation, to give you both a chance to think about where you want to go from here. How does that sound?"

Ana kept her head down because she didn't trust herself to speak. Lurleen reached for her handbag and drew out a sealed envelope. "This is a little gift from us, Brandon and me, so you can get away for a while, travel around a bit, see a bit more of Texas. Or you could go on north to New York or D.C. Would that friend of yours, that music teacher, be able to go with you?"

After Lurleen left, Ana opened the envelope to find ten bills of one hundred dollars each. Blinking back more tears, she picked up the telephone to call Harriet. There would be no tourist's adventure, no tossing of this money away. She had a gut feeling that she would need to hang on to every cent she could, because things were just not going her way.

Harriet came over at once, irate. "Oh, those people! They think they can just take over your life and turn you into a Texan, like you have no identity of your own. It's not right! They don't appreciate you, Ana, and that's the truth! You're just as special as they are, but in different ways, and that's the way it should be. Well, we'll make them sit up and take notice. That's what Jerry needs, too!"

As she had promised, she brought her latest copy of the union newspaper, *International Musician,* and she and Ana pored over the advertisements for temporary orchestra openings. They skipped over the major orchestras where the competition would be much too stiff for Ana to compete, and they settled on the San Sebastian Symphony. It was a midsized, West Coast orchestra.

"It's right on the Pacific Ocean," Harriet exulted, "so it will be like a vacation for you for a few months. I'll make a few calls and start the wheels rolling, and we'll get your application in by this afternoon, by fax. I'll bet my friend Walt Anderson in Austin can help you with a temporary work permit, because he knows everybody."

By the end of the week, Ana was packed and ready to leave for an audition in California. She left everything behind except for her clothes and her violin. She called Lurleen just before Harriet drove her to the airport in San Antonio, and her mother-in-law took her announcement in stride. "Well, Ana," she said, "if that's what you want to do. Now you take care of yourself out there, and *keep in touch.*"

Chapter Twelve

RYAN MARSHALL WAS in his office by 6:45 A.M. on Monday. Daniel Lessing would arrive for the Friday evening rehearsal, and there would only be enough time to do everything that must be done in the intervening week if he made every minute count. Because this concert was outside of the regular series, arrangements were not automatically in place, and must be checked one by one, to be sure he hadn't forgotten anything. It was so easy to do, and in the end, there would be no one to blame but himself. He woke up in the darkest hours of each night and went over everything again and again, doing a mental checklist and wondering why problems always seemed more acute in the middle of the night than they would in the morning. But he could handle it; he always had. Still, he had a hard time falling asleep again while his mind churned.

There was a Wednesday afternoon rehearsal, and just before Ana left her apartment, the mailman poked a small envelope through the slot in her door, along with a handful of junk mail. She turned the envelope over, and her heart flipped to read the postmark from Bautista, Texas. From Jerry, the note was brief: "My dear Ana, I'm truly sorry that it didn't work out for us. I am very fond of you, but we were just not right for each other. I hope you will find someone who will make you happy and you will continue to make your beautiful music. If I can help you in any way, please let me know. Jerry."

She stuffed the envelope into the drawer of the kitchen table as she blinked away the tears that were forming. No, she would not cry. That part of her life was over, and she would try to move on. She left for the rehearsal.

For Ryan, there was a finance meeting of the board at noon and a special meeting of the executive committee of the board at 1:00 P.M. He knew that the directors were concerned about the budget, and the need for this concert to fill a big projected gap and above all, they wanted it to be what they had called it—"Special." There had been such great publicity, and they had to live up to it or sacrifice any lasting benefit.

He called the box office and said, "Daphne, I'll need an up-to-the-minute ticket count by noon. Can do?"

"No problem. It's going very well. All the good seats are gone, and we've just the very front and the last three rows in the back to fill up. Looks like a sellout!"

"It had better be. Thanks, Daphne."

He checked with the florist. "Two large baskets, remember, and white wicker," he said. "I want them there by 5:00 P.M. Saturday, in place onstage. What are you using, gladioli? Well, use your own judgment, but make it impressive." The board wanted flowers and lots of them, and he didn't want to come up short.

He called the printer. "When will you have the final proof for Saturday's program? Don't make it the last minute, okay? I want to see the proof by Wednesday at the latest. How did the color come out on the fundraising graph? Is it a warm, rich green and a clear, bright red that will catch their eyes? Yes, I want to see it one more time. Wednesday, then."

There were three telephone messages from Ray Johnson, the percussionist and personnel manager. Two cases of flu in the second violin section. Well, that made sense, because they sat next to each other. The other message was annotated "Re: Ana Breckenridge." What could she want? She had never called the office and had never asked for anything. He dialed the personnel manager, but his line was busy and he set the messages aside for later.

He checked with the Bay View Hotel to confirm that Daniel Lessing's New York management had booked a Friday reservation. A suite of two rooms. All okay there. He looked at the clock. After ten already. He'd better update a new total for the finance committee and have enough copies run off. He stopped for a cup of coffee.

At noon he ate his lunch at his desk—a turkey sandwich on rye and iced tea delivered by the corner deli, although he didn't feel hungry because his stomach was burning. He hoped he wasn't getting an ulcer. Stress could do it.

The finance meeting went well, and the committee seemed pleased, so far. Afterward, those who were not on the executive committee left the meeting room, which was always made available by Vice President Foster Carswell. His law firm, Carswell, Montgomery, and Greuning, was a faithful supporter of the San Sebastian Symphony. The second meeting, too, went well. As past president, Carswell was automatically chairman of the executive committee, and he presided. They heard Ryan's optimistic report with pleased smiles and were congenial, anticipating the weekend's concert and a gala reception following at Vice President Lenore Perry's dramatic beachfront home of stone and glass. These social events were the most enjoyable part of being a board member. Carswell, tall and physically fit, looked lawyerly in a pin-striped three-piece gray suit with a light blue tie that accentuated his blue eyes and neatly trimmed white hair. Coming right to the point, as was his style, he asked the question all of them were thinking. "Well, then, Ryan. as I interpret your report, you can pretty much guarantee that we'll wipe out our deficit with this concert?"

Ryan felt a flash of fierce resentment. *Guarantee? Who could guarantee anything ahead of time, except the Almighty? We could have an earthquake, Lessing could catch the flu, or the hall could burn down. Why must I guarantee it? I've already done everything I humanly can.*

He glanced at Noelle, who smiled with gentle encouragement. Stay cool, her eyes coaxed.

Ryan took a moment to calm down. "Well, sir," he said, hoping that his forced smile didn't look that way, "as far as the fates permit, I can guarantee it!" They interpreted that as a joke and laughed. They were in a good mood, pushing back their chairs, and moving toward the door, chatting now of other matters.

At the rehearsal, Concertmaster Walker Fleming again played the soloist's part of the concerto that was considered to be one of the most difficult in the violin repertoire. The orchestra gave him another resounding ovation of stamped feet and bows tapped on instruments. He bowed and grinned, saying to Richter, "I could learn to like this."

When Ryan returned the calls from the personnel manager, Ray Johnson said, "Breckenridge, violin one, asks if you'll make an appointment so she can meet with the soloist. Says she knew him in Europe, and it's very important that she talk to him today. Can we set up a meeting for her?"

Ryan frowned, "Well, I'm sure he knows a lot of musicians in Europe, but we don't know that he would want to see her.

That's up to him, but he'll be really busy with interviews and rehearsals, so don't encourage her. Tell her she can leave a message for him at the Bay View Hotel, and the rest is up to him. Let her know that she's on her own. Sorry."

There was a message to call the head stagehand, Ken Carpenter, but Ryan put it aside. He didn't want to talk to Ken just then because he hadn't taken any action on the Tommy Barger question, and he felt very uneasy about this. The timing couldn't be worse. Instead, he called the piano tuner to confirm tunings before the Friday night and after the Saturday morning rehearsals. He checked with the auditorium management to confirm that the wine bar in the lobby would be well-stocked for Saturday evening's performance.

Tuesday morning on his way to the office, he spotted Emily and her blond friend jogging along the beach in short shorts and tank tops, and they answered his honking horn with a cheerful wave of hands. He felt a sudden urge to talk to Emily again, if only he had more time. It had been okay to tell himself, as he had for years, that he didn't need close ties with anyone, but after the dinners with Emily he had to admit that their time together had been remarkably pleasant. She had turned out to be so different than he had expected, more candid and honest, saying what she truly thought, someone he felt he could trust. He felt drawn to her and he admitted to himself that everyone needed at least one person to confide in, one person with whom one could be totally frank and open. He knew that this level of honesty was what had brought him and Emily closer together and changed their relationship, warming it considerably. He wondered if they could at least eat breakfast together the following day. He resolved to call her later in the day, if at all possible.

The courier from the printer waited at his office with the final program proof. The program would be easy to proof read, because there were only a few corrections to confirm. He signed off on it, and Lorene gave it to the courier to rush back to the printer.

He called the local arts critic, Julian Crandall, to confirm that the telephone interview with Daniel in San Francisco had taken place.

"Oh, yes," Crandall said. "We got it. He does a lively interview; not too much ego. Our photographer will be at the Friday rehearsal."

"Make it around 8:15, when they take a break. He'll be finished by then," Ryan said.

So that story, appearing in the Saturday morning editions, should generate enough walk-ins to sell those last few seats. A full house. He permitted himself a moment of euphoria.

He didn't, after all, find time for breakfast with Emily. Wednesday came and went, and where Thursday went, he couldn't afterward recall. Late on Friday afternoon, he drove to the airport to pick up Daniel Lessing and his priceless violin.

The soloist was easy to spot, not only with the help of publicity photos but because he grasped his violin case close to his chest for safety, one arm protecting it. He moved quickly down the escalator at his own frenetic pace. His dark eyes scanned the faces of those waiting at the bottom and quickly settled on Ryan, although they had never met. He had been through this action many times, and he always looked for someone who also seemed to be looking for someone. In the car for the return trip to the Bay View Hotel, Ryan asked about his San Francisco performance.

"Oh, great," he said. "A really nice audience. Generous and friendly, not like New York where they sit on their hands unless you play better than anyone they've ever heard. And then, some applause, but not too much."

He grinned at Ryan, "So, I was lucky." Ryan congratulated

him and meant it. A good New York review was like money in the bank for a performer, and his management could use it promotionally for years.

Ryan left him at the hotel after giving him a printed agenda and reminding him of a 7:00 P.M. pickup for rehearsal. Ryan grabbed a salad from the deli and returned to his office to check for any emergency calls and was grateful to find nothing critical. So far, so good.

At the rehearsal, Daniel spent ten minutes alone in his dressing room with the door shut to warm up with a little Brahms while Ryan waited in the hallway to introduce him to the music director, Lucas Richter. Backstage, Ana waited in the shadows, at a distance from other orchestra members who were warming up and tuning. She had made a special effort for her appearance that night, forgoing her usual blue jeans and T-shirt for her one decent casual outfit—the flowered skirt and yellow-knit T-shirt. She recognized Daniel's familiar voice from around the corner of the hall as he met Richter. They chatted and laughed for a few moments and then moved toward the stage where most of the orchestra members were already seated and waiting. As conductor and soloist came around the corner, Ana stepped into the light.

Daniel stopped dead in his tracks and stared at her. "Ana? Ana! Is it really you? I can't believe it! What are you doing here?"

Ana moved toward him quickly, laughing with delight. They couldn't fully embrace because each one held an instrument, but Daniel wrapped his bow arm enthusiastically around her shoulders and quickly kissed her on either cheek. His dark eyes flickered with the inner excitement she remembered so well. In disbelief, he shook his head, saying, "Ana, Ana, what a wonderful surprise!" They grinned at each other, remembering how close they had been, until Daniel quickly recalled why he was there. "La ʳ," he said, "let's talk!"

She nodded and he moved off purposefully toward the open stage door without looking back. The rehearsal went well. Daniel's tone was so strong and virile that it overwhelmed Ana. How far he had progressed since their days in Prague! No wonder his name was becoming known worldwide. She recognized, sadly, that he had moved on to a higher level that she was probably never going to reach. At intermission, he was immediately surrounded by excited string players, all vying for his attention and talking shop. Although she could see his eyes moving through the crowd around him, as if he was looking for her, she couldn't break through. Ryan signaled that the photographer was waiting in his dressing room, and Daniel followed him, again without looking back. This was business, and it must come first.

After the rehearsal, Daniel remained in his dressing room with the door shut, doing another interview. She waited for a half hour or so before writing a note to him that she left with Tommy Barger for delivery. "Danny, please call me at my number, 463-7790. Very important! I must talk to you! Your loving soul-mate, Ana."

Ana's spirits sank fast. The chance to talk to Danny had not happened, and perhaps it would not because they kept him so busy every minute. To be honest, she knew that their two worlds had moved far apart, like a glider and a jet. His career was on the ascendancy to rare heights, while hers drifted and was so uncertain that bare survival here was in question. And Danny owed her nothing. Her plan, which had seemed foolproof earlier, now seemed very much in doubt. She felt disconnected and uneasy, as if she was teetering on tiptoe at the top of a very deep abyss with only the unknown hovering at the bottom.

She left the rehearsal through a small door on the opposite side of the backstage area, wh e she had parked her car earlier to evade Karl Godwin. This past week, she had stopped answering her telephone that rang and rang. But as she left the parking lot on a small side street, she spotted Karl's car, still parked by the main stage door and she knew he was waiting for her. Her heart pounded as she watched for his car in her rearview mirror, and she began to breathe easier when she made it back to her apartment without being followed. As she had planned, she parked a half block away in the alley. She slipped quickly up the stairs, and once safely inside, she locked her door and pulled down the shades.

Quietly, she made a peanut butter sandwich and poured herself the last of the milk. She would rest a while to relieve the tension she felt and if Karl didn't show up, there would be time for one more run-through of the evening's music.

She was only halfway through her sandwich when she heard his footsteps on the staircase outside. She remained motionless, barely drawing a breath. He knocked, repeatedly and insistently, rattling the doorknob and calling softly in his most stern voice, "Ana! Answer this door!"

After another half an hour, she saw a folded sheet of white paper coming under her door, but she didn't move to pick it up until she heard Karl's descending footsteps. The note, in his resolute black script, read, "Ana, stop hiding from me! I know about your divorce. The Immigration will be looking for you. Shall I tell them where you are? I can help you, but you must talk to me, or you will regret it. K."

Ana felt a stab of anger at Beth's betrayal of her confidence. She had promised.

But Ana knew how Karl dominated his wife and that Beth was a bit afraid of him, so she shrugged it off, never having had much faith in anyone's integrity. Beth was just like all the rest—not to be trusted.

She opened her door carefully, listening for a full minute before she ventured out and went quietly down the stairs on tiptoe. Surely it was safe to bring her car from the alley. There was no one in sight. Holding her breath, she went around the back of the garage to nearly collide with Karl, who was waiting for her.

Chapter Thirteen

SHE ARRIVED EARLY for the concert in her long black
dress because she was too nervous to remain in the apartment
any longer, waiting for Danny's call that didn't come. The
parking lot was already filling up with patrons in their resplen-
dent best who liked to socialize with their friends at the wine
bar in the lobby before the concert. They seemed elated and
expectant.

A majority of the women wore long dresses that sparkled
and glittered, and most of the men were in tuxedos. They
laughed and chattered among themselves, their voices bright
with anticipation of pleasure to come. Hearing them, Ana
could not help but feel her own sense of pride growing. It was
an honor to be a part of an evening like this, she thought, no
matter what might happen later. Walking parallel to her was
Noelle Wright, who wore a full-length gown of sapphire blue
with pearls, accompanied by a woman friend in cerise chiffon
and long diamond earrings in pendants that swung slightly
when she turned her head. Although Ana had never spoken
directly to Dr. Wright, she thought that it would be very nice

to do so because her background indicated that she took music seriously.

As they approached the concert hall, their paths diverged—Ana's toward the backstage entrance, and Noelle Wright's toward the brightly lit lobby, which had tubs and baskets of flowers in every corner and near the wine bar, where the line waiting to be served was already long. Uniformed ushers were posted at each entrance to the inner concert hall, and their arms were piled high with the evening's programs that smelled of fresh ink.

Backstage was a cacophony of sound as the musicians warmed up, the oomp, oomp of the tuba mixing with breathy octave-to-octave runs and trills from the woodwinds and melodic murmurs from the strings. Onstage, the timpanist meticulously tuned his three large copper drums, bending his head so his ear was inches above their calfskin as he tightened their pitch, listened, and tightened again. His intense concentration shut out all the other sounds around him.

Ana watched from a distance as Ryan arrived with Daniel Lessing in full concert dress, white tie and tails. Ryan accompanied Daniel to his dressing room, where he left him alone and quietly closed the door behind him.

As she continued to warm up, Ana tried to imagine the stress the soloist had to endure before every concert when he knew that he had to perform at his peak—or close to it—or risk a bad review. Such a report would travel like wildfire among orchestra managers who book the artists. If it happened too often, a career may begin a devastating downward slide that could be difficult to reverse. She had often heard the axiom among performers that the unfortunate slide downward can be much more rapid than the happy climb up.

At exactly 8:00 P.M., the orchestra was in place onstage and waiting, alert and silent. The house lights dimmed, and the auditorium doors were closed against late arrivals. There was a ten-second, breathless hush before the concertmaster came onstage and bowed to applause. The orchestra tuned again to the oboist's A. After another pause of five seconds, Lucas Richter appeared and bowed to the increased applause as he mounted the podium and raised his baton. The instruments came up, and the concert began with the overture from Gluck's opera *Alceste.*

After the overture, the applause quieted, and Daniel Lessing appeared at the entrance to the stage. He was followed closely by the conductor, who had left the stage out of courtesy to permit the soloist to precede him. Lessing bowed solemnly to a storm of applause, bowed a second time, and waited. When there was complete silence, Richter raised his baton, and the instruments came up. And so, at last, the moment had arrived that the audience had anticipated since the moment they had purchased their tickets.

Program notes explained that the concerto, one of Brahms's finest works, was written in 1878 in the Austrian Alps and is regarded as one of simplicity and charm. Its rugged grandeur and its integration of the solo part with the orchestra made it a great challenge for most of the violinists of its time, whose skills would be no match for those of contemporary artists. Today, no fine virtuoso resists it, as it can be a chance for extroverted playing, or it can be played as Daniel Lessing played it—thoughtfully, deeply analytical, and tremendously moving.

The strings, bassoons, and horns introduced three song-like themes, and after almost a hundred measures, Lessing's solo violin made its strong entrance with delicate passages interwoven among the orchestra themes. In the second movement, the solo violin revealed a second theme that was tender and poetic, ornamental without excess, delicate, and lyrical.

The spirited final movement offered Lessing a great many hazards but also gave him his opportunity to dazzle his audience with difficult passage work, double stopping, and arpeggios, ending with such stunning vivacity that it brought the audience involuntarily to its feet in a storm of emotion.

For all who were present that evening (and more than a few who weren't present but later claimed they were), it was a concert that they never forgot. Daniel Lessing had delivered a stunning performance that transcended every expectation, electrifying his audience, notching their adrenaline upward to an almost unbearable level so they were transfixed and breathless in their seats until that final moment when they rose to their feet with eyes shining, deeply grateful to have been present for a unique performance of such genuine individual artistry.

Noelle Wright applauded until her hands were numb and her eyes were bright with unshed tears. Ryan Marshall closed his eyes and silently said a fervent prayer of thanks. The audience applauded until Daniel Lessing had returned to the stage four times. When he didn't return for a fifth, the applause slowly died out, but they were reluctant to move away. On their feet, they lingered between the rows of seats and talked among themselves, sharing their awe at Lessing's gloriously prodigious performance, so their exhilarated voices filled the hall with an energized buzzing sound that rose and fell.

Daniel rested in his dressing room for the second half of the concert, which the intercom piped in. As a rule, he did not escape to his hotel at intermissions because he truly enjoyed meeting and talking with members of the audience, especially the younger ones who were just learning to love classical music. He wanted to encourage them and to emphasize his lifelong conviction that fine music is a vital part of the civilized life and must not be missed. No truly educated person could disregard it. In addition, he didn't mind showing them the priceless violin and telling them why it was so special, although no one was allowed to touch it or pick it up.

When another standing ovation met the last lovely strains of *Shéhérazade*, Ryan slipped out the exit nearest his aisle seat and entered the backstage area by way of the Green Room, which he knew would soon be thronged with patrons who hoped to meet Daniel Lessing and who would momentarily besiege him in his dressing room. Directly opposite the dressing room door, a stairway led to the choral rehearsal room, and Ryan moved up five steps so he would have a vantage point for observing the crowd and keeping the rare violin within view. While he knew that all the extra publicity had sold out the concert hall, it had also given the patrons a feeling of familiarity with the soloist, almost as if they knew him personally. The intimacy of his playing had made them feel that the experience was incomplete until they had met him, shaken his hand, and told him how his performance had moved them deeply. No true artist tires of hearing this, because it is his or her *raison d'être*.

As Ryan had expected, he was only a minute ahead of the throng. The Green Room, the hall, and the dressing room area were soon bedlam. Among the crowd of patrons were many members of the orchestra who had helped make his performance a triumph and who felt, and rightly, that they had shared a privilege denied to those in the audience, whose participation was only in listening.

Ryan noticed Ana Breckenridge edging her way to the front of the throng with her violin already in its case. Because she was tiny, she slipped between and around many of those who waited, and she didn't hesitate to push a little if those ahead of her didn't give way.

From his vantage point, Ryan could clearly see Lessing's

incomparable instrument, gleaming in its open case on the counter of his dressing room where the soloist talked to three very young patrons who played in the youth orchestra. Lessing was willing to let them look at the violin all they wished, but he wouldn't let them pick it up and never moved more than a few steps away from it. He moved quickly between the instrument and any overly enthusiastic patron who might reach out to touch it.

Near the light board, Ryan saw that Tommy Barger stood immobile, with an avid expression and folded arms, instead of beginning to clear the stage setup. Then his attention was drawn from Barger to the tall blond man called Karl, who had been haunting the backstage area in recent weeks. Ryan intercepted a quick glance and a nod between the two men, and instantly, he tensed. His hair bristled along the back of his neck. The next moment, the entire area was thrown into utter blackness.

A woman screamed. Ryan tried to shove his way down the stairs, but no one moved out of his way because they didn't know where to move in the darkness. He heard a scrambling sound, a loud thump, and then the sound of running feet. Many voices shouted over one another.

Ryan began to shove people roughly out of his way. "Barger!" he shouted. "Get those lights on!"

After what seemed like a long time but could only have been minutes, the lights came back on, but it was Ken Carpenter who managed to do this. Out of the silence, an agonized wail arose, and Daniel moaned in agony, "My violin! My violin! Someone has my violin!"

The crowd was paralyzed with shock until the retired naval commander Grady Sommerfeld, who walked with a cane, pointed it toward the rear of the acoustical shell and shouted hoarsely, "There it is!"

All heads turned as if they were at some bizarre tennis match. Ryan recognized the stocky figure of Tommy Barger frantically scrambling near the top of the ladder that led to the roof of the acoustic shell. Barger clutched the side rail of the ladder with his right hand, while his left arm cradled a violin close to his body.

As Ryan ran toward the acoustic shell, he shouted, "Security! Security!" With his gun drawn, the uniformed guard rushed in from the rear exit where he'd been assigned. His attention was drawn instantly to the figure of Barger climbing the ladder in semidarkness, and he pointed his gun at him and shouted, "Stop! Hold it right there!"

Barger, now near the top, looked down in panic and grunted, "Uh . . . uh! No!" Because he was staring at the gun, he missed the next step and lost his footing. His other foot began to slip sideways, so he now was badly off balance. He continued to clutch the violin, but his remaining free hand was not sufficient to save him. One foot dangled in the air, and the other foot slipped off of its step so that he swung free with one hand for an instant before he fell, screaming in terror, turning slowly with his mouth open in an ugly grimace. Below him, two women shrieked and backed away in stupefied horror.

Tommy hit face-down on the concrete with a ghastly thud. Blood poured out of his ears and pooled around his head. His broken body was grotesquely twisted and covered a splatter of tiny scraps of wood where the irreplaceable instrument appeared to be splintered under him into a thousand pieces like matchsticks.

Daniel was near hysteria as he rushed to the spot and roughly shoved the stunned patrons aside. He collapsed to his knees, wailing and tearful. He covered his face with his hands and rocked back and forth, moaning, "Elohim . . . oh, Elohim!"

Behind him, a woman whose face had gone deathly white began to sob.

Chapter Fourteen

IT WAS 5:45 A.M. after Lessing's concert when Noelle
Wright's telephone woke her from what had been only a few
hours of groggy sleep, so it seemed at first to be part of her
troubled dream. A clipped voice said from a distance, "Dr.
Noelle Wright, please. Evan Frobisher here, *London Times.*"

Noelle shook her head to clear the fog of half-awareness.
"Yes . . . yes," she said. "Hello, Noelle Wright speaking."

"We'd like to have a statement from you, Dr. Wright," the
reporter said. "What will your organization do about the loss
of the irreplaceable Guarneri violin?"

She was stunned to realize that the news was already being
broadcast worldwide. "We . . . don't know, as yet. We're meeting shortly to determine exactly what the situation is. Give me
your number, and we'll get back to you."

"Right off, if you will! We've a deadline here, and the BBC
has already done the story once."

She had no sooner replaced the telephone than it rang
again. "Dr. Wright?" she heard.

"Allbritton here. Chief investigator for the Oxford Agency
here in London. As you know, we carry the insurance on the

Guarneri that Daniel Lessing has been playing. Did you also know that the instrument was on loan to him and that it actually belongs—or did belong—to Philippe Breton, who is now retired in Paris?"

"Yes," Noelle answered, writing everything down. "So I was told."

"Right. I'm on my way to the States, leaving from Heathrow in about an hour. My flight goes over the pole, so I should be there before too long. In the meantime, I must ask you to make no formal statements to the media. They will be avid for news, of course, but that's their problem. As you can imagine, Mr. Breton is quite disturbed about this." Was there an implicit reproach in his voice?

"Yes, of course. I understand." Actually, it was the first indication she had that the symphony association might face some liability over the theft of the violin. She felt her throat tighten, and that made it more difficult to keep her voice calm. "You'll contact me when you arrive?"

She scrambled out of bed, and the telephone rang again before she had tied the belt of her white wool robe around her waist. It was *The New York Times*, followed by the *Los Angeles Times*, then *Newsweek*, and then a spokesperson for Tom Brokaw. She took all of their numbers, declined to make any statement, and assured them that the association's manager would get back to them.

It was now nearly 8:00 A.M., and she tried to reach Ryan at his office but heard a busy signal on her first three tries.

Finally, Lorene picked up. "Oh, Dr. Wright," she wailed. "This is so awful! We're surrounded! There are three television trucks in the parking lot . . ."

"Lorene, I must speak to Ryan, right away! Will you put him on?"

"Oh, there's no way! All four of the other lines are on hold for him now. I'll have to hand him a note, and he'll call you back."

"Okay, but right away, please!"

When he finally got through to her, she alerted Ryan regarding Allbritton's warning about the media. "And Ryan," she said, "have Lorene set up an emergency meeting of the full board this morning around eleven, if the meeting room is available. Put the rest of the staff making the calls." Since Ryan's staff was a small one, the rest of the staff meant Miriam, who was bookkeeper and season ticket secretary, and Sarah, who handled production and was masterful on her computer. All of that would have to wait.

As soon as Noelle had completed that call, she took a break to put on the coffee. Foster Carswell's call came before she had time to take a cup from the cupboard. "Yes," she assured him, "Ryan will set up a meeting for the full board at eleven, if we can use your meeting room. The insurance investigator from London is on his way here. Foster, do you think we could be in any trouble over this?"

He was terse, not exactly reassuring. "Can't say, as yet. Have Ryan bring a copy of the contract he signed with Lessing's New York management with him to the meeting. And, Noelle, with your approval, I'll contact Chief Rossi downtown to see if we can get some help out of L.A. Do you recall that we're related, in a way? My wife and his wife are sisters. I'm sure the chief wants to do everything he can to help, because this whole affair makes our city look bad."

Within an hour, Foster called back and said, "It's all set. L.A. will send one of its best investigators, man by the name of Fitzgerald. He's already on his way."

"Oh, Foster, that's good news. What would I do without your cool good sense?"

She put her breakfast dishes in the dishwasher and folded

away the local paper, where giant headlines screamed about the concert disaster. She dashed for the shower before the telephone could ring again, but she thought she could still hear it with the water running and the bathroom door shut against it.

The rest of the morning was more of the same, and the emergency board meeting brought its members up to the minute on developments. "There's nothing we can do just yet," Noelle reported, "but I promise that we'll keep you posted. And we must all remember, no talking to the media!"

Lenore Perry, whose catered reception of the night before had turned out to be more like a mourning wake, raised her hand and asked, "Foster, do you think we board members can be held liable for the loss?"

"Don't know yet, but I doubt it. Don't worry ahead of time."

They left the meeting, subdued and concerned. Late in the evening, D. E. S. Allbritton called from his local hotel and asked for a meeting with Noelle and the association's attorney early the next morning at the symphony office. When Fitzgerald also reported in, she asked him to attend.

The meeting was devoted to setting strategy. Fitzgerald planned to begin his interrogations immediately, contacting every member of the orchestra, the security people, the ushers, the stagehands, and any patrons who were known to have been backstage on the night of the concert. First, however, he would call on the only witness whom he hoped was not impeachable—the victim, Daniel Lessing.

The young soloist appeared to be near collapse in his hotel room. Although Ryan had contacted him by telephone four times on the previous day, Daniel begged for a little more time to pull himself together. The hotel switchboard was holding his calls and was reluctant to admit Fitzgerald to his room until the lieutenant flashed his badge and refused to take no for an answer.

In his room, Daniel was still in his rumpled, black satin pajamas. His thick, dark hair fell over his forehead in a tangled mass and beneath it, his face was pale and tense. The draperies were drawn so the room was dim and stuffy. The television set was turned on, but the sound was off.

After Fitzgerald entered the room, Daniel locked the door and leaned against it. His voice shook. "I can't talk to people about this. Not yet. I just can't." He shook Fitzgerald's hand and then turned to the television set and increased the sound slightly. A news broadcast was underway. A blond news anchor from a Los Angeles television station was holding her microphone in front of Emily Murphy at what appeared to be Emily's front door. The newswoman wore a bright scarlet pantsuit, and her shaggy hairstyle left a swatch of hair falling across her forehead and into her eyes, so she peered out from under it.

"I don't know anything," Emily said, unsmiling. "I didn't see it happen, and I have nothing to say. You'll have to talk to our manager, Mr. Marshall."

"But what do you think might have happened?" the newswoman persisted. "Isn't it very unusual for such a valuable instrument to be heisted that way, in front of thousands of people?"

"It wasn't thousands," Emily said, annoyed.

Fitzgerald scowled. The telephone rang, and Daniel looked at it anxiously. "I told them . . ."

"Do you want me to take it?" Fitzgerald asked. "Might be something urgent."

Daniel nodded. Fitzgerald took the call, listened, and jotted notes on a pad he drew from the pocket of his dark blue suit. He turned to Daniel. "It's Paris," he said. "Somebody named Breton?"

Daniel bent his head and closed his eyes as if in pain. "Oh, how can I bear it? But I must talk to him. He called twice yesterday, and I couldn't talk." He brushed the back of his hand across his eyes, drawing a ragged breath and holding his hands together in a brief silent prayer. "He has always been so good to me," he said, "and so generous, trusting me with his most valued possession. And now . . ." Reluctantly, he picked up the telephone. "*Bonjour, mon ami,*" he began emotionally. His dark eyes rolled skyward, brimming with tears. Fitzgerald could hear a torrent of French in reply, to which Daniel replied repeatedly, "*Oh, non, monsieur. Non, non, non.*" He finally broke down completely and sank slowly to the floor as he sobbed and rocked his body back and forth, back and forth.

Fitzgerald knew that he might have gone out on the balcony to avoid witnessing this pathetic and emotional collapse, but he also knew that conversations under great stress often give up valuable clues, and he had been in law enforcement long enough to set sensitivity pretty far down the list of requirements for the job. He also wished, since he was eavesdropping, that he could remember more vocabulary from his high school French classes.

He picked up a magazine from Daniel's hotel coffee table so he could pretend to be reading rather than listening, but he was embarrassed to discover that the magazine was in a Semitic language—Hebrew he guessed—and its sentences read from right to left. He couldn't make out a word of it. Carefully, he replaced it, hoping Daniel hadn't noticed.

Daniel finished his conversation and rushed into the bathroom, where Fitzgerald could hear him losing his breakfast, but he showered and was calmer when he finally came out. He had changed from his pajamas to a pair of wrinkled shorts and a T-shirt, and he was barefoot. Fitzgerald, ever observant, noted that he had very long, thin, bony toes.

"That good man," Daniel said mistily. "Sometimes I call him *mon pere,* and I think he likes to think of himself as my papa. Would you believe, now he worries about me when you know his heart must be breaking over his Guarneri, now lost forever?" He wiped his nose again. "Of course, I will go see him, but when?" Again, he covered his face with his hands. "My God, I don't know what they'll tell me to do tomorrow, and as for another fiddle, no one says anything. Am I supposed to go out looking for one myself for tomorrow's performance with the L.A. Philharmonic? I know nothing. I'm a musical puppet, so I go when they say 'go' and stay when they say 'stay.' It's disgusting."

"Look," Fitzgerald said. "you're not performing tonight. How about if I order us a couple of tall, cold beers and we talk a bit? I've got a lot of questions for you."

As if he had forgotten why the police officer was there, Daniel looked startled. "Well, okay," he said, "if we must do this."

Fitzgerald was quickly on the telephone to room service, and after the cold beer had relaxed Daniel somewhat, he opened his notebook and began at the very beginning. Had Daniel met anyone at his San Francisco concert who had seemed unusually interested in the violin? How about on the plane? Who had sat next to him? What kind of questions had they asked?

They worked their way through each hour of each day since his San Francisco performance, and Fitzgerald wrote everything down in his own version of shorthand. When they reached those critical moments backstage when the lights had gone off, what exactly had happened? Daniel, who had been sitting beside Fitzgerald on the sofa, leapt to his feet and resumed his pacing. He clenched and unclenched his hands and held them out in front of himself; he noticed that his palms were wet with sweat. He wiped them on his rumpled shorts.

"I knew instantly," he said, "that someone was after the fiddle. Before I could protect it, someone—a body—hit me with both hands. I fell backward and hit my head on something—a cabinet, I think. I was disoriented, and it was an unfamiliar room. I thought I could make out a tiny pinprick of light where the violin was, but by the time I managed to stagger to my feet, the lights came back on. My violin was gone. Only the empty case was there." He stared at Fitzgerald with wide eyes. "I wonder why they didn't take the case?" Writing busily, Fitzgerald nodded and said, "I'm wondering that myself."

After he stood looking out the window for a while, Daniel said, "There's something else."

"Yes. Go ahead."

Daniel turned around. "I think someone tried to warn me. An orchestra member . . ."

Fitzgerald was instantly alert. "Who? Which orchestra member?"

Daniel hesitated, closed his eyes, and took a deep breath, wondering what his revelation would do, for good or evil. "I knew her as Ana Iliescu in Prague, but I think she goes by a married name now." He clenched and unclenched his hands repeatedly. "We didn't find a chance to talk, but her note said it was urgent."

Fitzgerald scribbled away in his notebook. "That's it?"

Daniel put his hands over his eyes. "That's all I can remember. Maybe later . . ." After ten minutes more of unproductive questioning, Fitzgerald left him and went directly to

Ryan's office. He was pleased to see Noelle Wright also there. He told them of his meeting with Daniel. "He gave me one lead." He looked at his notes and then asked Ryan, "Who is the young woman violinist from Europe who might have known Daniel Lessing?"

With raised eyebrows, Noelle and Ryan exchanged glances, and Ryan said, "We were just talking about her. We've had an inquiry from Europe that has been forwarded about four times. Seems that someone is looking for her."

Fitzgerald's head came up, "And . . . ?"

Noelle said, "I've been looking into it and have made contact. I thought I would place a telephone call when the time difference is right."

Fitzgerald, still writing, said, "This could be a real break. I want to discuss your telephone call with you before you make it. Was the inquiry from some sort of authority? Police? A foreign government? Interpol?"

Noelle shook her head. "Sorry, nothing like that. It was her mother."

Fitzgerald was out of the office within minutes. He had Ana's address, an apartment over a garage. He parked his car and walked across the graveled area behind the house where a woman was on her knees, weeding a scraggly flower bed. She wore a bright flowered housedress, a wide straw hat covered with a riot of faded cotton daisies, sandals with sport socks turned up, and floppy green gloves. She looked up as he approached but didn't stand. He introduced himself.

"Well," she said. "I'm Mrs. Janner, her landlady. She's not here."

Fitzgerald handed her his card, and she held it in her muddy gloves. He said, "I need to talk to her. Do you know when she'll be back or where I can find her?"

"She in some kind of trouble? I never trusted her a whole lot. She didn't talk to no one," Mrs. Janner said.

"She's not in any trouble that I know of, but I need to talk to her. When do you expect her back?"

"Good question." She wiped her nose with the back of her hand. "She got a registered letter early this morning, from someplace in Texas. I signed for it and brung it up to her, and she seemed real glad to get it. Must have been money in it because she sat down and wrote me a check for the rent she would owe for next month, in advance. Said she had to take a trip and could she leave her car here," she sniffed, "such as it is. When I come back from the grocery store, she was long gone. Left no forwarding address or nothing."

Fitzgerald realized with dismay that he was too late. Ana had, in fact, disappeared.

Chapter Fifteen

AT EIGHT THE next morning, Noelle's telephone rang. It was Allbritton, and he had news. "But not over the telephone. Okay if Fitzgerald and I bring some breakfast and meet with you, earliest possible, at your home?"

"Give me a half hour," she said. Her heart began to beat faster.

The two men arrived promptly and parked in the brick turn-around area behind her kitchen. She had opened the top of her Dutch door, and they could already smell the coffee brewing. Allbritton brought her a large, beautifully gift-wrapped package of imported teas, and she was glad she had remembered to put on the kettle for him. Fitzgerald contributed a carton of freshly baked croissants and a jar of home-made blueberry jelly from downtown's La Boulangerie. Because the early sun streamed into the room, she had decided that they would eat in the kitchen. After large glasses of fresh orange juice and their choice of coffee or tea, the men came right to the point. Fitzgerald glanced at Douglas with raised eyebrows, and the investigator nodded a go-ahead.

"Well, Dr. Wright," the lieutenant began, after a large and

bracing swallow of coffee. "We've had good news from our crime lab. Message came through late last night, but we'll want to keep it under wraps, for now." He took another drink of coffee, and Noelle tried to hide her impatience. "Well," he continued, "seems as if the instrument crushed under the body of the stagehand was a European-made, twentieth-century model of moderate value and therefore," he smiled at Noelle, "it was not . . . the Guarneri."

What extraordinary news! Incredible! Noelle was elated beyond words and immeasurably relieved. She called Ryan at once with the good news, and she asked him to set up an emergency board meeting as early as possible, which turned out to be at ten that morning. Noelle had already spoken to Foster Carswell, who was also pleased but cautious, uncertain as yet that they were entirely off the hook. At the meeting, the other board members were confused. If the priceless instrument had not been destroyed, where was it? Who had it, and why? What would happen next? Emotions ran high.

"Now we wait for a contact by the perpetrator," Fitzgerald said. "Someone has the instrument, and they'll demand some fancy bucks for it. You can be prepared for that."

"Another consideration," Carswell said, "is what the association's liability may be. Our contract with Lessing's New York management reads that we must provide adequate security. That might depend on what a judge decides is adequate, and did we have it?"

"Another question is," Allbritton said, "to what extent the Oxford Agency will continue to be involved in this investigation and what the reaction of the owner of the instrument, Mr. Philippe Breton in Paris, will be. Will he decide to file charges against you?"

"So," Carswell said, "for now, we wait. Stay close to your telephones."

The meeting wrapped up, and Allbritton walked out with Noelle. As they approached her car, he asked, "Are you free for dinner tonight? Fitzgerald is always off doing interrogations, and I'm getting frightfully bored talking to myself."

She was startled at the invitation, which was somehow different than their meetings up to that point—strictly business. But she decided it would be nice to have dinner with him, and after all, it would probably be only this one time.

He noticed her hesitation and was amused. "I'm quite harmless. Children, old ladies, and pets trust me, and I promise to bring you home by eleven, an hour earlier than Cinderella."

"Well," she said and laughed. "It's been a while since I've gone by Cinderella's rules. I'm flattered, and thank you. I would enjoy having dinner with you. About seven?"

She wore a sleeveless dress of cherry red silk that provided a nice contrast to her dark hair and reflected a faint glow on her face. In spite of her intentions, she felt a small buzz of excitement. It was nice to be going out with someone she liked so much. It seemed like a long time since she had done that. They had dinner at Appollinaire's on the bay, where fresh seafood was always on the menu. Over sea bass, fresh artichokes, and several glasses of fume blanc by candlelight, she found that he was easy to talk to. He told her about growing up in England, going to school, and playing in the school band. Although he used his three initials in the British manner, his full first names were Douglas Eames Stuart, following a family tradition. But his close friends called him "Brit." He had a little daughter named Heather, and his unmarried sister lived with him in the family home they had both grown up in near Canterbury. She cared for his daughter when he traveled. "I'm a single father," he said. "Did you know that? My wife Valerie died four years ago in a skiing accident at Val d'Isere."

Noelle drew a quick breath, "How dreadful! I'm so sorry. She must have been very young."

"Thirty-two. It was a tragic loss, and I was terribly bitter over it for years, mostly because Heather has to grow up without her mother." He was pensive, staring out the window. "Valerie was a very active sort of person. She loved things that went fast—fast cars, fast horses, dangerous ski runs. She wasn't nearly accomplished enough for the run she took that day, but nothing would stop her." He turned his wine glass around and around by its stem. "She once told me that she felt fully alive when she was risking everything for a few thrilling moments. The challenge was irresistible, and at those times she felt invincible, but it was very difficult for me to understand that, and it still is."

Quietly Noelle said, "I can't imagine what that must be like, that love of danger. I suppose it's what impels racing car drivers and test pilots in space, but I don't have that kind of courage."

"No, I'm sure that's not your style. But I don't believe that it's only a matter of courage. It can be ego-driven and therefore selfish toward those who love you and will suffer when you destroy yourself." Bitterness had crept into his voice.

There seemed to be no good answer to that. After an uncomfortable pause, she changed the subject. "I feel so much better now that the Guarneri has been resurrected."

"Yes," he said, smiling, "as do we all, especially the Oxford Agency." Over a strawberry mousse and coffee, he said, "Your Mr. Marshall has been to see me."

"Ryan? Really? He didn't mention it."

"It's about his music. He had told me recently about his concerto, and I asked him to let me take a look at it. I hope you don't mind?"

"Oh, surely not," Noelle assured him. "That is Ryan's

affair entirely. He composed it on his own time. We've tried to help him get it published, but it didn't work out, and that's as far as it's gone. Did he tell you that Hammersmith rejected it?"

"Oh, yes. He's quite devastated by that."

"Oh, I know."

"I had an idea," Douglas said. "I think I told you about my longtime friend in London who found the Purcell piece for me to throw my money at? His music publishing company specializes in works for students, youth orchestras, music academies, that sort of thing. I had wondered if Ryan's work might fit perfectly into this category. I took a look at it and I liked it very much. It's not a work of genius, but it has some very nice sections and it would be something that talented students could master. If no one has any objection, I'll ship it off to my friend Alistair in London. Can't hurt!"

"Oh, how good of you! I would be just delighted if he likes it."

"Well, Ryan won't become vastly rich, but it will bring him some nice steady income. And the best part is, once it's accepted, it will probably have a long life. There are always new music students coming along, year after year, and that's a good thing."

"That would be so rewarding for him, especially the money part of it," Noelle said.

He raised an eyebrow. "Oh? Money problems?"

Noelle was chagrined, "I shouldn't have said that. I found out by mistake, and I haven't told anyone."

Douglas was thoughtful. "Serious money problems?" He watched her intently.

She bit her lip. "Yes," she said reluctantly. "Fairly serious."

After a bit of thought, he asked, "Living beyond his means? Big cars, big house, parties, that sort of thing?"

"Oh, no, nothing like that. He lives quite simply, in an apartment."

"Women, then?"

"No, no."

"Well, what then? Gambling?"

She looked at him guiltily, and her silence gave him his answer. "Ah," he said. "Very interesting."

Noelle watched him closely as he talked. He had a very nice face, blue eyes that looked at her directly when he spoke, level brows, a sensitive mouth, and abundant sandy-colored hair that wanted to curl but was kept firmly brushed in place. Because her mind wandered, she missed some of what he was saying but was alerted by another mention of Ryan.

"He seems quite taken with that pretty little violist. When he brought the concerto to my hotel room, she came with him. While I studied it, they sat very close together on the sofa, holding hands and whispering, with their heads just inches apart."

"Really? Ryan?" She was delighted. "Which violist?"

He laughed, "Ah! I see that I've become an Irish biddy, free with the gossip. But that's as far as I go. You'll have to figure out the rest of it for yourself."

There was another urgent board meeting the following afternoon at Foster Carswell's offices. Fitzgerald had news. "Ladies and gentlemen," he announced, "we've had our contact from an intermediary of the perpetrator."

Everyone began talking at once, and Foster had to thump his empty coffee cup on the table to achieve silence.

Fitzgerald continued, "Their go-between is a guy who runs a little music store in Los Angeles. We've known of him in the past, and even though he's been badgered now and then by our department for fencing stolen property, I think the guy is being straight with us on this. He says he's been contacted by the party or parties who have the instrument and that it is safe and undamaged. He has not made any monetary demands—at least as yet. He wants to know if you will negotiate with this party. Do you agree to do this? Shall we tell him to proceed?"

Again, many excited voices spoke at once, but it was eventually voted that Fitzgerald should proceed and that another meeting would be called as soon as any further message was received. Foster said, "I move that these two gentlemen be authorized to represent us and that Dr. Wright, our capable president, take part in the negotiations with the intermediary and report back to us." That motion was immediately seconded and approval voted before Noelle could gather her thoughts enough to express her reluctance to undertake any such mission. Too late. It was a done deal.

That night, it took her a long time to fall asleep. Then she had a dream that was straight out of the late-night television crime shows, full of shadows and whispers and people she couldn't identify and didn't care to know. Threats and innuendo were implicit but vague, bulky men pressed near her, and she felt off-balance, disoriented, and confused. The scene shifted, and she was outside in a dark area where two men appeared suddenly in front of her. One of them said, "If you don 't have the money, give us your pearls." He grabbed her arm roughly.

She woke abruptly, shaken. Pearls? What pearls? Although the demand had seemed perfectly logical in her dream, as soon as she awoke, she knew it was ludicrous. The only pearls she possessed were in a single, modest strand that her parents had given her when she graduated from high school. Even so, her terror had been very real. A residue of it lingered, and she shuddered. The reasoning sector of her mind told her that the facts of the dream meant little and were only a sign of her subconscious revealing its anxiety. Nevertheless, she was relieved to hear Esperanza's old sedan pulling up the driveway, so she was no longer alone. She went into her bedroom, brought out the department store bags from the previous day's shopping, and dumped their contents in a large pile on the kitchen table.

When she came into the kitchen, the housekeeper guessed immediately what the items were—a jumble of children's clothing in every bright color and three pairs of shoes. "Oh, Ma'am," she cried. "What have you done?"

They began sorting them, two stacks for boys and one for a girl. Noelle said, "I wish we knew their sizes better."

"Angelina says they're different here, so she can't say. Oh, look at that pretty little skirt for Maria, with all those tiny flowers, and the little shirt with ruffles on the sleeves. How thrilled she will be!" Esperanza said.

"Now, remember, they must register for the new school term. They're very bright youngsters, and we're already halfway through their English books. Tell Angelina that she must do this."

Esperanza shook her head, "Sure, I tell her but she is very . . . shy."

Noelle was firm. "Education is their only way out of poverty. This is a good beginning, but that's all it is. They must be very determined."

Esperanza continued to look doubtful. "She is so . . . timid, afraid of everything."

Impatient and growing annoyed, Noelle heard herself say, "Never mind. I will take them for registration."

They heard the sound of a car climbing the brick driveway around the side of the house and into the parking area. She was surprised to see Douglas alone, parking his rental car. The two men had been coming for breakfast several times a week with their reports, and she had been expecting to hear from them.

He came to the half-open Dutch door and tapped. "Anybody home? Bakery delivery here," he said.

She went to the door and opened the lower half also, to admit him. "I was expecting Sherlock Holmes, and now I have a delivery man? Whatever has happened?"

"That's the breaks," he said. "Up one day and down the next." He carried a box with a label that read "La Boulangerie," from which floated delicious fragrances. Giggling, Esperanza scooped up the clothing meant for her niece's children and vanished to run the vacuum cleaner in the bedroom and hallway.

Noelle put two coffee cups, plates, forks, and small yellow linen napkins on the table. "What smells so delicious?"

"Beats me. She called it *gateau citron.*"

It was a very fine lemon cake, and Noelle cut two generous slices while Douglas chose Earl Grey from the package of tea bags and filled his own cup from the blue kettle that whistled faintly on the back burner of the stove.

"Where's the lieutenant this morning?" she asked. "Still interrogating?"

"Probably. Since this activity is winding down, we decided that it didn't take two of us to give this onerous daily report." When she raised an eyebrow at his choice of words, he said, "Actually, we flipped a coin." His eyes flickered with mischief. "He lost."

She looked at her serving of cake to hide a smile. "Anything new on the violin?"

"Still waiting for a reply, but I would guess it's only a matter of a day or two until we can meet with the intermediary, soon as we know time and place."

She nodded and tried to take her mind off of the shadowy

men and stolen pearls from her dream. As they chatted, she noticed that Douglas seemed preoccupied, tapping his index finger on the tabletop, an action she hadn't noticed in him before. She thought that perhaps he was growing restless since the investigation was nearing an end. She knew she would miss him when he returned to London, and she hoped that wouldn't happen for at least a few more weeks.

He glanced at his watch and folded his napkin neatly by his empty plate. Impulsively, she said, "Would you like to see my garden?"

"Love to," he said, following her out the kitchen door. "I'm a chap who loves to mess around in the dirt myself. I call my garden 'Haphazard Hill' because I plant anything and everything that attracts my attention at the local nursery, with no organizational plan whatever, but I kind of like it that way. Back to nature, and all that."

Douglas followed her up the winding hillside path that was thick with redwood shavings, past tile-covered concrete benches hidden away in shady spots and a miniature pool surrounded by velvety green moss, circulating its water endlessly and burbling at its work. At the top of the garden, Avery had built a cedar gazebo where four hanging baskets were lush with fuchsias, thriving in the cool moisture that came up every night from the sea.

"What a delightful spot," Douglas said. They sat on the bench to watch the sun sparkling around tiny sailboats maneuvering in the bay. They were quiet for a while, as if talking might break the spell of this peaceful place. Finally, he asked, "Did I ever tell you about our little village? We're in Kent, not too far from Canterbury. It's called Chilham, and we pride ourselves that it's the least tourist-spoiled village in Britain. The houses are mostly timber and brick, eighteenth-century Tudor and Jacobean, with dormer windows and projecting gables. We don't change things much around there, maybe every hundred years or so, if it's absolutely necessary. It's a tranquil area with small streams and wooded valleys, lots of pine trees in certain sections. You would like it there, since you love gardens. Have you been to the U.K., Noelle?"

"Yes, once," she said. "Avery and I toured Canterbury Cathedral and the town around it, but I wanted to spend much more time there." Embarrassed that she might sound as if she was angling for an invitation to visit, she flushed and continued hurriedly, "Well, we saw all the usual touristy things—the Tower, Hampton Court, Windsor Castle, St. Paul's, Westminster Abbey, Parliament, Greenwich. Let's see, have I forgotten any?"

"And did you enjoy it?"

"Loved it all!"

"Perhaps you'll come back for another visit?"

"Yes, perhaps."

Chapter Sixteen

EVENTS BEGAN MOVING rapidly and simultaneously, so Noelle felt that she wasn't properly in control of every detail, as she should be. The message from the intermediary at the music store came through on Wednesday, and the three of them were to go to Los Angeles on the following day. The lieutenant hoped to borrow a state car for the trip.

Ryan called to report with delight that the continuing flood of newspaper publicity had made the community newly aware of the fact that they had a symphony orchestra. Contributions poured in from donors who had never given before. Requests for season ticket brochures for the next season had their telephones ringing off the hook, with a renewal deadline still six months in the future. "Can we have a meeting to review all of this good news?" he asked.

"Oh yes," she said. "We must do that right away, but first I have to meet with the demon thieves—tomorrow as a matter of fact. Assuming that we return intact, how about meeting on the day after tomorrow?" It was agreed.

Allbritton and Fitzgerald arrived at her door just after six the next morning, with Fitzgerald at the wheel of the long black car with state seals on its doors. "I wouldn't have been authorized for this car," he said, laughing, "if your valuable stolen violin wasn't making news all over the world. The guys at the top are getting touchy about all the media attention. They want this matter resolved. The sooner the better, so they'll let us flash their authority today. Everybody comfortable?"

When Noelle spotted the highway sign indicating Los Angeles at fifty miles distance, Fitzgerald reviewed the facts as he knew them and cautioned them about taking any unnecessary risks. "We have no idea who these people might be, or if they're dangerous or armed, so be careful! Let the badges take the risk. That's what they get paid for, and they're very good at it." Then he dropped his bombshell. "A person directly involved may join us. Just stay cool."

Nick's Music Store was on a side street in a seedy section of east Los Angeles, and Fitzgerald, who knew every section of the sprawling metropolis, had little trouble finding it. Besides, he had been there before. It was on a street with other nondescript shops and some small stucco houses with old cars parked where their lawns should have been. The large plate-glass windows at the front of the shop were dusty. Glass display stands supported guitars of various brands and styles, including the regular ones of wood, the plastic ones in bright colors—some with pictures painted on them or rhinestones set in their bodies—and the electronic ones with sound amplifiers standing by at the ready. A few dusty harmonicas and a spread of faded sheet music completed the display.

Fitzgerald parked the black car directly in front. "Let 'em know we're legit," he said. "And that we actually showed up, on the level."

They were early. The shade was still drawn on the front door where a sign read "Closed," as it would remain for most of that day. Inside, they met Nick, who was jovial and keyed up to be playing a part in an event that had made so many newspaper, magazine, and television news stories. The controversy was definitely good for his business. He wore a red, plaid flannel shirt with wide yellow suspenders on top, and his baggy black pants had various bulky tools protruding from every pocket. His mop of curly black hair was unkempt, although he had shaved a two-day growth of beard, which he didn't always do. His black eyes glittered with excitement. He shook hands all around, twice with Noelle.

"We're all set, Lieutenant," he said. He spoke rapidly, with a slight accent. "Everything is just the way you told me to have it. Now remember," said as he waggled his index finger at Fitzgerald, "I don't have a clue as to who these guys are, and I want to be crystal clear on that." He watched Fitzgerald anxiously. "I know you guys think I fence stolen stuff, but I swear, my hands are clean on this. They just called me out of the blue. I wanna do the right thing but, I don't wanna get burned on it, see?"

Fitzgerald stared at him solemnly for a few moments to let him sweat before he answered, "At this moment, Nick, we believe you. Whether our trust is misguided remains to be seen, right?"

Nick frowned. Fitzgerald's wording made him nervous. Was there a trick hidden somewhere? He led them to the back section of the store where he did his instrument repairs and showed them the one-way mirror in the door between that area and the front of the shop. Douglas and Noelle remained there with the door shut. Fitzgerald returned to the front, where they could see him strapping on his underarm holster and gun and snapping a pair of handcuffs to his belt. The unmarked car had arrived across the street. Noelle looked at her watch. Twelve minutes to go. She looked up and saw

Douglas watching her. He moved closer and put his arm across her shoulders.

"You okay?" he asked softly.

She nodded but closed her eyes briefly. She had a queasy feeling in her stomach, and she hoped she wasn't going to lose her breakfast. How humiliating that would be.

She looked around the shadowy back room and spotted a dingy door with a faded sign that said "private," and she assumed that it was a lavatory. She could only imagine what it looked like inside and hoped she wouldn't need to use it. The minutes dragged by. The small room was stuffy, smelling of oil, glue, and other things she didn't want to think about. The meeting with the perpetrators had been set for 10:00 A.M., and when that time arrived, the tension in the shop reached a pitch. They spoke in whispers and stared at the closed front door. Noelle's throat felt dry and tight. Douglas reached for her hand, which trembled, and held it tightly in his own. She was glad of that firm pressure.

Five minutes dragged by. The only sound came from the ticking of a large, old-fashioned clock on the wall. Now, no one spoke. Everyone began to feel apprehensive. Was anyone actually going to appear, or was it all a hoax? At eight minutes past ten, the front door began to open very slowly. Nothing happened. Then a violin case came into view, followed by the small, wide-eyed figure who was carrying it. It was Ana Breckenridge.

NEITHER ANA NOR Noelle ever forgot that morning in the music store, when everything moved so quickly. Before Ana had time to close the door behind her, Fitzgerald had the violin out of her hands, and Douglas was out of the back room to receive it. Fitzgerald grasped Ana's right hand and drew it behind her back, snapping one cuff on and turning her around rather forcefully. He snapped the other cuff on her left hand as the four men from the unmarked car across the street came promptly through the front door. One blocked the front exit, and two others moved into the back room where they opened every visible cabinet and door. A fourth man went out the back door and searched the alley. Noelle, immobilized, stared in amazement, and they stared back at her. She hurried to the front of the shop to identify with the right side of the action.

Ana stared around the room with terrified eyes and her lips parted in shock. Never had she expected this reaction. She looked from one to the other in disbelief. *What is happening here? You people don't understand! You're making a mistake!*

"Sit down," Fitzgerald said, pushing a chair up behind her. "Ross, do you have the recorder?" A short and stocky officer with red hair and matching freckles moved up to the counter and placed his equipment on it. "Plug?" he said to the wide-eyed Nick, whose head had been swiveling around to follow the action but who managed to point out a plug under the counter.

"Ready to roll," said the redhead.

Fitzgerald stood in front of Ana with his open notebook and pencil ready. "You have the right to remain silent," he began, reading her Miranda rights and when he had finished, he said, "Do you understand that?"

Ana shook her head negatively. She didn't understand any of it. Hadn't she just brought the violin back, safe and sound, risking her own safety to do so? Were these people not grateful? Her wrists behind her back were beginning to grow painful. Her eyes moved questioningly from one to the other, settling on Noelle. Surely, this woman who she so admired would intercede for her? But Fitzgerald was in charge, and no one else interfered. He was talking to her again, something about a lawyer. She shook her head, uncomprehending, and he asked, "Are you willing to make a statement without having a lawyer present?"

Again, she looked from face to face. No one was helping her. Noelle's gaze fell when their eyes met, and Ana's heart sank in despair. Softly she said, "I have no lawyer, but I will tell you anything you want to know." She blinked back tears that stung her eyelids. "Could I please have my hands free? I won't run away, I promise you that."

Fitzgerald made a few notes. "Waives her rights," he said to no one in particular. "Okay. We'll take the cuffs off, but I expect a full statement from you and I want it straight. Understand?"

Ana nodded miserably. The situation was not working out at all. Was she in serious trouble? The way everyone in the room looked at her with suspicion, she was afraid this might be so. She had no idea how to help herself. She felt completely alone and vulnerable. How had it all come to this?

They all pulled up chairs and Red started his tape recorder. Fitzgerald read some details into it, such as their location, date, time, and the names of all of those who were present. He nodded to Ana, "Okay, young lady, start at the beginning."

"The beginning? When I came to the States?"

"No, no. Begin with your first contact with anyone about stealing this violin."

She began with the Godwins and the instruments and bows in their closet. The second night that she had eaten dinner with them, she said, Karl told her of his idea to steal the Guarneri, saying that it would not be damaged and only the rich insurance company would pay. He said he had done it before, and no one got hurt but there was money in it for everyone who helped him. She insisted that she wanted nothing to do with the idea, but he pursued her relentlessly and made vague threats about bad things that could happen. She was running short of money when the letter from Jerry's lawyers came with notification of the planned annulment of their marriage. She was uncertain whether or not she would have a job with the orchestra for the next season. If not, she had no idea where she might go, or if she could even remain in the States. In desperation and confusion, she had confided in Beth about the annulment, and Beth promptly betrayed her confidence to Karl.

After that, Karl gave her little peace, insisting that since she was no longer married to an American citizen, she had no right to a green card and therefore couldn't work. She would soon be deported, he said. He often followed her car when she went out, and she felt that he was always watching her, whether or not that was true. She had hopes of making contact with Daniel Lessing when he came to do his concert, and to warn him about the plot against his violin, but when he arrived, he was kept too busy, and she was unable to talk to him. He never called her. Reluctantly, seeing no other way out, she agreed at the very last minute to help Karl steal the Guarneri.

"He had it worked out to the minute," she said. "We all had our jobs to do, and we had to do them exactly as he planned. That stagehand—the one who fell—he was part of it. Tommy, you know? He was to get a small share when Karl sold the violin."

She paused and sat quietly with her eyes closed and her head drooping forward. Noelle brought her a glass of water, and she drank it gratefully, with a shy smile of appreciation. Ana continued, "I was to work my way to Daniel's dressing room. At the proper moment, Tommy was to throw the switch and put out all the lights, at which time I was to come into Daniel's dressing room very fast. And I did that. Karl had given me a tiny flashlight, just a dot of light, and I had it in my pocket. I could see the violin—right there in its open case on the counter in front of me. I shoved both of my hands against Daniel's chest, very hard, and he fell backward and hit his head. I felt so bad about that—but I didn't dare stop to see if he was hurt. I snatched his violin, took my own out of its case, and put Daniel's violin in my case. When I came out, Tommy was waiting. I passed off my violin to him so I wouldn't be seen with two violins if the lights came on too soon. Tommy was to climb the ladder of the acoustic shell, hide my violin up there, and get it back for me after everyone had left. In that same time, I ran toward the backstage door with Daniel's violin in my case, but the lights came on too soon. That was Ken Christopher! I stopped running and walked very calmly out the backstage door, right past that guard with a gun. He didn't pay any attention to me because the manager was shouting for him and he began running in that direction. Karl was waiting at the stage door in his car with the motor running and the lights off. I jumped in with the violin, and we drove slowly away. No one stopped us."

Red held up his hand and said, "Hold it a sec. Gotta change the tape."

Ana again looked at Noelle, who nodded at her and offered a smile of encouragement.

Fitzgerald said, "Want to stretch a minute?" She did. After a ten-minute break when no one in the room spoke much, she continued, "Karl said we must all go about our business as usual so no one would suspect us, so we did. You know, he kept that priceless violin in his closet and no one guessed. They were searching all over the world, and it was hidden only blocks away. But after two days, Karl, Beth, and I left in their car for Los Angeles at two in the morning. I didn't want to go anywhere with him because I didn't trust him—and now, not her either. I suspected if he could sell the violin quickly, he would be gone and I would never see a penny, which I needed very much."

She gave Fitzgerald a measuring glance, wondering if she was about to implicate herself even further. Having little choice, she continued. "We all shared two rooms in a shabby motel, where they took the bedroom and I had to sleep on a lumpy sofa in the front room. Karl didn't leave the flat or let the violin out of his sight, and he sent Beth out for food and to get cash or whatever he needed. Always, he was the boss. I feel sure she is afraid of him, and she always does what he tells her to. Maybe she loves him, I don't know." She made a face of disgust and shrugged. "On the second day, I decided that I was truly ashamed of what we had done to Daniel and how I had behaved in this country, where I had always dreamed of coming and making a good life in music. Most of all, I wanted nothing to happen to Daniel's violin, and I worried about how I could get it away from Karl and . . . " her eyes glittered with tears . . . "give it back."

Fitzgerald was not sympathetic. "Go on," he said.

He ignored the look of resentment she flashed at him. "Well," she continued, "on the first day there, Karl was still tired from driving all night and not sleeping much. He fell asleep sitting up in a straight chair that he had propped against the front door. He was holding the violin case in his lap to be sure nothing happened to it, and when he fell asleep, it slowly slipped from his hands and slid to the carpet below. Beth was out buying groceries, and I just decided, at that moment, to do it. Without packing anything, of which I didn't have much, I grabbed the violin and climbed out through the only window, which opened right on to the sidewalk. I ran downstairs and saw a taxicab going by. I waved for it to stop, and I asked the driver to take me to some nicer area at a good distance from there, which he did—a long way." She looked around the room at the others. "The amount of that taxicab fare was a big shock!" Two of the officers laughed at the expression on her face.

"Then," she said, "I called the musicians' union here and got some names of other violinists. I talked to them and one way and another I was given the name of Mr. Nick at this store. He called you, and now," she extended her open hands, "here we are." She exhaled a long, heartfelt sigh and closed her eyes. Her shoulders slumped with exhaustion. Noelle brought her another glass of cold water while the officers consulted.

Then, Fitzgerald signaled to Noelle and Douglas, and the three of them went into the back room to consult. When they came out, Fitzgerald said to the officers, "Okay, I think we've got enough for now, with your expert help. We're going to head back and book her in the jurisdiction where the crime took place." He shook hands all around and then snapped one cuff on Ana's right wrist and the other on his own wrist until they got back to their car. Douglas carried the violin and sat in front with Fitzgerald, while Noelle sat in back with Ana, who had been released from the handcuffs. The back doors were locked from the outside.

When they were about five miles out on the freeway going north, Noelle reached toward Ana, who sat slumped in a small and woebegone heap in her corner of the seat. Noelle put her hand on Ana's arm and said softly, "You did the right thing at the last. You can always be proud of that."

Ana tried to smile, but her face felt numb. She closed her eyes and leaned her head back against the leather seat where she almost instantly fell fast asleep.

Chapter Seventeen

BY THE FOLLOWING day, the huge black cloud that had seemed to hang over the symphony association, and to some extent, over the entire city, had lifted. It was a new day, especially for the directors who arrived at Foster Carswell's offices with light hearts and the knowledge that they might reclaim their private lives. They laughed and talked among themselves about the miracle of the day before, when the elusive Guarneri had been almost magically retrieved.

Carswell, Noelle, Fitzgerald, and Allbritton each gave their reports. On arrival back in San Sebastián, the big state car had been driven directly to the police station, where Ana, much to her dismay, had been fingerprinted and booked as an accessory to a crime.

By that time, Carswell had arrived at the station. "We did not file charges against her, at least not yet," he said, "and it will depend on whether or not anyone else does—Lessing, Breton, or the Oxford Agency—and then the district attorney will decide if he will pursue it. Since the girl has returned the violin voluntarily and has not asked for any money, we prevailed upon them to release her on her own recognizance, which they did, but they insisted that she surrender her passport and her green card, without which she cannot work in the U.S. The lieutenant took care of that." He nodded at Fitzgerald.

The burly officer continued their account. "We drove her back to her garage apartment, and I went upstairs to take possession of the documents." He glanced at the other two who had waited downstairs in the car, "I must admit, we had all begun to have a bit of sympathy for the young woman, and from the looks of that little apartment, she is in a pretty sad state, all around. Doesn't look like she has the wherewithal to go much of anywhere."

Noelle, who had no intention of including this fact in her report, had turned to Douglas as they waited in the car, "Poor little Ana. I think she's been more a victim than a perpetrator, and she seems so alone here. I wonder if I . . . "

Douglas had shaken his head. "No. Let her squirm for a while. She's not been totally innocent in this affair, and she needs to recognize what a huge mistake she made. Think of it. If Godwin had been a bit swifter, the Guarneri would be long gone."

"I suppose you're right," she said, looking anxiously up at Ana's apartment door.

Now Carswell continued, "The young lady has serious problems with the immigration people, and perhaps we'll look into that."

The meeting broke up with everyone in a pleased and relaxed mood. Noelle remembered her promise to meet with Ryan, and she drove directly there, feeling exactly as she had years before when school was out for the summer. What magic days might lie ahead?

When she entered Ryan's outer office, she was surprised to see that it was not Lorene who was at the desk, busily typing on the computer, although the young woman looked vaguely familiar. Her auburn hair was cut short and worn straight, barely touching the top of gold hoop earrings. Her lime-green dress looked as cool and crisp as young lettuce, and she glowed under a nice tan. She swiveled her chair to face Noelle.

"Good morning, Dr. Wright. May I help you?" she asked.

Noelle hesitated and said, "Good morning. Is Lorene . . ."

"She's out with the flu, and Ryan—Mr. Marshall—was just swamped, so he asked me to fill in for a day or two."

"How very good of you! But don't I know you?"

"Emily Murphy, second chair in the violas."

"Ah, of course! But you've changed . . . your hair?"

The young woman laughed easily. "Yes, among other things." She glanced at the telephone console. "Mr. Marshall is on one line, and there are two others on hold, so it will be just a minute."

Noelle nodded and sat down on the chair near the receptionist's desk, where Emily didn't at once resume her typing on the computer but sat smiling at Noelle. The awkwardness seemed to call for some sort of comment, so Noelle said, "That's a lovely tan you have. Been spending lots of time at the beach?"

Emily's smile broadened. "Oh, I've been on a cruise to Mexico with my mother." She touched a large, gold medallion of an intricate Aztec design that was at least two inches across and hung on a heavy gold chain around her neck. "She bought this medallion for me in Cancun, and I adore it, gaudy as it might be."

Noelle said, "I've been admiring that. It's quite lovely."

"You know," Emily said emotionally, "we had such a glorious trip, and so much fun together. It was the first trip we've ever made, just the two of us."

Noelle wondered why that was so, but she thought better

of asking. Better not go there. Emily, still smiling to herself, turned back to the computer and resumed her work. It was almost ten minutes before all the lights on the telephone console had blinked out and she was able to buzz through to Ryan.

He came out of his office with both hands extended to Noelle, which was a much warmer welcome than she had ever received from him in the past. She was startled to notice that he, too, seemed changed. A corduroy jacket in a warm, mustard yellow color over an open-necked knit shirt of olive green and darker olive green trousers had replaced the three-piece vested suit. His light brown hair that he usually parted and brushed smooth looked fuller, as if it had been blown dry, and it fell slightly over his forehead. He looked younger, more relaxed, more comfortable with himself.

As Noelle rose to take his hands and then follow him into the office, she turned toward Emily to thank her with a smile, but the young woman's attention was fully on Ryan. The two of them exchanged swift glances of such warmth and intimacy that Noelle felt herself an outsider. Not that she minded. Something nice was happening here.

Ryan's office, too, seemed changed. An opaque white bowl of milk glass overflowed with white lilacs that were at the height of their glory and drooped from their own weight to the glass top of his desk. Their delightful fragrance drifted throughout the office on the soft breeze that came in through the open window. Noelle was amazed because she had never seen flowers on Ryan's desk before, nor had the window ever been wide open. Ryan himself appeared to be completely free of his usually constant stress, and she thought that this more informal person would be much easier to like. She smiled at him. "So, now it's happy days all around?"

He grinned at her and passed his open hand above his

littered desk. "Isn't this phenomenal?" he asked. "All these are new ticket orders, and we've had more than thirty new telephone pledges for business contributions next season! Can you believe it? At last the community has discovered that we exist, so it seems, as if there's some good that can come from an event that began so badly." He crossed his arms and continued to grin at her. "Best of all, my dear Madam President, is that the special concert with Daniel Lessing did what we had hoped for, and we'll be in balance at the end of the fiscal year."

She couldn't resist moving around his desk and giving him a warm hug. "Congratulations, Ryan! I'm so pleased,"

As she co-signed the monthly checks, Ryan said casually, "It looks like Mr. Allbritton's friend, the British publisher, is quite interested in my concerto, and we might have a deal there."

"Oh, that's wonderful news!"

"So," he said, fiddling with a pencil on his desk, "if all goes well, I might ask for an extra couple of weeks for my vacation this summer. We . . . I want to go to the music festivals in Europe. What do you think?"

She wanted to laugh with pure pleasure, feeling fairly certain that he didn't plan to go alone, but she restrained herself to an enthusiastic, "Ryan, you must count on it!"

Chapter Eighteen

ESPERANZA HAD PUT the coffee on before she went downstairs to begin washing windows in the spare bedroom, and she had left a collection of colored pictures on the kitchen table for Noelle, done in the watercolors on the sheets of art paper that Noelle had given her young students, Luis, Maria, and Miguel. The imaginative paintings totally charmed Noelle. One, by Maria, was of their shaggy pepper tree with tiny happy faces hidden among its leaves, like fruit. Luis had painted the stray dog that they had adopted, with a crown on his head and a laughing mouthful of human-looking teeth. The dog wore a tiny sign around his neck that said in fractured English, "Luis I love." Miguel, being the youngest, had contented himself with drawing his house with one side in pink, one in blue. Noelle felt sure that the other two sides, not shown, would surely have been green and yellow. Laughing as she poured herself a cup of coffee, she studied the paintings carefully. How enchanting these bright-eyed children were. She would always have a nice feeling about having helped them get a start, but she was also convinced that they would have managed to make it one way or another and a little bit of struggle made them stronger for whatever lay ahead. They were quick and intelligent, they wanted to learn, they had a lot of spirit, and so much joy in just being alive.

She heard cars climbing her driveway, and she felt a little skip of a heartbeat. Douglas had called the night before to say that Fitzgerald had been recalled to his precinct and would be returning on the following day, so they would both like to come for breakfast. She went to the cupboard for cups and saucers and some oranges for fresh juice.

As the two men left their cars, Noelle noticed through the kitchen window that both had the appearance of men beginning a holiday. For the first time since she had met him, Fitzgerald was not wearing his dark blue suit, but instead, faded blue jeans and a blue cotton shirt with a tiny white pattern and an open neck. Douglas wore gray flannel trousers and a knit shirt of lighter gray, with no tie. They laughed together, and she knew how relieved both men were to have the Guarneri theft put nearly behind them. They came into her kitchen as casually and comfortably as if they had been doing it for a long time, and she liked that.

The lieutenant carried two brown paper bags that he placed on a chair. Turning to Noelle, he gave her a broad smile, "I took a half-day off yesterday and drove to the little town of La Mesa in the valley, about thirty miles from here. Seems they were having a model train fair, and I couldn't miss that. I also found some nice fruit." He opened one bag and handed Noelle a giant mango, plump and pink, six whiskery kiwi fruits, and nicely wrapped packages of moist, fresh valley dates and locally grown walnuts.

Noelle said, "Such treasures! This calls for my Italian platters." When the juice was poured and the fresh fruits cut into generous slices, Douglas contributed a baker's box of fresh blueberry muffins. Noelle produced a large platter of scrambled eggs and bacon. She poured tea and coffee, and they all sat down.

Fitzgerald reached into his second brown bag. "See what I found at the train fair!" In the middle of the table, like a unique centerpiece, he placed an exquisite miniature steam locomotive and two matching antique freight cars. "Baltimore and Ohio," he said proudly. "1828. First railroad company in the United States and authentic in every detail." Noelle picked up the tiny engine, and she was surprised at how heavy it was, and was fascinated at how much detail the little engine had.

"All steel," Fitzgerald said. "No plastic anywhere."

"I would hate to ask how much something like this costs," she said.

Fitzgerald laughed. "Well, you can just say that I'm spending the inheritance I would leave to my children, if we had been blessed with any." Noelle and Douglas exchanged smiles upon seeing the jubilance reflected on the lieutenant's ruddy face, and she thought that these beautiful little models were his substitute for family. She was happy to see that, for him, the trains seemed to fill what would have been a great void in his life.

Douglas said, "Now, to get on with our final report. The Oxford Agency has contacted Daniel Lessing, who is bursting with such boundless joy that suing anyone is the last thing on his mind. He has also prevailed on his mentor, Phillipe Breton, to do the same, since the violin is intact and no permanent harm was done, other than to our collective nervous systems. Barring unforeseen circumstances, this seems to be winding down satisfactorily."

Fitzgerald pulled his attention away from his steam engine to add, "The district attorney is willing to drop charges against little Ana, with the understanding that she is to leave the country almost immediately. The immigration people, after

Foster Carswell's intercession, have agreed not to deport her if she goes on her own and surrenders her green card. She agrees to all those conditions and is very happy that she will not have the black mark of deportation on her record. She was terribly upset to think that this was going to happen to her." He looked at his bulky watch on its heavy black leather band. "Time for me to hit the road." Lovingly, he wrapped his engine and two cars in their tissue paper and replaced them in the brown paper bag. They all stood, and he reached for both of Noelle's hands and placed them together between his own. "It's been a pleasure knowing you, Madam President, and not just for the very fine breakfasts." He bent and lightly kissed her cheek, but she threw both arms around him.

"Donal, you've been wonderful!" she said. "We will miss you. Promise me that you will come by for dinner any time you're in the area?"

"That's a promise," he said, shaking hands with Douglas and moving quickly out the door with a little salute. She was sad to see him go, because, realistically, she knew that she would probably never see this very nice man again.

Douglas seemed preoccupied and declined a second cup of tea, checking his own watch, a slender gold Rolex. "I've got to get back to my room for a call from London," he said. "Something seems to be cooking. Can we talk later this afternoon, say around two?"

A flush of unexpected emotion crept upward in Noelle, and her heart began to beat fast enough that she could feel it pulsing at the base of her throat. "I'll be here," she said.

A few miles away, in her garage apartment, Ana was packing. She was determined not to return to Europe carrying the same decrepit duffel bag that she had left with. She went shopping and was thrilled to find one she could afford, a roomy black nylon with many zippered compartments and little wheels at one end for easy pulling. She had never had a suit-case of her own. It now lay open on her bed, with neat stacks of her belongings already in place. How lovely and clean everything looked, and it was all because of her landlady.

Mrs. Janner had spotted the long, black car with the state seals on its doors when they had brought Ana home from Los Angeles, and the following morning, all of her avid questions were answered across the front page of the local newspaper and on the television news. In her mind, Ana was not only a celebrity, but a heroine. As soon as the shades were open in the garage apartment the next morning, Mrs. Janner was tapping on Ana's door with a plate of zucchini muffins, still warm from the oven and covered with a plaid napkin.

Ana was surprised and pleased, and she invited her landla-dy in for a cup of tea. Before they could use the chairs, she had to remove the piles of clothing she was preparing to hand-wash in the kitchen sink.

"Oh, no, no," Mrs. Janner protested. "You must come and use my washer and dryer, and I'll set up my ironing board and iron for you, too." So, after all, the two women struck up a belated friendship and now all of Ana's clothing was bright, crisp, and folded in the black nylon bag. The only question remaining was—where was she to go? There was no question of returning to her homeland, and in any case, she hadn't heard a word from Marie since that last, ugly morning when she told Ana to leave. Nor was it possible to rejoin her friends in the quartet because they had replaced her first violin posi-tion and were now playing the circuit in England. The last card she had received from Heidi was mailed from a rather seedy-looking vacation hotel at Brighton.

She decided that she would sleep on it and the next day, just go to the airport, and choose a ticket she could afford for a European destination in Germany, Austria, or Switzerland.

Once there, she hoped to find a job after she had located another violin. She had to make a new start somewhere, and the location didn't matter much at this point in her life.

To pass the time of her last day here, and because she hadn't slept much the night before, she decided to take an afternoon nap. She curled up with the nylon bag still beside her on the bed and was just dozing off when she heard ascending footsteps. As she pounded on the door, Mrs. Janner's excited voice called through it. "Ana, Ana, open quickly! It's a cable for you from Europe!"

Chapter Nineteen

NOELLE WAS RESTLESS, wandering through her house without much purpose, and then climbing her garden path to enjoy the sparkling view and to wonder where she was going from here. Her indefinite leave of absence from the university had to be resolved soon, but she wasn't sure what this resolution would be. Nor was she clear as to what direction the rest of her life was going to take.

She enjoyed the warm sun for an hour or so, but her mind raced and she returned to the house where she changed into a new jade green knit pantsuit that she had recently bought but not yet worn. She freshened her makeup, adding a few drops of her longtime favorite Chanel No. 5 behind her ears and at her throat. There was no denying a sense of anticipation that something fine was about to happen to her, and she recalled this same emotion from her childhood when she usually woke each day to the sure knowledge that this day would be special.

Douglas returned promptly at two with a large florist's box of yellow roses. "For your prodigious hospitality," he said, "and for you, especially." They were magnificent, their long stems hidden in a lush bed of green fern. It seemed like a long time since anyone had given her such flowers. She buried her nose in their velvety fragrance. "How very nice you are," she said. "And extravagant, too!" Opening a cabinet where her collection of vases stood, she stretched on tiptoes to reach for the tall white one with a fluted top.

Douglas came up behind her, and by reaching around her, easily put his hands on the vase and brought it down in front of her. His move left her within the circle of his arms. She stood silently and unmoving, though her heart had begun to pound. After a moment, he stepped away, freeing her, and he leaned against the table with his arms crossed and his eyes sparkling with mischief. "Well," he said, as if nothing had happened, "our friends the Godwins may be at it again. Another of Oxford's insured instruments, a rare cello this time, has been stolen at a concert in Edinburgh."

She was appalled. "So soon? Are you sure?"

"Nothing is sure at this point. Interpol has come into this matter, and Godwin, if he is indeed the thief, may soon reach the end of the line. In any event," he looked glum, "I must return to London on today's late flight."

She felt regret at two levels. First that he was leaving, but also that young Beth was about to be trapped by the nefarious activities of a ruthless husband. She didn't deserve that.

"Shall we go into the living room?" She was disturbed by his preoccupied expression that seemed to be combination of anticipation and concern. Carrying her vase of precious yellow roses, she led the way into the large room, where the afternoon sun came flooding in through the panoramic west window. She paused there, as she always did, for a moment of pleasure from the view. The sunlight shone on her dark hair and brought an additional warm glow to the vase of yellow roses she held close to the jade green of her knitted suit.

"Hold it!" Douglas said. "Don't move!"

She was startled; she did move, turning to him in surprise, but he was awestruck, staring at her. "What a lovely scene!" he said. "I hope I can always remember it. If only we had an artist here . . . Monet, or perhaps Vermeer?" Then he laughed at himself. "I know what. Just hold that pose, and I'll take up oil painting myself. Won't take a minute!"

They both laughed, and, relieved, she put the vase of roses on the table. He came up beside her to share the view. After a few moments, he put his hand on her shoulder and gently turned her around so she faced him. His gaze intense, he said softly, "We need to talk."

"Yes."

He brushed a wisp of dark hair from her forehead with his index finger and then slowly followed the contour of her face downward until he could lift her chin with the tip of his finger. "I've wanted to tell you, for days now, what kind of emotions you stir up in me. Not just passionate emotions, although I have those too. But most importantly, you project for me a pure, unspoiled quietness, a feeling of peace and . . . tranquility of such depth that I can scarcely endure going off and leaving you here. These past few years have been such turmoil for me and Heather, because we've hit some mighty rough seas. Now you've filled a void in my life that I had nearly despaired of filling." He placed a hand on either side of her face. "Dear Noelle, will you spend the summer with us at Chilham, and get to know Heather?"

This calm request took her breath away. She stared at him with wide eyes.

"I'm serious, you know," he said.

"Douglas . . . I . . . don't know what to say."

"Just say you'll come. I promised Heather I'd ask you, and she's waiting . . . we're waiting . . . for our answer." He drew her closer and wrapped his arms around her with his face pressed against hers. His words very gentle, just below her ear. "You aren't going to disappoint that sweet little girl, are you, Noelle?"

She pulled back and looked up at him. "Douglas," she said softly, "I will come to Chilham with the greatest pleasure. Just tell me when."

He crushed her in a bear hug. "Bravo! How about tomorrow?"

She sobered and said, with a straight face, "I do have one condition, however."

He looked surprised, "And that is . . . ?"

"That Heather and I get a private performance of your Purcell manuscript on your flügelhorn. And I'll need a pompom."

He burst into laughter, insouciant. "Oh, you drive a hard bargain, wicked woman!" he said. "And you will be punished by actually getting your wish." He pinched her cheek lightly. "But you already knew there was no escape, didn't you?" He bent over her, and she knew that, at last, she was going to be kissed.

The doorbell rang.

He groaned, "My God. What absolutely rotten timing!"

She felt a bit shaky as she moved to answer the door, releasing his hand at the last possible moment. When she opened the heavy oak door, Ana waited there.

"Well, hello!" Noelle said. "Come in, come in."

She did, hesitantly. She was dressed in her traveling clothes—bright skirt and knit blouse with sandals, her long hair brushed back, and held in place with a velvet ribbon. She seemed a very changed person. Her eyes and her color were bright. They had never seen her so elated. Noelle urged her to sit down, and she perched on the very front edge of a blue floral chair with her feet neatly together and flat on the floor in front of her. Fascinated, they watched her. She said, "I'm so glad to see Mr. Allbritton here, too. Now I can say goodbye to both of you, who have been so kind to me and so fair, even when I didn't deserve it. I can't tell you how much that has meant to me." She blinked back tears that threatened. "So, today I'm leaving for Europe. Everything here has been settled and I may go, but I will miss all of you. You've been true friends to me."

Anxiously, Noelle asked, "But where will you go?"

Ana inched even further forward on the chair, and her soft voice rose in pitch to match her fervor. "But that's the most wonderful part, I must tell you!" She reached into her small handbag on a gold chain and withdrew a yellow envelope. "Look! A cable from my mother! She's been searching everywhere for me, and now she wants me to come to her in Salzburg and live with her and the organist Marcel, whom she has married. They have this little stone house on the hill—very old, just below the Hohensalzburg fortress. From their front window, they can see the yellow house of Mozart on Getreidegasse. Imagine!" She looked from one to the other and they were enchanted at her ebullience. "I may stay as long as I wish, and my mother will arrange an audition for me with the festival orchestra, where they both play. Oh, how happy I will be to see her again, my beautiful mother! And to think, she spent all this time searching for me. And this long cable—it must have cost her a great deal of money, no?"

Noelle thought fleetingly of her own enormous long-distance telephone bill for multiple calls to Austria during the past few weeks. Douglas gave her a questioning look, but she shook her head slightly. *No, let Ana believe that her mother has done all this herself. She needs this now.* "Do you have your ticket for the flight to Europe?" she asked. "Is everything taken care of?"

"Oh, yes," Ana said. She was proud of herself. "My friend Mrs. Janner took me to see a travel agent in the shopping mall near where she lives. Everything is fixed, and I've paid for it. Also, I have twenty-two dollars left for food, so I won't starve."

"Oh, wait," Noelle said as she hurried to her kitchen, where the scent of warm cinnamon still lingered from Esperanza's weekly cookie bake. She found a flowered shopping bag and put in a small block of cheese, some crackers, an apple, some napkins, and a full dozen of her favorite snickerdoodles. When she returned to the living room, Ana was holding a small package of her own that she had wrapped in wrinkled white tissue paper.

"I want to give you a tiny something, Dr. Wright—not a real gift, but just something to remember me by. I brought this from home when I came to this country." She handed the small package to Noelle, who opened it to discover a fine white linen handkerchief, not new but newly laundered and pressed, the corners embroidered with delicate *edelweiss* in the European fashion.

Noelle was touched and said, "Ana, this is very dear and I will treasure it. But no matter what, I could never forget you." She went to the younger woman and put her arms around her shoulders. Shyly, Ana returned her embrace, and both of them laughed.

Douglas watched and smiled tolerantly at the two women hugging each other. Being a man, he thought in more practical terms. "What about your car?"

"I will give it to the first person at the airport who is fool enough to take it," Ana said.

"No, no," he said. "You shouldn't do it that way. Do you have the title with you?"

She nodded.

"Then you should sign that over to . . . whoever, and get one dollar in exchange. That makes it legal and clears your name off the title."

"Ah," she said. "So that's how it's done. I will do it that way." She cared not a whit about the fate of her troublesome car. "Now," she said, "I must start for the airport as I drive very slowly and keep out of everyone's way."

After more farewells and good wishes, she ran happily down the front steps to where she had parked her car on the street below. Douglas and Noelle went outside on the terrace to watch her progress, which, unfortunately, wasn't far. After about twenty yards, a huge amount of steam poured out from under the hood of the Renault, and she let the car drift forlornly to the curb.

"Uh, oh," Douglas said. "There went the radiator hoses."

A furious Ana emerged and stood glaring at the little car with her hands on her hips. Douglas guessed that if Ana knew any profanity, she was now making good use of it.

"I'd better go help her," he said, smothering his laughter. "And I'll have to drive her to the airport, because that pathetic vehicle isn't going anywhere." He put his arm across Noelle's shoulders and said, "I'll be back, earliest possible. We have some unfinished business?"

"Yes," she said, jubilantly. "I'll be here."

He drove his car down to the disconsolate Ana. On inspection, he decided that they would abandon her no-account car where it stood, for the time being. He transferred Ana's black nylon suitcase to his car, and she climbed happily into the front seat. He beeped the horn twice as they drove off. Ana's small hand waved energetically from the right window as Douglas's hand performed an equally high-spirited salute from the left window. Noelle laughed at their antics and watched until the car was out of sight. Exultant, humming bits from Mozart's *Magic Flute,* she went inside, where her living room was suffused with the scent of yellow roses.